Desire for Dominance

ALLY MARR

Book 1 of The Playhouse Series

First Edition June 2023
Cover Design by BookCoverZone
Editing by Shana Grogan

ISBN 979-8-9882811-0-8 (paperback)
ISBN 979-8-9882811-1-5 (ebook)

Published by Daphnis
AllyMarr.com

Hello there!

I wanted to write a romance story grounded in the lives of every day kinksters. This includes mismatched kinks, negotiations, and consent at all times. I also wanted to write a book that introduces kink to the reader through the eyes of a character new to the scene in a way that is genuine and unrushed. My hope is that Lily and Mark take you on a journey that could happen to any one of us

***

The safeword is *gimbal*, but to be sure you won't have to use it, let me give you a tiny dip into the novel. This is a spicy book, so I get into all the details of what goes where and how it feels. This is a kinky book, so I go into all the details about how *that* feels too. Kinks in this book include but aren't limited to (in alphabetical order): Bratting, Breeding, Consensual Non Consent (CNC), Ethical (and maybe some questionable) non monogamy, Impact, Orgasm Control, Pet Play, and Pussy Worship.

Now if that's gotten your fingers wet, turn the page, and let's go on an adventure.

Chapter 1

Lily expects the alarm but still jumps when it goes off. It's happening! Jeff grins and nudges her shoulder. She smiles and refocuses on the rocket in front of her. Lily takes a deep breath and leans up on her toes to get a few precious inches closer. Four years of hard work has brought her to this static fire, and Lily isn't going to miss a second of it.

Before the big launches that get covered on TV, some companies run a static fire to make sure everything is working. It's the last real test for the equipment, or at least as close as they can get without actually sending test rockets into space. Lily won't be able to get this close on launch day. She'll be working on other projects and it'll be someone else's big day. Despite the fact that the rocket is sideways and there is only one stage, this is her big day.

With the crackle of the speaker, the countdown officially begins. Lily crosses her fingers. She glances at the nozzle as the countdown reaches zero and fire spews out of it. A roaring sound, not unlike thunder, rolls over the group a second later, bringing a hot wind that sends Lily's dark brown hair flying around her. She lets out a startled breath as the area almost trembles with the force of ignition, and she tightens her grip on the railing in front of her for stability.

A voice comes over the loudspeaker. "We have ignition."

Ally Marr

Black smoke rolls from the giant plume of fire in front of her. Lily's gaze flicks to the screen, back, and to the screen again. The nozzle burns white, and it's difficult to look at directly. Behind her, the different teams talk about their checks, but it all fades into the background.

"We're looking good so far," Lily squeezes the bar and bounces on her toes.

Jeff nods. "Let's hope we stay good."

The loudspeaker crackles. "T plus ten seconds."

Jeff crosses his arms. "They're doing all the checks now."

Lily lets out a long breath to calm down. These next twenty seconds are the most critical in determining if the last few years of work are right. Dozens of engineers have worked on their small part of this rocket, but as the project engineer at Aerospace Actuation she was one of the few lucky enough to be able to come witness the test in person. She's worked on a few different rockets in the past seven years, but this one is hers. It's the first one she's been trusted with completely. As the lead designer, Jeff was able to grab a spot as well. She listens for each of the verbal cues that indicate successful checks and her smile grows wider with each one. It goes exactly as planned.

"T plus thirty seconds."

"Yes!" Lily jumps up and down as she shouts and gives Jeff a high five.

Jeff grins. "We're golden."

If she could take an image back to her younger self for motivation, this would be it. This would be the image that helped her through every microaggression about her dark skin and Puerto Rican descent. Every sleepless night in college led her here. All those years paid off. She builds rockets now, she built *this* rocket. The fire and noise dwindle until all that is left is black smoke clouds. The people around them erupt into claps and cheers, the voice on the speaker declares the test successful, and Lily lets out a sigh of relief.

"Is that it?" Jeff asks. "That's a bit anticlimactic."

"Be thankful it is, anything exciting means more work," Jeff lifts his hands in surrender and they both turn to see the celebrations. Some people are already leaving, and others pose for pictures. Maybe it is a bit anticlimactic. It was a long trip to get here from California, and a long trip back tomorrow. The only other thing Lily plans to do in Mississippi is get catfish. "What would make it feel better?"

"Make a wish." He grins, turning back to the rocket.

It's not a star, but she shrugs. If he wants to make a wish, who is she to stop him? She should make one too, in case it works. Lily hums as she looks over the rocket, thinking about all that it took to get it here. If it could grant wishes, she would surely deserve one. What does she want? Her mother would wish her a husband, her best friend Tala would wish for a wife, and she's sure Jeff is wishing for his dream house.

This is her dream. Well, it's half of her dream. The other half left her after a conversation she thought was leading up to a proposal. She won't wish for a partner though, or for him back, that would sour the moment in her memories. It doesn't have to be about love. Look at what she was able to do on her own.

My wish is to learn something new, something I never knew about myself.

***

The first project she's been in charge of, and it's in danger of not finishing.

Lily shakes her head as she tries to refocus on the conversation in front of her but the words all sound like she's underwater. She takes a deep breath. They had a successful test on Wednesday. They spent Thursday celebrating. How could everything have changed so quickly?

Lily flattens the paper in front of her on the table. The part number is written in bold font and highlighted. She underlines it again with her pen, the short stroke gouging the paper. One of the electrical components in the controller popped up on the government's 'do not fly' list. Just like that, all the work over the past four years becomes suspect and this project could be over.

Finally, Jeff's words start becoming understandable, and Lily focuses as he goes on to list all the ways that their testing is inadequate. It's like a death sentence for the program. Each avenue of recovery is shot down by the assembled team.

Despite the sinking feeling in her chest, and the need to blame herself for not having the foresight to pick a different part, there is nothing she could have done to prevent this. This isn't her fault. It's all out of control.

As the project engineer, it's her job to reign in any technical hiccups and gain control.

"Flight hardware is almost out the door. How soon can we get estimates to change the part?" Lily's going to have to push back on them. Everyone is going to want to take their time to get it right, and they should, but they don't have any time left. The static fire was supposed to be the final test. "We're supposed to be shipping hardware next week."

Jeff makes a non-committal sound. No one can hold eye contact with her.

"We have to set up a call today to tell the customer. A lot of eyes are going to be turned onto the program, so we need to be ready for it." No one says anything. There is more they aren't telling her. "What are you most worried about?" Lily tries a different tactic, and the room bursts into conversation.

Lily's unsure about what the team can really do in a few hours, but she'll be ready to fight for the program. She needs to. Otherwise, all of her work vanishes into smoke, along with all of theirs.

***

"I heard your program is in trouble." Tala bluntly skips any pleasantries as she approaches Lily's cubical. Lily groans as she stands and leans into Tala's side for a hug, careful not to wrinkle Tala's designer dress. Tala smooths Lily's curly hair down with a soft smile as she pulls back. Lily looks up to her Filipino friend who is only taller because of the high heels she favors at work. She was Lily's roommate in college, and it was probably the only time in their school's history that the algorithm worked in pairing its students up. Tala left after her bachelor's degree, making the big move from the east to west coast with her boyfriend. Lily followed a year and half later with a master's degree and her boyfriend. Neither of those relationships lasted, but this one did.

"The static fire went so well, and now all we can talk about are recovery plans."

"We've had to scrap the affected parts on our board, it was cheaper than spending all the hours trying to change the hardware or code around it." Tala glances at the part drawing on Lily's computer screen. Lily steps back and runs a hand through her hair as Tala skims over the drawing and slides into Lily's seat.

"We are delivering flight hardware soon."

"See that sounds like a problem."

Lily rolled her eyes. No kidding. "A problem I have to solve."

"That's why I'm a designer. I get bossed around, but I don't have to tackle the hard problems."

"Thanks, Tala." Lily deadpans, not thankful in the least, and Tala smiles. After a moment of silence, Tala leans back and shakes her head.

"Sorry hun, nothing comes to mind for a replacement. You'd have to redesign the whole board or how the controller works."

That's what the team thought too. Lily rubs her forehead, where she's beginning to feel her heartbeat thud against her eyes. "I'm going to need a drink. Do you want to go out tonight?"

"Not tonight." Tala shrugs, being unusually vague.

"Is something going on?"

"I've got a date."

Lily shakes her head with a small laugh and then puts her fingers to her lips, gasping. "A secret date? With who?" She leans against her desk so Tala can't avoid her gaze.

"Aleeyah." Tala blushes. "I'm meeting her at a club, so it's not like you can't come, it's just a different type of club than the ones we used to go to."

"You know I'm down for anything," Lily insists and Tala lets out a deep breath. They had some pretty wild days in undergrad before settling down. Sure, they haven't been really fun in a while, but it's not like they're boring.

"It's a swinger's club." Tala admits in a low voice, and Lily furrows her eyebrows. Okay. That's a bit more exciting than the clubs they used to go to.

"That, uh, that is a different type of club." It's not like she hasn't heard of the lifestyle and the popular books, but it always just seemed like fiction to her. "Is it just like a sex club?"

"Don't judge. Just think about it as trying something new." Tala winks. "Or someone new."

It's like her wish. Lily laughs and shakes her head. It's not like she's a prude, why shouldn't she check out a swinging club? Plus, it's been a year since her last breakup, she's due some crazy sex if she wants some. Worst case scenario, she gets embarrassed and spends the whole night on her phone. Best case scenario, well, maybe she learns something new or finds a one-night stand. "Let's do it." Lily hopes she's not biting off more than she can chew. "What's the worst that can happen?"

"The elderly orgy." Tala deadpans and Lily bursts out laughing.

"Seriously though, a swinging club? How come you never mentioned this in the years we've known each other?"

"I've mentioned it before; I just didn't mention it was a swinger's club. I like it better than other clubs. People are honest about wanting to sleep with you, so things are a lot more straightforward. I think you'll like it."

"Really?" Lily's skeptical.

"It's no crazier than making out with random girls at pride." Tala shrugs. Lily only remembers half of that day, to be honest, but she has lots of pictures that she hopes never sees the light of day. "You were way more fun before David had you trying to be Mrs. Wife."

"Can you not?" Lily's mood sours instantly, as it does anytime her ex is brought up. Tala doesn't think the end of her five-year relationship was something to really mourn, but Lily wanted a lifetime and now it's gone.

"I'm just saying, you don't have to be celibate forever."

"I haven't been celibate..." Lily argues, but it's not like having one one-night stand is that far from it. Sure, she let go of a lot of fun for stability before, but that's not unusual for relationships. Especially ones that last long enough where marriage is on the table. She glances at her bare left hand. She's not in a relationship anymore.

"We'll take one car, and you can be my designated driver." Tala decides. Lily mock salutes.

What did she just get herself into?

<u>Chapter 2</u>

Lily's not totally naïve, but she also has no idea what she should be expecting. A nightclub and a lot of leather would match what she's absorbed through popular media, but instead of driving downtown the directions lead her towards the outskirts of the city, where not many people are on the road this late. Nine on a Friday in June should be packed with traffic, but most of the traffic is heading the other way.

Lily taps her fingers on the steering wheel as they pass yet another street of large dark buildings. What if she's not cut out for the party life anymore? Lily glances at Tala as Tala changes the song in the car. Lily wouldn't have gotten through engineering school without her. This club is a piece of cake in comparison. Her nerves fade into excitement as the low base in Tala's song fills the car.

The GPS directs Lily into one of the parking lots and Lily quickly scans all of the buildings. They are all large, connected, and rectangular, but only one of them has their lights on. It's nondescript among the other buildings on the block. She drives towards it.

"We're here!" Tala exclaims as she grabs a backpack from the backseat and checks her hair.

"You look gorgeous as always." It's true. Tala is a slim beauty with a soft face and very long straight light brown hair. Her skin is beautifully clear and a few shades lighter than Lily's. Neither of them were lucky enough to break the 5'4" height mark, but Tala is petite to Lily's curves.

"Anything I should be expecting?" It didn't seem important to ask before, but Tala brought a backpack. Should Lily have brought supplies? There is an old condom in her purse, but maybe that's expired by now.

"It's too late to back out now." Tala laughs as she opens the car door. "It's a clothing optional kind of place, so you'll see naked people."

Lily's not sure how to react to that so she laughs. She's seen naked people before, maybe not so openly, but that should be fine.

"You might even see people having sex." Tala shrugs and Lily's laughter stutters to a stop.

"Tala."

"Okay, I probably should have warned you more, but you said you were down, and I feel like you'd actually like this place. You'll certainly get lucky if you want to. I know you haven't really been looking since David."

"Ay Dios mio." Lily groans. David would never have stepped foot in a place like this. David wasn't a fan of PDA any further than a kiss hello or holding hands. It's probably part of the reason Tala was glad for the breakup, she didn't see the love that happened in private, but who really declares their feelings out in the open? The very thought of her ex brings back her headache from this morning. "Yeah, I'll need a drink for this."

Tala gestures to her backpack. "I got you, girl." They reach the gray metal door of the club and Lily takes a deep breath. Excitement and nervousness create a perfect cocktail of butterflies in her stomach. Tala turns to her, her hand on the door but keeping it closed. "Seriously, no worries, no one is going to do anything you don't want them to. In this respect, it's much better than a dance club. If you need out, then we'll leave, just like that. I'll meet Aleeyah another day."

"You sure?"

"One hundred percent. I think you'd really enjoy some of the stuff that goes on in here." Tala grabs Lily's shoulder. "I'm pushing because I love you, and it is time, girl. Ready?"

It's time, Lily repeats in her head. *It's time.* "Let's do it." Do it while she still has the confidence.

Tala opens the door to reveal a dimly lit pool room with the start of a hallway in the back corner. Lily waves at the two middle aged men playing pool in the middle of the room, and they stop to wave back.

"Hey ladies, I can sign you in," one greets. He waves them over to a large wooden table in the corner. "I'll sign them in. Will, take your shot."

"Hi Thorn," Tala guides Lily over to the table. "Lily, this is Thorn, he's a dungeon master here, which we'll explain in a bit. Thorn, this is Lily, it's her first time." Lily nods as Tala places her hand on her shoulders. Thorn is a tall man. Not fat, but not quite fit either. His beard is patchy and his head is shaved. He looks like he's someone's dad.

"Yes, that's me, Lily," Lily waves with her fingers and he laughs.

"Welcome to The Playhouse! First things first, I'll need some contact info from you." He picks up a tablet and turns it on.

"I'm vouching," Tala adds and he nods, pressing the screen.

"So, I'm guessing you haven't been to a munch?"

"A munch?" Lily parrots back as she takes the tablet to enter in her info and Tala shakes her head. There is a waver and a few attachments she has to make, and this seems like a bit much for just sex. Wait. Tala said Dungeon Master. Is she in a dungeon? Lily takes another look at Thorn, but nothing about him screams kinky sex. The other man playing is just in jeans. Was she really expecting red lighting and men in nothing but chains?

"She's not on any of sites. I just dragged her out with me." Tala nudges Lily, and Lily returns her attention to the tablet. Hopefully she wasn't staring too hard. Her face warms as she digitally signs a waiver.

He perked up. "Kicking and screaming?"

Tala slowly grins as she shimmies her shoulders. Lily's never seen her with that look on her face. What else doesn't she know about Tala?

"I don't even know who you are anymore," Lily jokes, mostly to ease her own nervousness. Goosebumps rush up her arms and down her body. Tala wouldn't bring her anywhere dangerous. Tala sticks her tongue out at her, but she glances down the hall with an excitement Lily rarely sees on her.

"Okay, so once we've gotten that from you, I'll collect the door fee. Then I can give you a tour and explain the rules. Then you're off the leash and can go have fun." Thorn reaches out and Lily hands back the tablet. Tala hands over a twenty-dollar bill.

"This one's on me." Tala explains as Thorn takes it. "I'm going to go change, but you can drop her off with me by the dance floor when she's done."

"Abandoning me already?" Lily holds her hand over her heart with an exaggerated frown.

"It's a cold and lonely world woman, you'll learn." Tala kisses Lily's cheek. Lily laughs, and her nerves seem to settle, leaving her with curiosity. What is a dungeon like? What does Tala like about this place? Will she like it? "We'll start drinking when you're done with your tour." She waves before disappearing down the hall.

Lily hands the tablet back to Thorn, and then follows him down the hallway. "So, the bathrooms are on the left and this is the locker room." He opens one of the small lockers for her. It's enough room for a backpack, but not much else. "You have to leave your cell phone in here. There are no pictures allowed in The Playhouse. There is a level of anonymity that is expected here, so if you see anyone you know, don't expect that they'll be happy to talk to you about this outside."

"Right. No need to out anyone." Lily thinks of Tala. She rubs her sweaty hands on her jeans and shoves her bag in the open locker.

"Exactly." He taps the closed door before handing her the little key bracelet. "The first room on the right is the viewing room."

Lily puts the bracelet on and glances into the room. She freezes. A few men are lounging on a couch together and watching—blood rushes to her face as it warms. The TV fills the room with a moan and the slick sound of a certain kind of movement. One of the men glances up and catches her gaze. Lily's stomach jumps, a squeak escaping her. She darts her gaze away from his, wishing like hell that her pounding heart would slow down.

"That's uh, allowed here?" Lily steps to the side of the doorway and crosses her arms. She shifted from one foot to the other. Where is Tala?

Thorn nods. "Yeah, that's the viewing room. People use it to watch porn, masturbate, or engage in some mutual masturbation."

"Ah, yes, right. That… makes… sense." Lily's cheeks heat further as she clears her throat. That seems like something best to do alone at home, but then again maybe not. Tala did warn her about naked people so she'll have to get a much better poker face in the next ten minutes or she'll be flushed all night. Thorn shows her a lounge and a few bedrooms, but her mind is stuck on the viewing room until he stops so suddenly she almost runs into his back.

"Next we have the Dungeon." He points to a doorway in front of them but stands in the way of it. "You are not allowed to drink in here, and you can't play if you've had anything to drink. If you decide this is something you are interested in, you'll have to talk to a DM. Either Ronnie, me, Will, or Darius. A DM is a Dungeon Master, we're responsible for enforcing rules, making sure things are done properly, and making sure everyone is safe." Would she not be safe without them? Lily wants to ask, but she doesn't want to look stupid. She'll wait for Tala.

"You picked a great night to come, it's our monthly kink night." Thorn steps aside but Lily isn't ready to peek into another room yet.

"What's that?"

"Well, you are technically allowed to do a scene at any party, but kink night is just a way to get all the kinksters in at once. We'll have dedicated DMs all over to facilitate scenes." That doesn't make it any clearer, but she nods anyway. Is it just role playing sex? Or is a scene something different in the kinky world? He gestures to the door. Is she ready to see more? She'd never needed orientation for a club before. She takes a deep breath and peeks into this room.

Lily's instantly drawn to the figure in the center of the room. She's only got a side view, but he's stunning. This is already her favorite room.

He's stretched out across a giant wooden X behind him in a way that shows off shadows of his well-defined muscles. His wrists and ankles are tied to the wood behind him with leather cuffs, with the black leather popping against his light beige, ecru, skin, but he stands confidently. His biceps flex as he pulls on the restraints and as he relaxes them she traces her gaze down his sides. His whole body is on display, with absolutely nothing to hide behind. It's like a photoshoot.

The only thing hidden to her are his eyes, but Lily can almost feel the sharp jawline and slight stubble on her fingers. He's wearing an earring, and the studded diamond is the only thing he's wearing.

He's looking away from her at first, in deep conversation with another middle-aged man, which allows her to just stare. Even Thorn has stopped speaking; either that or she's stopped listening. She's not sure how long she stands there, just that she spends every second tracing his figure with her eyes. He really is gorgeous. In the middle of tracing the curve of his ass, she glances up to his face. He's watching her. A shiver shoots down Lily's spine, hardening her nipples and stealing her breath at once. His brown eyes are so dark that Lily could fall into their depths all night. Are his lips as soft as they look? He winks at her and smirks. She's been caught.

"Oh," she breathes, and Thorn chuckles. His smirk shifts into a smile, maintaining eye contact, and Lily licks her lips. Tala was right. She's already happy she came out tonight. His eyes drop, eying her up and down, but he never makes his way back up to her face.

"Pay attention!" The other man scolds as he hits him in the stomach with a riding crop. Lily flinches at the impact, and the man turns away from her with a surprised laugh.

"Let me show you the rest of the place, after that, you can come watch this as long as you'd like," Thorn motions down the hallway. "Don't worry, I've only got a few more spots to show you."

The rest of the tour seems rather uneventful in comparison, except for the comfortable absurdity of it all. Once they make their way further down the hallway to an area with couches, where music drifts in from the main room, he shows her the main area with a dance floor that no one is dancing on, no less than ten bare bedrooms that people make use of all night—that she is free to use whenever—so long as they clean up afterwards, and a sex swing that people apparently use in the open. There is also an upstairs lounge for watching and a bathroom that has no doors. Lily's still processing the swing when he leads her back to the dance floor.

"So that's the overall gist of everything. Tala said she'd meet you here, so I'll leave you for her to find. If you made your way back to the dungeon, I'm sure she'd still find you."

Lily's face grows warm again, but she only nods. "People may come up to you and ask you for all kinds of stuff, just do what you want. No scat, blood play, or waterworks in here, just for sanitary purposes. Bring your own condoms, but people usually have spares. Uh, if anyone is bothering you, come tell someone right away. We don't play around with consent here. No is no, maybe is no, I don't know is no. Anything but an enthusiastic yes is a no. Tala can probably answer any questions you have but feel free to flag us down to ask us anything."

"Sure," Lily glances around the room. "Thanks for the tour." Some people are wearing some of the leather outfits she was expecting. A few people are walking around in club attire. One man crawls across the floor in a dog costume.

"I'm glad that Tala brought me."

"I hope we'll see you around after today." Thorn steps back and disappears down the hall as Lily smooths her shirt down and checks her breath to make sure it doesn't stink. Two steps into the hallway, Tala appears with a smile.

She's dressed in barely anything, and nothing's *wrong* with it, but Lily's never seen this much of her outside of her house. Lily boldly wore a shirt that showed off her cleavage. Tala's lacey lingerie barely counts as a bra.

"How do I look?" Tala puts her hands on her hips.

"You look great and, um, really confident." Lily glances at the booty shorts and then up to the lace that barely covers Tala's nipples. Honestly, a lot of the people here are in similar stages of undress. "Should I?" she gestures to her jeans and flats. Tala shakes her head.

"No! Not at all. Stay as you are." Tala grabs Lily's arms. Not that it seems like such a bad idea. It's not often she gets to show off how great her tits look in a push up bra. Maybe next time. Maybe she can work up to it once she stops blushing.

"So how was your tour?"

"I have questions. Do people really use the showers here without a door? Did you know there is a room where people just watch porn together? What's a scene? Do the DMs need to watch you having sex? What's scat play?" Lily counts them off and Tala smiles at her, amused.

"Yes, the showers are fun. The porn room is a little weird to me. A scene is whenever people engage in BDSM play, I think. What were the other questions?"

"Scat?"

"Poop."

"Literally?" Lily shudders. "That's a no."

Tala laughs again. "Well, did you see anything you liked?"

"There was something," Lily confesses, "or rather someone. He was in the dungeon when Thorn was giving me the tour."

"Oh?"

Lily bites her lip before lowering her voice to a whisper. "He was just stretched across the wooden X like a work of art. He had a little scruff and these super dark brown eyes. His hair looked so soft and long enough to really play with. All he was wearing was an earring!" Lily can't believe she's saying this out loud but she can't stop. "Then he smirked at me! I think my nipples are still hard from looking at him. I mean I just wanted to trace his abs with my tongue." Lily blurts, and then covers her mouth with her hand to stop the words from escaping.

"You're drooling on the floor," Tala pretends to wipe her chin and Lily rolls her eyes. "Was he Chinese? Tall, pale, and gorgeous?" Tala asks and Lily nods, hoping that Tala hasn't already slept with him. "That's

Derrick's sub, he's a real cutie. I'll introduce you guys later. I think his name is Mark."

"Sub?"

"He's a submissive, it's the kinky term for the bottom. The one who gets spanked and stuff."

"Well he's, um, in there now and I'd like to go see him," Lily gestures towards the dungeon, but Tala locks their arms together and walks them over to the snack area, where she pulls out a bag from the fridge.

"Yeah, sure, just take a drink with me first. Aleeyah should be here any minute, and I am going to need the liquid courage."

"You don't need any of that, and I thought Thorn said we couldn't drink."

Tala hums as she starts to pour vodka into two cups. "That's if you are playing in the dungeon, which I never do and you're certainly not doing." She pours cranberry juice into the cups and hands one to Lily. "If you're doing anything else, well, just don't get hammered and you'll be fine. Well, except tonight, because you are driving us home."

Lily sips on her cup slowly as Tala nervously drinks two cups. Any minute turns into ten, and then fifteen. Maybe they should go wait in the dungeon. She can't leave Tala alone, but she doesn't want to miss Mark. She grabs a second drink.

"Excuse me, are you Tala?" Both Lily and Tala turn to see another woman. She's tall, beautiful, and wearing a short white dress that pops against her dark skin. This must be her.

"Only if you are Aleeyah," Tala steps closer to look up at the other woman, who beams.

"Then I guess it's my lucky day." They hug, and Tala stays under her arm as she turns to face Lily. "Want to move to the couches?"

"You two should get to know each other. I'm going to see if I can find Mark," Lily doesn't want to be a third wheel. She can't help the smile as she heads towards the dungeon. She pushes her curls behind her shoulder and squares her shoulders. What is he up to now? Would he smile for her again? She grabs the doorway as she enters it, but he's not here. Her smile shrinks. He's not by the X, the chairs, or standing around the edges of the room. He must have left while she was with Tala. She didn't see him on the way over either. Did he already leave?

In his place, there is a man in boxers kneeling on the floor with his arms chained up to the ceiling. Behind him is a woman in a leather top and jeans, holding a leather tool. She runs her hands through his hair and the man murmurs something to her and the hairs on Lily's neck stand up like he's murmuring in her ear. Lily leans against the doorway and takes in the sight. When was the last time she had sex? When was the last time she watched porn? She's reacting like a horny teen to the seductive whispers between them. She's reminded of her first boyfriend, and how they would have sex in reckless places. She used to think she wanted people to catch them, but she could never have imagined putting on a direct show. Is that something she could do?

"Such a good boy," the woman in leather purrs, "letting me beat you up in front of all your friends. How did I ever get so lucky?"

Lily reluctantly backs away as soon as the DM in the dungeon motions towards her drink. She walks past the bedrooms in the hall, some of which sound like they're being put to use, and into one of the lounges. Was Mark in any of those rooms? Could she have been with him had she stuck around in the dungeon? She takes a seat on an empty couch, taking another sip of her drink and glancing around to see if Tala is nearby.

Lily sighs. Imagine all those muscles being put to use to please her. His pale hand against the dark skin of her hip as he pulls her close. His soft hair between her fingers as his dark eyes look up at her as his tongue—

A tall and willowy man flops down next to her, letting out a heavy breath. His blue skirt pools around the whole couch. "Sorry about that," he readjusts to pull his skirt back under him as he settles into the other half of the couch, "I am just a mess today!" He pauses, looking her up and down. "I don't recognize you." He leans into her space. "Are you new?"

"Today's my first time here."

"Yes! Love it. My name is Dominick, but you can just call me slut."

Lily snorts at his overly serious expression, and he cackles before giving her a playful nudge. "Kidding!" He cackles, "but since Dom means something here that I am totally not," he winks, "people call me Nick."

"Hi Nick," she shakes his offered hand with its manicured baby blue nails. "I'm Lily."

"So Lily, what's your poison?"

"Oh, no," Lily shakes her head, "I'm not—I'm just here just to watch."

"Well, there is a great orgy happening in the big room if that's your thing. I think you could still join if you wanted." He points towards the room. Lily nods, trying her best to act like this is normal for her to talk about. "Or the Sybian is in the side room. There are usually a lot of women in there."

"Right," Lily shifts in the sofa. "I haven't decided what to watch yet, so I'm just enjoying my drink."

"Well, I'm beat." He throws his feet up onto the ottoman in front of him, "heels are a beast."

Lily agrees as she eyes his tall pink heels, and leans back to settle into the couch.

"Hey, Nick," A man greets. He's a tanned man in a white polo shirt and jeans. He has a strikingly handsome face and a full 5 o' clock shadow. He looks down the hall and shifts on his feet. What's distracting him? "Have you seen Ronnie?"

"Amos," Nick greets in a light and flirty tone, "I didn't know you were coming out today."

"Me neither." His voice is deep. Would Mark's voice be as deep? He turns to Lily and extends his hand. "I don't believe we've met."

"I'm Lily." She shakes his hand. It's calloused and rough, but warm and firm in her hands.

"Are you new around here?" Even Amos' voice is calloused and rough. He must work with his hands.

"I am."

"Good, it's nice to see new people. I hope to see you around in the future."

"I haven't seen Ronnie, but she's probably upstairs." Nick offers, and Amos nods.

"See you later, Nick. Nice to meet you, Lily." He heads to the staircase.

"He's a single Dom, if you're looking." Nick bumps her shoulder. "Although he seems a bit cranky today."

Lily shrugs.

"Super broad shoulders though, as you saw. Great to throw your legs over. I can set you guys up." He winks and Lily bites her lip.

"No, no. Thanks for the offer, though. I'm really just here to watch today." Unless she gets to see Mark again, then she might make use of one of those bedrooms and throw her legs over *his* shoulders.

"Speaking of, I hear Master Maya is going to take a turn on the swing, want to watch her?" Nick asks as a commotion starts up in the main room.

"Sure," Lily ends up saying, still stuck on the thought of getting Mark into one of those bedrooms and not really processing the full implications of watching until she is in front of the sex swing watching a woman get eaten out. So *that's* what the swing is for. Lily blushes and turns away, but everyone nearby is watching. Master Maya seems happy to let them watch. It would be more awkward to leave than stay, probably, and she's not *so* opposed to that. She turns back. Maya runs a hand through the man's hair and her other hand grips the straps that hold the swing up.

"Look at this little crowd that's gathered to watch us, pet." Maya cackles wickedly, tossing her head back before locking eyes with one of the others watching. "Of course you can't look, you're much too busy."

Lily swallows as the man moans out. A man drops to his knees in front of Maya. Is this hot? Lily hasn't decided yet, but her body has. A wave of arousal settles in her core. Unbidden, Mark pops into her mind. If he kneeled in front of her, would he be wearing that sly smirk or would he—

"Sometimes she gets three or four tributes." Nick whispers. "She only comes once in a while, so it's always a show whenever she's here." Lily can't imagine being so bold, but remove the crowd and change the man...

Lily stays the entire time. Maya gets tired of the one man and uses her foot to shove him away. The next man begs for a chance. "Master Maya," he drops to his knees. "Please let this worthless slave serve you. I promise to worship you as best as I can until you no longer have need of me."

Such desperation. Could she ever inspire that in someone?

"I never have need of slaves."

Lily liked to think she had enough confidence in her life. She'd never been too shy to tell lovers what she liked, or stand up for herself, but she never dared to imagine commanding that much respect, inspiring that much desire, or being daring enough to take lovers like toys. Something about what's happening strikes her as being perfect, but she doesn't know what that is. When it's over, Lily's not sure what to do with herself, but there is a bit of a buzz in the back of her mind.

"You'll have to come back one of these weekends. Will's agreed to set me on fire for my birthday." Nick says, once the crowd has dispersed. They make their way to the couches by the dance floor, where a few people are dancing. Mark is still nowhere to be found. She's missed her chance.

"I just may." Is that literal fire, or is this slang she hasn't heard yet?

"Take me home, darling." Tala startles Lily by hugging her from behind and kissing her cheek.

"Hi Tala," Lily greets, after realizing who it is. "Was it that good? You two seemed to hit it off."

Tala comes around the couch to sit across Lily's lap. "I'm in love," she sighs out and Lily laughs, wrapping an arm around Tala to prevent her from falling off. "Seriously, I thought we hit it off online but seeing her in person was so much better."

Lily sends an apologetic look towards Nick, but he looks amused at the interruption.

"Did you see her? You saw her. That cute little dress, her pretty face, and oh! her dark lipstick." Tala continues on her rant, kicking her legs up to take up the rest of the couch, "I love that she came with her natural hair today. I liked the box braids but her natural hair just frames her face so much better." Tala runs her fingers through her own pin straight hair and sighs longingly.

"Hi Tala," Nick grins, and Tala gives him a little wave.

"Hi Nick, having fun with Lily?"

"You know me, always hanging out with newbies. If you don't mind though, I'm going to go out for a smoke." Nick winks as he struts away, and Lily can't help but be impressed by how confident his strides are in his heels.

"So are you going to see her again?"

"She's taking me to the movies next Saturday. I'm thinking of surprising her with dinner afterwards, so we can spend some time talking to each other more."

"Did she already leave?" Lily looks around the main area, but doesn't see her.

"Yeah, I walked her to the door before coming to find you. Did you get to talk to Mark?"

"I missed him." Lily sags. Tala nuzzles into Lily's neck.

"That's just as well. It's probably better to meet him at a munch. You should come to the one this week, he'll be there."

"What's a munch?"

"It's like a meet and greet, but for kinky people."

"I do want to meet him," Lily hums as if she's debating going, but Tala yawns instead of teasing her. "Are you ready to go?"

"Can I sleepover?" Tala stands and stretches.

Lily stands. "Of course, I'd be disappointed if you didn't." Lily follows Tala into the hallway.

"Oh, are you leaving too?" An unfamiliar but incredibly smooth voice says from behind them in the hallway. Lily lets the smooth voice roll over her shoulders and debates looking back towards it. She would hate to turn and be disappointed to find an average man behind it. Tala turns with a flourish.

"Mark!"

"Mark?" Lily spins around to see him. He's dressed this time, in a tight red workout shirt and loose black shorts. "Hi." Her voice is breathy and high pitched.

"Hey," he smiles down at her as their eyes lock again.

It's a stupid thing to think, but the whole drive and night was worth it for the few seconds of eye contact they make. His eyes are dark brown, deep and rich, like she could fall and fall and never emerge. It fits perfectly on his handsome face. She looks lower. His smile is easy and wide and kissable. His jaw is sharp, but his skin is likely soft beneath his slight stubble. His shoulders are broad and muscular and the image of throwing her legs over his shoulders returns to her, unbidden. His shirt has no sleeves, so she's treated to miles of defined muscles and lines on his arms.

"Mark, this is Lily. Lily, this is Mark."

Lily exhales, meeting his eyes again as she smiles. Hopefully, she hasn't been caught staring.

"Lily." Mark repeats, extending a hand to shake hers. His hand is warm and calloused, and squeezes with just a slight amount of pressure. Lily beams up at him and the warmth lingers on her fingertips for a precious few seconds after he pulls back. Mark's smile shifts away from her to Tala, but returns for a quick glance.

"Are you heading out too, then?" Tala asks.

"Yeah, I've got a gig tomorrow afternoon, so I didn't want to stay too late today."

"A gig?" Lily asks.

"Yeah, Mark's a super sexy model." Tala nudges Lily and winks and Mark's face lights up in a beautiful light blush as he looks away.

"Thanks, Tala. I keep telling people, it's mostly editing."

"It's not." Lily blurts, and she straightens as he shifts his gaze back to her. "I just—I saw you in there," Lily broadly gestures down the hall, not sure if the dungeon is even in that direction. "You look great."

"Thanks, Lily." Mark glances behind them and frowns. "I'd love to catch up more, but I really do have to go. I'll see you around?"

"We'll be at the munch." Lily decides. He nods before hiking his backpack up and walking away from them. "So, when *is* the munch?"

Tala only laughs.

Chapter 3

"It's Mami." Tala groans as she tosses a pillow in Lily's direction.

Lily rolls towards the edge of the bed. "Already?" Her phone buzzes again and she blindly reaches for it. Lily groans as she catches the charging cord, and she pulls the phone closer as she sits up and answers the video call.

"Liliana," Carlos, her older brother, grins into the camera. "How are you doing?"

Lily yawns and shakes her head. "I just woke up."

"I can see that." He places the phone down and steps back to offer Lily a view of the living room behind him. "You've got drool all over your face."

"What?" Lily rubs at her face and narrows her eyes as Carlos laughs. "Ugh."

"Hey Carlos!" Tala leans over to squeeze into view. Lily tilts the phone so she can wave to him.

Mami pops into view, smiling. "Look at you, Liliana, you look so tired!"

"I'm okay, Mami. How are you doing?"

"I'm always better when you come over... when I have you and your brother here. This old house is too big for just me."

Papi died on a beautiful summer day, his favorite type of day. They played in the park and were talking about what to have for dinner. Lily wanted ice cream. He turned to her with a grin, but his face morphed into pain and he collapsed. Everything after that is a blur, but she remembered screaming that she had to see him and refusing to go to bed that night. Mami promised that they could go to the hospital and see him in the morning, but by the morning he was gone. Mami tried to pretend that it didn't matter, that she could support two children on her receptionist salary, and threw herself into debt to keep their schooling and Lily's skating. At one point, when Lily was old enough to realize the financial hole Mami kept digging herself into, she stopped asking for things. She got a part time job and tried to ease some of the burden.

"You could always sell it, Mami."

"Ah," she dismisses, "this is the family house, Liliana, it's for you and your brother when I go to Jesus. Then it goes to the grandchildren." Mami's eyes shift to Tala.

"So, Liliana, are you going to give me grandchildren?" Mami asks suddenly, startling Lily into sitting back against her headboard. She might've already if David had followed her plan instead of breaking up with her. As it is now, she doesn't think they are coming anytime soon.

"Hasn't Carlos given you enough?" Lily tries to laugh about it, but Mami shakes her head.

"Don't be stupid," Mami chides, not unkindly, "it's never enough." Lily sighs and Mami grabs the phone. The screen darkens as Mami's hand covers the camera. "What about that young man, um, what was his name?"

"David and I broke up like a year ago." Lily waves her hand to dismiss the thought. She was too busy trying to micromanage her own engagement that she missed the signs of him pulling away from her and deciding she wasn't worth it.

"No, no, not David, the new one."

"He didn't work out either."

Mami huffs and then the phone shows Mami and her sister in law, Megan, with her niece. Megan bounces Luisa on her lap and makes her wave to Lily.

"It's because you were always telling them what to do, mija."

"I know," Lily sighs, "Anyway, I kind of want a husband before I start having kids."

Her mom waves her hand around. "So who's the new one?"

"I don't have a new one!"

Tala cackles next to her. "His name is Mark, Mami."

Lily shoots Tala a look of betrayal, but Tala only grins in response. "We met him when we went out dancing yesterday."

Mami smiles, and Lily groans out. Mami is going to want all the details, then she's going to get her hopes up and it'll be all the worse when it doesn't work out. "Oh, tell me all about Mark, mija!"

"They're having dinner together on Wednesday," Tala continues, "so Lily should be able to tell you all about him next week."

"Good. Good." Mami grabs Luisa from Megan to set her on her lap. Behind Mami, Megan mouths the word 'sorry'. Mami must have been talking about grandchildren before the call. "You're not getting younger mija, when I was your age, I already had both you and Carlos."

Lily looks away. She'd probably be pregnant right now, if everything had gone according to plan. She wanted a house and kids and a dog and all of that but she had to do it right. She had to be sure. David wasn't as much of a planner. Lily had to be sure she could do it on her own too, in case anything ever happened. Maybe that's what drove him away.

"Aye Mami, let her be. Unless you don't love all my children." Carlos breaks her train of thought as takes the seat on the other side of Mami. "I can try to make more."

"No way, I'm done!" Megan interrupts. "Beyond done."

"Ay no, I just want to know," Mami laughs, "and when are you going to give me grandchildren, Talita?"

Tala laughs. "Right after Lily does."

"So done." Megan repeats.

***

After four meetings, six hours, and one yelling match, Lily doesn't bother to try and hide her sigh as she rubs her temples with her fingers in an attempt to mitigate the pounding. Her first major project is dead before leaving the ground. Four years of work will just be canceled like they never happened. Every meeting seems to come to the same conclusion. As they did on Monday. As they did on Tuesday. There has to be something in here, some way to account for this that she is missing, but she hasn't found anything yet. There's been no reward for the overtime effort she's put in this week.

"We aren't going to be able to fly," Jeff is quiet in a way that manages to silence everyone in the conference room. "There isn't another way to look at it."

"There has to be." Lily counters, again, "we can't just not fly. We had a successful static fire." She looks at the half a dozen engineers desperately. They look as disheartened as she is.

"We can't really model this, so we can't design it out." One insists.

"And we can't account for it without redesigning the controller." Jeff adds.

"Which blows cost and schedule out of proportion." Lily sighs.

Her team continues to talk in circles, and are only interrupted by the sound of her head hitting the table. They must all be looking at her, so she waves her hands before resting her elbows back on the table.

"I'm tired." She confesses, hidden by the curtain of her hair. "We can talk about this more tomorrow. I have to go talk to our customer."

"We'll figure this out, Lily, you just have to trust us." Jeff places his hand on her shoulder. Lily nods, but she's silent as she grabs her laptop and makes her way back to her cubicle. She makes a last minute detour to Tala.

"Maybe I shouldn't go today," Lily sighs.

"Leave work at work," Tala's response is immediate. She looks up at Lily and frowns. "That bad?"

"We're having daily meetings with the customer now, and they are not happy. Do you think they'll cancel the program?"

"This far into it? I doubt it." Tala hums. "Unless this results in you starting over, they're not going to look somewhere else. It wouldn't be cheaper, or faster, and there has to be a mostly salvageable product even with the one bad part. You'll be fine. You need to trust your team."

"You're right," Lily admits after a few seconds of silence. "Are you going?"

Thankfully, Tala accepts the change of subject. "Yeah. Just me though, Aleeyah can't make it."

"You can't ditch me like you did Friday."

"Okay, how was I supposed to say no to her?" Tala stands and makes a dramatic face. "Sorry, my Sapphic goddess, I have to go make sure my friend hasn't melted into a puddle of nerves. Besides, I saw you watching Maya. You weren't so bad off on your own."

"It was fun. I had more fun than I thought I would." Lily admits. Is this the caffeine and painkillers or is Tala the headache repellant?

"There you go, the munch is a lot less intense, and I would've started you there if I could do it over, but hey," she shrugs, "it's working out."

"Sure."

"I checked. Mark said he'd be at the munch. He RSVP'd online."

"Oh, I didn't RSVP. I should have asked."

"I did for us both. It's at Rosie's anyway, so there's usually enough space for extras." Tala stops talking as another engineer leans over her cube wall. Tala frowns apologetically, "I'll message you, okay?"

"Okay."

Her last meeting for the day is in another 30 minutes, and she has to figure out some way to make this situation more than hopeless. Instead, Lily's distracted. She looks Rosie's up on her phone. Will she get to talk to him more? Maybe they can get to know each other over drinks and spend some more time together, even if it's just for the night. She's not trying to date him.

Chapter 4

So far, the munch at Rosie's seems like a regular night at any restaurant. No leather or half-dressed people. No heavy rock playlist and red lights. She is just pointed to a back room that has a bunch of tables by a bar. There are about a dozen people sitting at the bar, and more are scattered around a few smaller tables, having conversation. This could be a birthday party. She shifts her weight and takes another look around, trying to spot a familiar face.

Is she in the wrong place?

Lily glances towards the entrance and debates leaving. Tala's message said she was already here, so she should see her if this is the right place. She scans the group again, but she doesn't see Tala anywhere. She pulls out her phone and re-reads her last message. Maybe she should just go home and spend some more brain power on work.

"Are you Lily?"

"Yes." Lily looks up from her phone.

There is a white middle aged man smiling down at her. He's in jeans and a polo and he offers his hand for a handshake to her. "I'm Derrick, welcome to your first munch."

Relief fills her, and Lily shakes his hand. "Thanks, I was sure I was in the wrong place."

"No, no, this is it. Tala said you'd be here, she asked me to introduce you to Mark." Busted. She's not mad about it, though. "So it's pretty casual, you may see some of the same people you saw at The Playhouse here, so feel free to say hello."

"Okay, yeah." Lily nods.

"Ronnie's going around to vet people, so you'll want to be sure to talk to her if you want to stop by next time without Tala."

"Vet people?"

"Yeah, don't worry about it. It's just a conversation to be sure you're someone we would trust in our space."

"Sure, I can do that." She pauses. "Um, have you seen Tala?" Lily follows Derrick as he guides her to a side booth. Her seat gives her a view of the entrance, and Lily tries not to stare at it.

"I asked her to run out and grab something from my car with Mark, but they'll be here in a second." Derrick huffs as he sits and Lily shifts her attention to the door, hoping to catch a glimpse of him. "He's always at the munches looking for new faces."

"Thanks. Derrick, right?" Lily double checks before she repeats it in realization. Tala mentioned him. "You're his," she fumbles around the word, "Dom?"

He nods. "Tala told me you saw Mark and I doing a scene when you first walked in. I was the one working him."

Lily shifts in her seat as she spots Mark by the entrance holding a cardboard box. He's wearing blue jeans and a tight black shirt that his biceps pop out of. It hides all of the finer details of his chest, but Lily remembers what's underneath. She can't pull her eyes away from him, even as she continues talking to Derrick.

"I liked watching," she confesses, "but I don't know how into this I really am." Lily just knows that she's into Mark, and would love to get Mark into her. He spots her and smiles and Lily gives him a little wave.

"Different people like different things." He shrugs. "My wife, Michelle, isn't a huge fan of impact play either." Derrick turns and waves Mark over. "I'm free to answer any questions you have. Tala told me you were new at this, but you are not alone. If there is anything that I can do for you, please let me know."

Mark arrives and silently puts the box on the table in between them. He steps back and puts his hands behind his back as he looks down. It puffs out his chest and pulls the shirt tight against his shoulders. "Anything." Derrick repeats as he reaches for the box.

"I will let you know if I can think of anything." Lily eyes Mark out of the corner of her eyes. Derrick smirks as he opens the box.

"Did you peek?" Derrick asks and Mark nods.

"Yes, sir. I had to make sure it's the right box." Mark's voice is soft in deference. She smiles even as Derrick shakes his head.

"You can only train them so well." He turns to Mark. "Naughty boy." Derrick chides.

"I'm sorry, sir." Mark drops to his knees and bows his head. Lily shakes her head and stammers out as her cheeks heat. She's not even trying to say anything, and shuts her mouth in embarrassment. Derrick places his hand on Mark's head before looking back to her.

"It's okay, but I will need to figure out how to keep you from ruining the surprise."

"Does he really have to *kneel*?" Lily can't take her eyes off of him. Somehow it's even better to look at him from this angle. Soft hair and an angular face, and close enough to touch. Derrick pulls his hand back. Instead of standing up, Mark lowers to sit on his heels, puts his hands on the floor in front of him, and then bends forward to place his head on his hands. The other people at the munch are staring. Derrick spots her blush and grins.

"He is a pretty boy, isn't he?"

"That's not…" Lily can't finish her thoughts because it's true. It sounds demeaning but it's true. He is so pretty. "It's—"

"Lily, this is Mark, Mark, this is Lily."

"Nice to meet you," Mark says to the ground. Lily can't say anything at all. She's saved from an awkward silence as Derrick continues talking.

"Today, you will service our new guest in whatever capacity she'd like."

"Yes, Sir. Whatever you need today, just tell me and I'll get it." Mark is eager and still *facing the ground.* "I'm at your service."

Lily swallows and shakes her head. Is normal behavior or a faux pas? She can't rip her eyes away from him long enough to tell what everyone else is doing. She continues to shake her head and clears her throat. "Get up." Her voice comes out soft. She clenches her hands together to resist the temptation to run her fingers through his black hair. She wants him but he isn't hers to take, despite what Derrick and Tala seem to have schemed up. He lifts his head from his hands first, looking up at her with a cheeky smile and a fire in his eyes, before he rises back to his knees. She rips her eyes away from him to look back to Derrick, who is grinning. "Get up." She repeats, stronger, not knowing how much longer she can resist.

"Would you like a glass of water?" Derrick offers.

Lily nods. "Yeah, I'll be—"

"I'll get it." Mark interrupts. "Ice?"

"No. Thank you." He walks away and she doesn't stare, but it's a close call.

"I will leave you both to it." Derrick stands, "but please, feel free to meet some other people. They are all involved in this one way or the other. And feel free to come to other events, Mark can bring you. It's good to be curious." He winks and turns away, taking the box with him. Tala leans against the table and grins.

"So," Tala teases. "How's it going?"

"Shut up!" Lily hisses.

"So demanding, it's only your first munch," Tala winks, "we may have a new baby domme on our hands here."

"Ay Dios mío." Lily hides her blushing face in her hands. "Did you see that?"

"I did." She's still smiling as she sits across from Lily. "Kneeling on the first date. Super kinky! It seems like you're getting along pretty well, maybe you'll get to see him naked again."

Lily blinks as a glass of water is placed in front of her. If Mark heard Tala's comment, he doesn't show it.

"I'm glad you seem less stressed out."

"Thank you." Lily turns to Mark and he bows his head.

"Can I get you anything else? Derrick said he'd put your first drink on his tab."

"Well that's sweet." Tala comments, "No one bought me a drink my first time."

"I'm a cosmo girl, and I'd hardly turn down a free drink."

"Tala?"

"Tequila sunrise."

"I'll be right back." He smiles, and only after he leaves does Lily frown.

"So now he's our waiter?" She groans. "I wanted to make a good impression. Giving him drink orders wasn't my idea of a good meeting."

"I mean, taking orders from you is probably his idea of a good time." Tala shrugs. Lily's idea of a good time has a lot less talking, unless he's talking to her while buried inside of her. It's a lot more active than having him kneel in front of her and Derrick.

"He's with Derrick." Coño! She's been fantasizing about a taken man.

"They're not exclusive. Derrick's been married for like 10 years. You could ask him out. You never know what could happen."

"I know I'm a catch, but he seems to want something a bit more..." Lily hesitates. She's only heard the one term… "Chocolate?"

"Chocolate?" Tala questions, before laughing. "You mean not vanilla?" She laughs again. "I'll remember this." Tala grabs Lily's water and drinks from it. "I'll remember this forever." She wheezes and Lily looks away. "When you get married, I'll mention this in my speech, I'll make it the dessert at your baby showers," Tala laces her hands together. Lily rolls her eyes but it's true. Lily is very much an outsider here. She doesn't really have plans to stay either. She's really here for Mark, all the other stuff is in the background. He looked nice kneeling, but she doesn't

33

want to put him there while she eats dinner with her friends. It's just weird.

"Who's Ronnie?" Lily tries to shift the conversation. "I'm supposed to talk to her to be vetted."

"Mm sure," Tala glances around the room. "I haven't seen her yet. By the way, I want you to know I was watching you at the party, not in a creepy way, but just to make sure no one did anything. I didn't want you to feel like a third wheel, but I also didn't want to leave you totally alone. Aleeyah thought that it might've come off wrong if you thought I didn't care enough to stay with you."

"Oh, yeah. That's good to know."

"Here's your drinks ladies." Mark places them down, acting the perfect part of a waiter. He gestures to Tala drinking Lily's water. "Lily, would you like another water?"

"No, no, it's fine. Really." She stresses. "I know Derrick said you had to, but you don't *have* to."

"It's my pleasure," he sounds so scripted that Lily raises her eyebrow. "Do you want to sit with us?"

"If you want me to," he chuckles.

"Do you want to?" Lily repeats, eyeing him warily. She'd love to spend more time with him, a lot more time with him if she's honest, but not because he's forced to.

"I'd like to, yeah." He sounds honest, so Lily slides down the booth so he can sit next to her. "I would've said no if I didn't want to get to know you a little better."

"Well don't let me get in the way of that," Tala stands up. "I'm going to make the rounds. Don't be too rough with each other." Tala eyes twinkle as she grabs her drink and exits.

Mark shifts spots, moving from next to her to across from her in Tala's spot. Lily mourns the opportunity for contact. She takes a slow sip of her drink and smiles into it, and Mark leans forward and rests his arms on the table.

"What brought you out to The Playhouse?" He's close enough to kiss now, if she just leaned over to him. She could just pull on his shirt and bring him closer. "I've never seen you before."

"Tala did," Lily leans forward. Her fingers tighten around the glass as his lips twitch. He looks her up and down and she licks her lips. "I'd had a pretty rough day at work and told Tala I'd be down to go anywhere."

"That's pretty cool. Tala's been on the scene for a while, so she can certainly help you with the swinging aspect of it all."

"I don't know what aspect of it all I'd like," Lily admits, "but it was fun to watch."

"You didn't stay to watch me," Mark teases, leaning back in his seat "and I put on such a good show."

"I wanted to." Lily sits back as well, and hopes she's not blushing. "Thorn was giving me a tour, by the time I got back to the room, you were gone."

"Next time," he shrugs, as if they weren't talking about her looking at his naked body with a dozen other strangers.

"Next time," she agrees, not sure if she's dreaming.

"So are you an engineer too?"

"Yeah, Tala and I work together." Lily details her job to Mark, unable to help but gush about how cool it is to work on electronics for the International Space Station. She's in the middle of detailing a launch party the firm had last year when Mark stops her.

"Wait," Mark shakes his head, "you're a rocket scientist. An actual rocket scientist." He whistles.

"Technically, a rocket engineer." Does he like smart girls? His whole face softens and his eyes light up as he takes her in. "Tala is too."

"Wow. That's—that's awesome."

"Thanks," Lily returns his smile. She gestures to him across the table. "Tala said you were a model."

"I am." Mark squares his shoulders, but then they fall as he takes it back. "Well I'm trying, but gigs don't come as often as I'd like. I'm a personal trainer down at Iron Bar Gym."

35

"I don't think I could go to a gym every day. They always stink." Lily shakes her head. Mark laughs before pretending to sniff himself. Lily waves her hands in front of her. "Not you! I mean, I'm sure you smell fine. Good even. I—" Lily clears her throat, stopping her ramble and putting her hands in her lap, but the grin on his face tells her he knows she's flustered. She can't smell him now, not over the smell of the food and alcohol, but she wants to reach over and take a sniff.

"I like knowing that my body is in tip top shape, that way I know I can always perform at my best."

His words sound innocent enough, but his voice lowers and she doesn't hear it so much as feel it. Lily reaches out for her drink so that she doesn't reach for him. She squirms in her seat, taking a deep breath before taking a sip that she can barely taste. She blinks, and the moment is gone. He's waving his arms around and continuing his point.

"It's one of the reasons I'm always trying new sports to test myself. Working in the gym is just perfect for me because I love helping people see improvements in their life." He gives her a few examples, and in the middle of talking about a woman he took from a midlife crisis to a powerlifter, her phone buzzes.

She doesn't check it, but she can only imagine its Tala telling her to ask for his number. She could ask for his business card, but what if he thinks she's only interested in him as a trainer? She can just wait until later to ask for his number. She takes another sip. He's not drinking. Does he drink? Maybe he's just not drinking today. Maybe he's only with her because of Derrick, so maybe he didn't get a drink because he's not here to have fun.

"I like ice skating."

"You'll have to teach me someday." He taps the table. "Then, in return, I can teach you how to rock climb."

Lily agrees. Somehow, she's managed to successfully get two dates while trying to figure out how to ask for his number. "I know Derrick said you had to serve me," Lily practically purrs, to her surprise, "but he didn't say all night. You are free to leave me if you want."

"Am I boring you?" Mark retorts, using that lowered seductive voice that makes Lily want to take him home and make him trace all of the goosebumps erupting on her skin with his tongue. Her heart races in her chest, and the absurd thought that he can hear it dances across her mind.

"I don't think you could," Lily flirts back, but now that she's thought about the fact that Derrick has engineered this conversation, she can't help but make sure he wants to be here too. "But I notice you didn't get a drink, and that you've been with me since I got here, so I wanted to offer you an out."

"And if I want an in?"

Lily's nipples harden against her bra. "Then you should ask for my number."

"Lily, my darling," he grabs her hand across the table. It's exaggerated, like he expects her to laugh at him even as he does it, and she would, if she weren't already blushing and out of words. He lifts it to his lips and gives her knuckles a gentle kiss. His kiss lingers too long for it to be polite. His breath is hot on her skin. Would it be that hot on her neck? He smiles as her lips part, and she stares at him, speechless. "Would you do me the honor of giving me your number?"

Lily clears her throat as he looks up from her hand to her face, and she licks her lips. "Oh, is that the best you can do?" Lily's still breathless. If his kiss on her hand could do this, what about when he finally kisses her lips… her neck…her stomach? How amazing would it feel for him to trail kisses down her stomach until he's at her lips and kissing her there?

"Do you want me to sink to my knees and beg you for it?" He asks, with an earnest and yet sinful smile, as if all he could ever want was to kneel in front of her and beg.

"And if I did?"

The fire in Mark's eyes causes her breath to catch. He would. The heat of his hand around hers begins to burn with implication, and Lily pulls her hand back while letting a breath out. "Not that I do."

Mark smirks, and leans back in his own chair as Lily fumbles for her phone to exchange numbers.

"Thank you. I'll be sure to treasure it."

"Be sure to use it." Lily says, firmer than she intends to. He licks his lips as they lock eyes again, and she flushes under his gaze but won't look away. She spends minutes and yet days in the tension between them.

"I can do that. Anything else I can do for you?"

He could go down on her, right here.

"There is." Lily leans back into her chair and crossing her arms. "I have to meet with Ronnie before she leaves so I can come to The Playhouse without Tala, do you know where she is?

Mark stands. "I'll go find her for you," He walks away, and Lily watches him go this time. His shirt pulls across his back, showing off his muscular shoulders almost as well as when he was wearing nothing. She thinks back to the beginning of their night, when he kneeled in front of her. She was embarrassed in the instant it happened, thinking it both extraordinary and ridiculous, but now that he's not here she's thinking about it more. She felt a rush as he went down. An odd mixture of excitement, curiosity, and arousal that was stifled by embarrassment, but now that the embarrassment has left she feels it again. She wants to see him kneel again and, surprisingly, she wants to be the one he is kneeling for. That way, he can look up at her, and she can run her hands through his hair.

He grabs the attention of another woman and talks to her for a moment. This whole night is mostly a result of Derrick telling him to *serve* her. Would he do this for her without Derrick telling him to, would he *serve* her because he wants to? It's such a provocative term, which only makes her want to use it more. Mark gestures in Lily's direction and Ronnie makes her way over to Lily.

"Ronnie?" Lily asks as she gets close enough.

Ronnie nods. "Mark sent me over. Welcome to the community, Lily."

"Thanks, I'm really enjoying it so far."

"Good, I'm glad. Usually we recommend a munch before a play party, but hey, either way works."

"I didn't plan on being at either, but things happen." Lily shrugs. Mark happened.

"I hear that. Derrick mentioned that I should come meet you, but I didn't want to interrupt your conversation."

"Thanks."

"So, can you tell me a little bit about yourself?" Ronnie sits across from her, and it turns out that vetting is as simple as a casual conversation.

When Ronnie finally says her goodbyes, Mark slides back into the seat. "Have you been vetted?"

"No, I'm a terrible person, you should stay very far away."

He smiles. "That's too bad, I was hoping to see more of you around."

"At the club?"

"In general, as friends." His eyes drop to her lips, she can't help but bite her lips, and there is no way either of them mean friends.

"Great. We can plan to go skating."

<u>Chapter 5</u>

"I just want to make sure I understand this correctly. We have a list of concerns and no solutions, and the best ideas we have to move forward haven't yielded results," the customer summarizes. Lily grimaces as she looks at the phone in the middle of the table. They've gotten results, just not good ones.

"Yes." Lily answers. "We've been updating the team daily with our thoughts."

None of which seem promising.

"We've been exploring options," Jeff goes through a couple of potential options Lily already knows won't work. Her eyes throb as she drags her pencil across her notepad. This isn't a problem she can stay up all night to solve, and it's starting to really bother her. She hates sitting in this meeting without the answers; that there isn't even a direction she knows to explore. Everything is in the hands of her team. As she texts one of her engineers about an idea, her personal phone lights up with a text from Mark.

Are you going to The Playhouse tomorrow?

He wants to see her again, and the thought makes her smile as her skin tingles at the thought of being around him again. The phone goes dark but the words stay in her head. She wants to see Mark again and it would be nice to explore The Playhouse without every single thing being new and overwhelming. Maybe she could end up cuddled against him on one of the couches, or she could kiss him goodnight on the cheek. Maybe it'll be more than a kiss, and she'll have to decide whose house they are going to head to.

Or it could be more overwhelming the second time around, and she'll make a bad impression. She rubs her forehead as Jeff and the customer continue talking, and Lily forces herself to focus so she can take note of their suggestions to give them to the team. It doesn't look good, and the conversation quickly shifts to the financial implications. Once that starts, Lily picks up her phone to reread Mark's message. Tala is going to be with her girlfriend this weekend, so Lily will have to go alone.

Tala isn't going, so I haven't decided. She responds. His reply is immediate.

I'll protect you ;)
I'll have to think about it.
Just let me know!

If Mark wants to go with her, then maybe she should go. It'll be good to spend more time with him, and who knows where that might lead. Maybe she'll even get to throw her legs over Mark's shoulders and really get to know him. Then again, maybe this is where she finds out he wants her to join Derrick and him, or that he's not looking for anything outside his relationship. Derrick has a wife though, so surely?

Lily listens to the end of the financial conversation with scattered thoughts. and the other engineers in the meeting type away on their laptops. She's not sure what to say, to Mark or her team. The only way forward is to get more information. She could use a break. She messages Mark before she can chicken out.

I'm in.

Sure, Tala won't be there, but she kind of knows Mark, and she can always leave if it becomes too much. Something about the club and the people there has her feeling bolder than normal. Mark has her feeling bolder than normal. He's flirty and fun and unafraid to kiss her hand in public or look at her as if she's the only girl in the room. The bold flirtations will never last past the first time they sleep together, but she can enjoy it while it lasts. If Mark ends up ditching her she can hopefully find some of the people she spoke to the first time.

Awesome! I'll meet you there at 11

***

Lily arrives ten minutes early, making sure to give herself a few minutes to check her hair and lipstick before he arrives. She leans against the back of her car and waits. A few cars come into the lot and park, and people make their way into The Playhouse. Eventually, she sees Mark step out of an old sedan, and she makes her way over to him with a flutter in her heart. He's dressed in jeans and a tight-fitting T shirt. He's stunningly handsome, but casual, like her jeans and low-cut crop top.

"Thanks for coming out," he says as she catches up to him. He turns to her with open arms, and Lily steps into them without a thought. His strong arms wrap around her in a warm hug, and her whole body relaxes into it. She hugs him back and listens to the steady thumping of his heart. She inhales, and he smells like fresh laundry detergent and a hint of cologne. Her fingers trail along his muscular back and she has to say something before he pulls back.

"You can't leave me alone, okay?" Lily barely refrains from nuzzling into his chest. It rumbles with soft laughter that barely makes its way to her ears.

"I promise; I'll be with you all night." His hand is hot against her skin as he rubs it against her back. "No need to be nervous."

"That's what Tala said." Lily mock pouts. "Then she left me to go hang out with her girlfriend."

"I guess we can stay out here and hug for a few hours instead," he teases, "but you might get cold in that cute little shirt of yours."

"We can't have that now, can we?" Lily pulls back from the hug and a shiver crawls up her spine as his hand falls lower on her back before releasing her.

"You've been here before, you know the place is pretty chill, no one's going to do anything you don't want them to." Mark opens the door.

Thorn is sitting at the table, typing on his phone, when they walk in. He doesn't look up at them.

"No pool?" Mark walks forward, taking the tablet to sign in.

"Will's in the Dungeon." He explains, not looking up from the phone. Mark shrugs and then hands the tablet over to Lily. She types in her info and, with the warmth of Mark's hug lingering on her skin, impulsively clicks on the button to sign up for a membership. She'll probably be here often, if things work out. That, or she can come with Tala. She pays him for the membership and then Thorn digs around for a card for her.

"Ready to go?" Mark offers her his arm. He could mean it as a joke, but she already wants to touch him again. She wraps her hand around his bicep, giving it a slight squeeze, and he gestures down the hall.

"What a gentleman." Lily can't help but tease. He doesn't take his arm back, and so she leans into him a little as they head into the main hall. They only make it a few steps down the hallway before a middle-aged woman stops in front of them. Mark introduces them, but the woman doesn't even glance at Lily.

"I didn't know you were coming today," she purrs to Mark, stepping closer into Mark's space. "I'm happy to see you."

"It's nice to see you too," he inclines his head politely.

"You playing?" The other says, a hint of a flirt on her tone as she steps closer. Lily tightens her fingers a little, hoping he's not going to ditch her so soon, and Mark takes in breath and smiles before shaking his head.

"No, I'm just an escort tonight, maybe next time." He winks and the other girl leans in, and then leaves her lipstick smudged on his cheek as she kisses him. Lily wants to wipe it off, but she refrains. She also wants to reach up and leave her lipstick smudged on his cheek, or his neck, like a warning sign, but she can't do that either.

What's wrong with her? She barely knows Mark and she's already feeling possessive of someone who's not hers. Instead of saying anything, she gently squeezes her fingers around his bicep, feeling the solid muscle of his arms. He straightens next to her and says goodbye, something Lily doesn't bother to do, and then turns to lead the way to the back rooms.

He leads her into the dungeon, which is empty. It must only be full on those monthly kink nights. The back wall is full of different tools of many different colors. There is lots of leather, some feathers, and some bottles that probably have lube. The side walls have some other tables and chairs and what looks like the table at a gynecologist's office. The wooden X is larger up close, and she sees that there are holes, cuffs, and a bar on top of it.

"Tala's more of a swinger than a kinkster, so there's probably some more questions you have. Ask away."

"You were right here last time," Lily reaches up to touch the wooden X, "tied up." *And naked,* but she doesn't say that part. How many times has Mark been tied up here for everyone to look at? Will she get to see him naked again? "What is it?"

"It's a Saint Andrew's cross," he runs his fingers over the wood slowly. A small smile stretches across his face and Lily drops her hand from his arm. She already misses the contact. If she reaches her hand up, she could slip it between his and the wood, and they'd be holding hands. Would he pull away, or would he close his hand around hers, duck his head into the junction between her shoulder and her neck and run his sharp jaw down until his lips press against her—

"It's basically used in the way you saw us use it last time. Bondage. Impact." Mark's voice drops into a husky tone that only fuels the image in her mind. If she took one step, he could dip his head and send his husky growl down her shoulder. Lily pulls back and turns away from him. Could he see her blush in the dim light? Lily gestures to the back wall. "So what are these?"

"These are actually for sale." He steps closer to her. The heat of his body is there for a breath before he walks to the back wall. Lily doesn't say anything, she can't, not without sounding like a breathless mess. "These are mostly impact toys. They're for pain play."

"You like pain?" How could anyone like pain? The instruments on the wall all looked vastly different, and only some of them looked like they were for pain.

"Love it. Pain is the best way to take pleasure."

"I'll take your word for it." Lily grabs a whip and lets it unravel. She wants to try it out, but she'll probably hurt herself and she doesn't like pain. Does it crack like it does in the movies? She curls her fingers around the leather handle and flicks it gently, but it doesn't move much. She really wants to crack it. Is there someone here that can teach her?

"Whips aren't really for beginners," he warns, holding his hands up and out like she's about to hurt herself in a bad way. Lily reluctantly coils it back up.

"Which ones are?"

"Probably floggers, paddles, and just your bare hands." He gestures to them as Lily reaches up to put the whip back. "If you are interested in this, you'll certainly want to find a Dom to help you with it." He comments as she continues to look at the wall, she spots a flogger and runs her fingers over the handle. She likes the leather handle of this one too. "There are quite a few who would put you on the cross if you asked, and I'm sure Derrick wouldn't mind giving you a soft introduction to impact play."

"Oh no," Lily lets her fingers slide through the cool leather strips of the flogger. They are smooth against her skin, and the contrast draws her eyes to the leather. She wants one, even though she has no use for it. "I'm not interested in anyone hitting me."

"Oh," Mark says, softly, as his eyebrows lift.

"Tell me more."

"There are different levels of pain." Mark leans against the wall. "Some of these have more of a thudding sensation to them." He picks up a leather paddle and hands it to Lily. She turns it over in her hands and runs her fingers over the material. It's awkward in her hands. "It's one of the easier ones to use. Although depending on what it's made out of it can hurt a lot."

"What about this one?" Lily picks up a riding crop. She likes it in her hands, light yet durable, and it reminds her of equestrians. It's a bright red color that matches her favorite nail polish.

"Crops are fun," the corner of Mark's mouth lifts, "it depends on how you use it, but they can be gentle taps or really sharp pain. The rod part feels like a cane, but not nearly as bad."

She probably can't hurt herself with this one, so she swings it in the air in front of her. It's even better than the flogger. Her lips twitch as she swings it again in the air. "Which one is your favorite?" She runs her fingers along the crop and settles them at the rounded tip.

"I like just about all of them." He shifts to face the wall with a half shrug. She doesn't really want to put the crop down, but she does once she spots what looks like a flogger made of chains. It's too high for her to reach, so she points to it.

"What about that one?"

"That is only a tool you'd use if you hated me." He shakes his head. "Don't even look at it anymore!" He leaps forward to cover her eyes and she reaches up to pull his hand down.

"Let me see!" She laughs.

"I'm afraid that's a hard limit."

"A what?"

He wraps his other arm around her back to lift her off the ground—which is way sexier than it should be. "Put me down!" Her giggle betrays the sternness of her tone, but she's hoping he doesn't. His skin is fire against her own, especially where his shirt has risen up against her back.

"I'm afraid that's a hard limit as well." He hikes Lily higher up and she cannot say anything at all. He's all hard muscle and hot skin and this is not something she's going to fight. "Oh, would you look at that. It's time to leave the dungeon." He chuckles. Lily squeals as he carries her out of the room and Mark removes his hand from her eyes to wrap it around her waist.

Ronnie is standing outside the door. "So this is the dungeon." She must be giving the couple with her a tour.

"Hi Ronnie." Lily laughs at the absurdity. She hasn't had this much fun in too long.

"Hello," Ronnie grins. The other woman with Ronnie is wearing nothing but a thick leather choker, despite the man being fully dressed. "As I was saying," Ronnie continues as she leads them into the dungeon.

Lily shifts her gaze to Mark's face, which is closer than she expected it to be. If she leans forward, she could scratch her breasts on the stubble of his face. He glances up at her and his brown eyes seem so bright even in this dim lighting. Would he taste sweet? Does he kiss softly or harshly?

"That's a collar." He lowers her to the ground slowly, and she wants to tell him to pick her back up. He doesn't back away and she doesn't care about collars now, she just wants to fist her hand in his shirt and pull him down to kiss her. "It signifies their commitment to each other."

"As a dom and a sub?" She stays in his space and looks up at him.

"Yes," He's still looking at it, almost longingly. She glances at the collar before looking back at him.

"Isn't Derrick your dom? Aren't you a sub?"

Tala had called him Derrick's sub. Derrick had claimed him at the munch. She watched him kneel.

"I am." He looks down at her and seems to be searching for the right thing to say next, so Lily takes the initiative to point out the obvious.

"You don't have a collar."

"No, I don't." He gazes at the collar that prompted the initial question, frowning. "At least not yet." Disappointment coats his words, and Lily frowns as well. Should Derrick have done that for him? His shoulders slump and he keeps his gaze on the couple. She doesn't bring it back up until he does.

"Hopefully I'll get one soon. Derrick and I talked about it."

"Why do you want one?"

"When you have a collar, you belong to someone. It's a lot more serious than just playing around."

"How serious?" Is she stepping on an established relationship? Tala implied it was open, and they've been flirting, but if Mark is taken then she has to step back. "Is it like a marriage?" He shakes his head. Relief washes over her.

"Not that serious." He brings up his other hand to lightly brush against his neck. "It must be nice though, to belong that way."

"Do you think he will?"

He shrugs. "I've been the perfect sub, and he hasn't yet." Mark shakes his head as he turns back to her. "It's okay though. I don't need one." He may say that, but it's clear he wants one. Does he feel the need to be perfect in general, or just as a sub? She doesn't know him nearly well enough to ask, but she wants to. The perfect sub, the perfect gentleman, the perfect waiter. How much of it is real?

He leads her out of the dungeon into the main room. Nick waves to her from one of the couches and then taps the space next to him to beckon them forward. Mark gestures to the couch and they walk over. Nick immediately launches into gossip as they sit with him. Mark laughs but doesn't comment, so Lily doesn't either. Nick doesn't mind and is happy to continue talking. True to his word, Mark stays by her side as they snack and Lily guides the conversation to more general topics.

"We should get up on the cross and do a scene," Derrick says from behind her, "or I can hang you from the ceiling. It's a good crowd today." They both turn to see Derrick standing behind the couch. "They'd love to see you." He says to Mark. "Do you want to?"

Mark smiles but shakes his head. "It's tempting, but I promised Lily that I would stay with her today, and I don't want to go back on that."

"Well, if I go with you, you'd still be with me, right?"

Derrick smiles.

"I guess so." Mark turns to her. "You'd see a lot of stuff, and it's not exactly a slow introduction to the scene. It's up to you."

"I imagine I'll see it one way or the other." The thought of seeing him against that cross again is something she doesn't want to pass up. Already, her heart quickens at the mental image of last time. "As long as no one does anything to me, I'm good."

"You heard the lady," Derrick puts his hand on Mark's shoulder, and Mark nods. "I'll go talk to a DM so we can use the room. I'll meet you there."

"Yes, sir," Mark lowers his head to gaze at his chest. Derrick nods again, and Lily must have missed some part of the conversation they'd had. Derrick heads down into the hallway and Lily turns back to Nick. Mark stands and stretches his arms above his head, revealing a sliver of skin above his shorts at her eye line. There's no hair that she can see, not even as she follows the indent of his V cut down where it disappears in his shorts. "Are you coming, Nick?"

"Oh, yes," Nick stands with a flourish. "I love watching boys get beat up."

Mark laughs and Lily stands as well. "Wait." Lily takes a clean tissue out from her pocket to finally wipe that lipstick off of his cheek. Mark doesn't say anything, but he turns his cheek to give her access to the smudge. He smiles down at her when she pulls back.

"Better?" He flirts and turns his head so she can get a good look at it.

"Much better." She crushes the tissue in her hand.

Mark offers his arm to her again, she takes it silently, and he leads her into the dungeon. He reaches up to tug on the leather cuffs in front of the St. Andrew's cross. A few moments later, Derrick enters the room with one of the DMs. Lily takes a step back as the three of them talk. Derrick points to the ceiling and Mark nods. The DM takes a step back and Derrick tells Mark to strip.

This time, she gets to see the preamble to the image that fuels her fantasies. She sits by the wall and her eyes are glued to him as he takes off his clothes, revealing his beautifully sculpted body. He's not bulky, but he is muscular, and the shadows on his chest show off each ab muscle he has. It makes sense, now that she thinks about it, that he's a personal trainer. Who else has the time to work out as much as it must take to maintain that shape? He cracks his neck while talking to Derrick, and she can't believe someone would be so confident, so unashamed, to stand in the center of a room stark naked on display. It's inspiring actually. Derrick lays out tools on the table and she recognizes a riding crop and a flogger, and winces as he pulls out a chain.

The DM, Will, goes over the rules briefly, reminding them about a few policies and making sure they are using safewords. People file into the room, having quiet conversations with each other that add up to a hum of background noise. The room fills until its standing room only, but Mark looks excited instead of nervous.

"No penetration, but I do plan to let him come at the end of the scene." Derrick unpacks his bag and Lily's mouth waters at the thought of seeing Mark in such a state.

"That's fine, Derrick." Will waves his arm around, like it's nothing new to him, and makes his way over to a seat on the side to watch.

Mark turns to her and winks at her playfully before he's blindfolded. That's twice now. Almost like a switch, the blindfold causes the nearby conversations to quiet, so that the only sound in the room is Derrick's voice. Now she can stare at him all she wants without him knowing. They forgo the cross this time, sliding leather cuffs over his wrists and ankles. The wrist cuffs are attached to hooks hanging above him, and stretch his body as his hands are pulled high. It's somehow even better this way, as she gets to see everything about him without any barriers.

Derrick picks up a riding crop, sliding the flat leather down Mark's chest and to his thighs. He slides them back up until he gets to Mark's face. Mark is already breathing heavily, and his hands twist in the restraints to hold onto the strap coming down from the ceiling.

"Where are we?" Derrick's voice is demanding, even when he's speaking softly. "How are you feeling?"

"Green."

Derrick hums, moving the crop all over his body. Mark squirms into it as his cock hardens, and then finally he seems to give in. He rises onto his toes to lean into it, whimpering. "Please."

Derrick snaps his wrist, bringing the crop down onto his skin. A light smacking sound fills the air.

"Thank you."

"Good boy." Derrick praises, and Lily leans forward in her seat to watch the pattern continue. Teasing and then hitting. Mark starts panting and Lily finds herself out of breath as well. Her skin prickles at the rise and fall of Mark's chest. Goosebumps erupt over her skin and desire pools in her core. Derrick moves to the other side, sliding the crop over his backside, giving light taps to the bottom of his ass cheeks. Mark whines and bucks against the cuffs.

"Where are we?" Derrick asks again and Mark moans. Lily stiffens in her seat as the sound travels straight to her core. He could be making those sounds for her. "Warmed up?"

"Yes, yes, green. I'm ready." Mark pants. Lily glances at the table. Is the flogger next? Instead, Derrick draws back and smacks his hand against Mark's ass cheek. Lily flinches, Mark cries out in pain, but Derrick doesn't stop. He slaps him again, and again. Mark jerks against his restraints and Derrick stops, just runs his fingers lightly over the red skin. This is what he likes?

"Green." Mark says, unprompted, and Derrick brushes the hair on Mark's face back.

"I know. I know. It hurts so good, doesn't it?"

"Yes, sir."

Lily sits back in her seat with wide eyes and a gaping mouth.

"Are you ready for more?"

"Yes, Sir. Please, Sir."

Lily flinches again at the sound the leather makes as it strikes his ass and looks around to gauge if this is normal. It must be, as no one rushes in to stop it. If anything, they look excited to watch. Two people start making out in the corner. It continues. Derrick whips him with the crop over and over until bruises and angry welts start to form. Lily squirms in her seat, arousal fading to anxiousness. Is it enough now? Mark cries and moans and doesn't say anything but more and please and green. Lily folds her hands in her lap. Derrick switches to a paddle, then his hand, then back again. The marks begin to litter his body, until he is a panting mess and Derrick puts all of his tools down.

"You're doing so well," Derrick praises. "How are you feeling?"

"Yellow," Mark grunts. "I need a minute."

"Okay," Derrick places his hand on Mark's colorful chest, and murmurs something Lily can't hear. Mark nods, and Derrick softly holds the back of his neck, leaning forward so that Mark's head rests on his chest. Lily swallows, chews on her lip, and bounces her leg.

"Green," Mark rolls his shoulders. Derrick steps back and uses the riding crop to lift Mark's now soft cock.

"You couldn't stay hard for me," Derrick sounds disappointed, and Mark rushes to apologize. Derrick lowers the crop and Mark continues apologizing. Derrick shushes Mark before murmuring again, and then he gestures to Will.

Turning back to Mark, he lifts the crop to his cock again. "Do you know what happens now?"

"No, Sir."

"Now I let everyone touch you, anywhere they want except here." Derrick lowers the crop again. Mark whimpers. Derrick places it on the table. "If you can get hard and pretty for me, then maybe I'll let you come."

"Yes, sir, please sir."

"Go ahead Michi," Derrick says to a woman in the corner, and she nods as she steps forward and rakes her nails across a welt on his side. Mark whimpers. Derrick gives others permission to touch Mark as well. People touch him almost everywhere, but no one kisses him. Those lips deserve to be kissed, but maybe it is against the rules. She doesn't remember that part of the talk earlier, but maybe she zoned it out. Then again, maybe it's good that they aren't kissing him, and she can have the honor.

"Do you want to touch him?" Derrick approaches Lily. Michi joins him; smiling like she's got a secret.

"I do," Lily admits. Touching doesn't even scratch the surface of what she wants. Mark shudders against a rougher grab on his ass and his cock hardens again as it bobs in front of him.

"I know he likes you, why don't you finish him off?" Derrick whispers as he intertwines his fingers with Michi's.

"What?" Lily's pretty sure she knows what he means, but she has to be sure. He doesn't answer and Lily turns her gaze from Mark to Derrick. "Is that okay?" She wants to watch him fall apart under her touch, but she barely knows him. "He's blindfolded; he wouldn't know it's me." They've been flirting, but it hasn't gone further than that.

"That's kind of the point." Derrick grins. Lily takes a breath as she looks around the room. This is a place with a different set of rules and different idea about what normal is. She lets herself absorb the energy of the room and shift into a world in which this is normal. It's exciting.

"Okay," Lily nods. It's not her ideal first time with him, but if it's now or never, she'll do it now. "I'll do it."

She inches towards him, hands shaking, and the people touching him pull away. He whimpers at the loss of sensation. She circles him slowly, letting her fingers trace over some of the more noticeable welts, marks, and forming bruises. They look painful, but Mark makes soft mewling sounds as she touches them. Lily traces the puckered skin next to a small cut on his hip, and tries not to smile too widely at the sounds he makes in response. It might as well just be them, as everyone else fades to the background. Finally, in front of him, she takes him into her hand, and he's hard and throbbing in her grip. She's imagined languid make out sessions on the couch with him, but she smiles as she tightens her grip around his cock.

The groan Mark makes is broken, and echoes in her body. She gives his cock a few slow teasing strokes; her nipples harden as arousal settling in her stomach. "Yes, please, thank you," he murmurs and she continues, growing bolder with each stroke. She loses herself in watching him, and doesn't think about the fact that she is jerking him off in front of a dozen people; that people are getting off on watching this. She wants to drop to her knees and take him into her mouth, but before she decides to go down he trembles in her hands.

"Please," he begs, "please can I come?" His whimper makes her bold and brave and confident. No one's asked her to come before.

"No." She answers, testing the waters, and he whimpers again. It's a beautiful sound. Such a big strong man and it is her touch that makes him whimper. All of those people giving him attention before couldn't get him to make that broken sound, but she can. It's her permission that separates him from release. She's never been this in control of anything before. "Lily?" Mark whispers huskily. She freezes. Her confidence vanishes with her anonymity gone. What is she doing? She lets go of him.

"Lily, please." He begs and it's like lightning. He knows and wants her. He knows and wants more. She can do this. This is normal. He's hers for the taking. She moves her hand into his hair, which is soft and silky, and pulls his mouth to hers as her other hand starts stroking him again. He moans out wantonly and jerks towards her. For all the playing she's seen, no one's kissed him in front of her before and it's a shame, given how desperate he is for it.

The kiss is incredible. She licks his lips with her tongue, and he parts his soft sweet mouth for her instantly. He surrenders to her tongue and this borrowed power is fire in her veins. His breath hitches in her mouth and she inhales him. He tastes like lust and fire and his cock pulses in her hands. He moans. Her name? It's hard to tell with her tongue in his mouth, but he knows it's her. She strokes his cock as she bites his lip and pulls. She tightens her hand in his hair before she pulls away, lips tingling, so he can't follow her. His mouth stays open and she is tempted to remove the blindfold. Would the look in his eyes showcase his desperation? He trembles.

"Come." Just this once, she can order him. His face softens at the command and his body clenches against their restraints.

"Thank you," he mumbles. He calls out to God, calls out to her, and then spills out all over her hand.

Like a balloon popping, everything returns to her at once. The cooling cum on her hands, all the people watching her look at it, and the fact that she just jerked off a relative stranger in front of a dozen other strangers.

Before she can panic about it, Will approaches her, putting a hand on her shoulder and leading her away to a sink.

What was she thinking? Her heart pounds in her ears as she follows Will. She's had one night stands with strangers, but this is levels beyond that. She hadn't even taken any of her clothes off, but she's never felt more exposed. Thank goodness Tala wasn't here to watch that. Oh, God, what is Tala going to say? Probably congratulations. Lily's face flushes with heat and she glances back at Mark. Derrick releases him from his restraints and reaches for his blindfold. Lily turns away. She's not ready to look into Mark's eyes and confront what she did.

The sound of running water causes her to blink. The cool water over her hands does nothing to stop the warmth spreading all over her body. She is in way over her head. She can pretend that it was spur of the moment, that this isn't who she is, but the truth is that it was incredibly hot, and she wants to do it again. She wants to do it to Mark again, and she wants him to know it was her the whole time.

"My beautiful boy," Derrick coos behind her as she lathers her hands with soap. "That was amazing."

Lily dries her hands with a paper towel and Mark hums as Derrick runs his hands through his hair. They are paying attention to only each other, and Lily is thankful even as she is jealous. She wants Mark's attention, but she's not ready for it. She's not ready for any attention at the moment. Lily glances around the room, but people are clearing out of the dungeon, and no one is looking at her. Despite putting on a show, she fades into obscurity at the end. Slowly, she nods and lets out a sigh. She's okay.

"I did good?" Mark asks.

"Yes, so good. My good boy. Beautiful." Derrick supports Mark's weight as he stumbles forward. Derrick then guides Mark to a medical gurney on the side and gets him to sit down. She should help. She should make sure Mark is okay with what she did to him. Lily takes a step forward to join them but stops at the hand on her shoulder. Will points to

Michi, who waves her over. Lily glances back at the two men, but her borrowed moment of intimacy is over, and Will walks her over to Michi.

"He's going to aftercare, it's usually private." Will explains and Lily nods, even though Lily's not sure what that is. She can ask later. Lily sits next to Michi. Derrick cleans and addresses a few small cuts. Then he makes Mark drink water and leads him out of the room. She forces herself to stay and not to follow.

"You can hang out with me for a bit. Aftercare happens in private, but he'll be out soon." Michi tilts her head, gesturing out of the room.

"What's aftercare?" Lily follows Michi out into the main hall with couches.

Michi takes a seat and taps on the one next to her. "After a scene like that, feelings can get kind of intense, so aftercare is a way to bring that intensity back down."

Lily sits. She can't imagine willingly spending a minute more with someone who hit her like that. "So, Derrick will do some of the things that will comfort Mark in order to return to normal. Different people like different things, and so what you need for aftercare is part of your initial negotiation with someone."

Negotiation? Lily narrows her eyes but Michi keeps talking. "Derrick is helping Mark, and then afterwards, I'll take Derrick to another room and make sure he's okay. There can be a lot of guilt when playing like that, especially since I don't like playing like that, so a top drop is something to watch out for too."

"Wait. You're Michelle. Derrick's wife." Michi nods and crosses her legs.

"Call me Michi,"

"I'm Lily," Lily offers her hand and Michi shakes it.

"I know; I've heard a little bit about you. It's nice to officially meet you. How are you enjoying The Playhouse?"

"It's certainly interesting," Lily starts. She spots a few people in leather, some with collars, and one man wearing nothing at all. "I think I like watching more than anything else at this point."

"Good, I'm glad. Well, let me know if you have any questions about this. Derrick said you were new."

"That I am." Lily agrees. "So, what do you do outside of all of this?"

"I teach kindergarteners."

"Oh, that's pretty cool. I think I would just be tired if I had to do that all day. My brother has three children and I'm ready for a nap after a few hours with them."

"I wish I had nap time too," Michi laughs, "Do you want children?"

"I want a bunch of children too, but not for some time." Lily smiles as memories of her nieces and nephew come to mind. "Especially given how busy my brother's life is now."

"I hear you! My mom had four children, bless her heart!"

"Do you have any?" Lily asks and a wistful look comes over Michi's face.

"Not yet. We're trying." She crosses her fingers. "I can't wait to be a mom."

Mark comes out of the aftercare room in a sweatshirt and blanket, still talking to Derrick. When Mark spots her, she waves him over and he shuffles over to the couch. Next to her, Michi stands and stretches. She tells Mark he can have her seat as she walks over to Derrick and takes his hand. Mark collapses into the seat next to her, and Lily waves to Michi before turning to Mark. He yawns.

"How are you feeling?"

Mark snuggles into the blanket. Lily understands why Tala thought cutie and not hunk when she described him if this is what Tala always saw of him. After all that intensity he comes down to this softness. "Warm."

"You are under multiple layers of fluff." Lily takes the opportunity to move some of the blanket to further encase him and maybe just sit a little closer. "Does it hurt?"

"Not as much anymore, it's just warm." He looks sedated, and so cute, and she really wants to kiss him again. "There's a little throbbing."

Lily nods, and there's a moment of silence as he sighs and settles further into the couch. "How long have you and Derrick been together?"

He turns to her. "A little over two years, we met through his wife."
"Are you dating?"
"No, just playing."
"It's just, and I don't want to come off as being judgmental, but he's a lot older than you," Lily shifts to face him, "and he's married."
"Well, he's not my dream guy," Mark shrugs, "but he's a great Dom." He stretches across the couch, "and I already know I can't be in a relationship without the kink, so this is what I'm doing right now."
"What do you mean without the kink?" She's asking a lot of questions, but no one's told her to shut up yet.
"I mean I've done the vanilla thing, and it's great for a while, but I'm just not satisfied without the kink. I feel a need to submit, to serve, and I can't be with someone who won't let me." Like her, because she couldn't imagine hurting him the way Derrick did, even if it results in this happy, sated man. "That's why I want the collar. It feels like more of a commitment than just meeting up to have fun."
So he's looking for commitment from Derrick, which means she's just fun on the side if anything. She can be okay with that. Mark continues to talk, but Lily interrupts him. "Is it weird for you that I jerked you off?" Lily has to ask, because it's weird for her that they aren't talking about it. Did she go too far? Derrick said she could but Mark didn't. No one said she could kiss him.
"No." He yawns, adorable and cat-like in his sudden need to lounge, "I'm pretty happy it was you, but it's pretty casual for me." He waits a second, and when she doesn't respond, he straightens in his seat. "Was it weird for you?"
"I didn't ask you." Lily explains. "I know Derrick said I could, but I didn't ask you."
"Is that all?" He laughs, but it's soft, and it's not making fun of her. "You have my permission to do it whenever you want." Mark shifts. "Derrick has permission to let anyone do it to me as well." He leans back again. "Sometimes part of the fun is not knowing who's touching me."

"I want you to know." Lily's unsure of where her boldness is coming from, unsure how long it will stay. "When it's me, I want you to know." Her hands clam up. Has she taken this a step too far in claiming him? He looks up at her with wide eyes but Lily doesn't back down. He swallows and nods.

"So tell me."

Ally Marr

Chapter 6

"He's in a relationship, Mami." Lily pouts as soon as Mami's face pops up on the screen. In this moment, she wishes she was back home, so she could lay down on the couch and put her head in Mami's lap. Instead she pops a bagel in the toaster and leans over the counter in the kitchen.

"That's too bad. You sound like you like him."

"I do," Lily whines. She tells her mom just a little bit about the conversation at the munch, but omits everything that happened last night. "I don't want to try and take him away from his partner, because that's terrible to them. Also, it's not a great way to start a relationship. He's amazing. He's caring and sweet and not afraid to show his feelings."

"Well, if it is meant to be, it will happen mija. I'm glad you went to dinner, even if it was only to meet his girlfriend." Lily doesn't correct her, "and if she won't commit to him, he may eventually leave on his own."

"Right, I don't want to stick around and hope for that, though."

"Of course not."

"It was a nice dinner." Lily admits. The toaster splits out her bagel and she slathers it with some room temperature butter.

"Good. I'm proud of you. I was worried after David."

"Mami…" Lily groans.

"What? I have a right to be worried. You date the man for five years, start planning children, and then poof! He's gone. When you called me in

60

tears I was expecting the ring! After that I was worried you'd swear off men forever. You and Talita—"

"Mami!"

"I am joking; pero I am proud of you for getting out there. There is a man out there for you, I know this. Oh! Say hi to your brother."

"So he's already dating someone else?" Carlos asks and Lily waves her butter knife back and forth.

"He didn't hide it, so I guess Tala didn't know."

"That sucks," Megan frowns, "at least you know now, and not after you started to really like him."

"True," Lily tilts her head, "but I was already starting to like him. I know I'm not the type to break up a couple, so nothing's going to happen." Nothing serious at least, but she won't talk about one night stands in front of them. "Maybe we'll be friends." She takes an angry bite as Mami sighs.

***

"I was at the customer meeting this morning, and they are considering canceling the program." Silence answers the project manager.

Jeff slams his hand on the table. "Are they out of their minds?" Jeff swings his gaze to the others in the room. "We are at the finish line right now, what could possibly be worse than pulling the plug?"

Lily looks past him to stare at the whiteboard behind his head. Dread churns in her stomach as nausea settles in. The project is done. Her project is done. "They're questioning the worth of continuing."

"This is nuts. It's going to take us what, a month, maybe two to come up with options."

"They don't want to chance it."

"But they want to flush millions of dollars down the drain?"

The voices sound muddled in her head, and Lily takes a deep breath. What can she do to save this project? Can she save it? "Can we change their mind? I think we all want to see this fly, so it's a matter of making sure that's possible."

"They haven't stopped us yet," their manager confirms. "If we can make a plan, we may be able to salvage this."

Jeff sighs. "So what's the plan? Everything I've heard about has already failed."

"That's the problem, we have no more ideas at this point."

Lily holds the conference room all day, and she listens in as different groups on the project come in to speculate on potential solutions. None of them seem especially promising, but each team promises to keep working on it, with Jeff going so far as to ask for her trust as he leaves the room at the end of his meeting. She tells him she does, but she can't help but to stare at the design to try and see if she can spot what they couldn't.

A few hours later, as Lily sits alone in the conference room, her phone vibrates on the table. She flips it over to see Mark has sent her a message.

Got a free day pass for the climbing gym today. Interested?

She could use some stress relief for sure, and seeing Mark will be sure to put her in a good mood. She looks up to the whiteboard and sighs. She really should stay and try to figure this out. No one's been able to come up with decent starting points today, and she really wants to come up with one before she leaves for the day. Her phone vibrates again.

Are you finishing up work soon? I can meet you there after work if you want, but we could go later too.

Lily types out her response, including a maybe next time so he doesn't think she isn't interested in spending time with him, but there is a knock at the door before she hits send. Tala opens the door.

"I came to say goodnight. Working late again?"

Lily checks the time on her phone before sighing. "Apparently, I'm not coming up with anything new though."

"I don't think that's going to work," Tala walks towards the whiteboard.

"Jeff said it wouldn't, but I was trying to come up with some ideas based on the premise."

"Girl, go home." Tala's still looking at the whiteboard.

"Mark invited me to go climbing."

"Are you going?"

"I was debating staying to work on this some more, that way I can give everyone instructions tomorrow," Lily raises her hands in surrender as Tala turns around to look at her. "I hadn't decided yet."

"Well, I'm going shopping with Aleeyah. She has a wedding to go to that she wants a new dress for."

"Sounds like a cute date."

"It sounds much better than getting sweaty climbing." Tala gives her a kiss on the cheek before heading out of the conference room. "Don't stay too late."

Lily doesn't really want to stay at all, and so when she lifts her phone up to send the message to Mark, she deletes it and sends a different one instead. She didn't correct Tala, but this really can't be a date. It's just friends. Friends having fun.

What would I need to go climbing?

***

Lily arrives at the gym before Mark does, but she heads inside early to fill out the waiver and anything else she'd need in order to climb. The gym actually smells nice. Well, for a gym. It smells like chalk but not sweat. The entrance is brightly lit, and the air conditioning is turned on enough that the air is a little chilly. Lily spots a sign-in desk but she turns her attention to the TVs behind it. It's displaying a climbing competition. A climber jumps off of a piece to catch another and Lily can't help but to make a small sound of surprise. The woman at the sign up desk hands her a tablet to fill out the waiver and Lily sits down to read it. On the TV, a different climber misses a piece and slams into the matts below. He gets up and immediately returns to climbing. Lily whistles as she turns her attention to the waiver which she finishes as Mark walks in the doors.

"There you are," Mark walks over to her and she's blessed with another hug. She squeezes him tight, but releases him after a second and steps back. He's in a red sleeveless shirt and black knee-length shorts with his backpack slung over his shoulders. She tries not to stare, but she can't help her lingering gaze.

"Here I am, signing my life away," Lily waves the tablet around before placing it on the counter.

"You're going to be fine." He uses a hand on her shoulder to guide her to the other table. "I'll protect you."

Lily gets her rentals and Mark slips into his climbing shoes, and they move further into the gym. "I'm surprised it smells so nice."

"It smells like chalk." Mark slings his bag back over his shoulder.

"It doesn't smell like sweat."

"Fair." His eyes connect with hers. "Thanks for coming out today, I know it was last minute, but I was hoping you'd be free."

"I was debating staying late at work, so you got me at the right time. I haven't eaten dinner yet though, so I'll have to get something after this."

"Sounds good. I know a couple spots in the area." A couple climbers make their way up the shorter walls in front of her. Others are tied to the taller walls. Mark explains the difficulty levels to her and the starting and finishing rules as he fills up his water bottle and chalks his hands up.

He holds the bag out to her and Lily chalks her hands up with determination as Mark picks an easy warm up wall to start with. She certainly isn't going to out climb him, but she doesn't want to fail at the first one.

"Let me do it first, just to show you how." Mark stretches out his hands and then crouches against the wall to grab the starting holds. He climbs slowly and deliberately, commenting on different climbing techniques as he does, like flagging and crimping, and with each new technique comes a new group of muscles that pop out and grab her attention. It seems effortless when he does it and within no time at all he's waving to her from the top of the wall.

Then it's her turn. The wall is a lot taller up close, but she takes a deep breath and reaches for the first piece. It's pretty easy, until she turns to wave to him and realizes how high she is. 15 feet? 20 feet? She turns back to the wall and clenches the pieces, and she doesn't hear whatever he's saying up to her. *Downclimb*. Climb down. She takes another deep breath very slowly makes her way down.

She beams up at him from where she lands on the mat after jumping off the wall. That wasn't so bad, not once she could move again. Mark nudges her as they walk to a new one and mentions getting her a timer, to which she giggles and lightly shoves him ahead, leaving a white handprint on his back.

Each wall gets progressively harder, but Lily's determination grows with each climb. Mark mentions a higher level one she could try on the other side of the building if she wants a challenge. Lily shakes her arms out and accepts. On the way there, though, Mark pauses to check out one of the routes on a side wall.

"Oh, it looks like they reset this wall!" He turns to the side, "can I climb this problem first?"

"Sure," Lily motions for him to go ahead. He presses himself against the wall, and then somehow grabs a piece smaller than his fingertips. She's only a little jealous of the wall, and for a second she imagines what it would feel like for him to press up against her. Maybe he'd pin her to a wall, and she'd get to make a breathless joke about being between a rock and a hard place. He'll probably laugh at it, and then she would be able to lean up and capture his lip. Friends with benefits are still friends, right?

She is sure he won't be able to, but Mark uses a tiny hold to bring himself up higher. His arm flexes as he grabs another piece and moves his feet up. It's impressive and hot. He picked a good date for them. He struggles a bit on one of the final moves, but manages to catch his balance and grabs the top of the wall to finish. He turns to her to wave and then begins downclimbing. Lily gives him a high five when he gets down, and he grins as he shows her the next boulder problem.

Lily gets to the top by following his instructions, and she's panting a bit by the time she gets there. Her feet hurt in the shoes, her hands feel raw, and there's a tension in her forearms that won't dissipate, no matter how many times she tries to shake them. She's at the top of the wall, but she sees the piece marked finish to her left.

"You have to get both hands on that piece." Mark comments from below. "Just get a little swing and grab it with the left, then you can match with your right."

It's going to take a bit more than a little swing, but she wants to be impressive, and it looks within reach. She gauges the distance and then pushes off the wall, holding her breath and reaching for the piece.

Her fingers lock onto the side of it with triumph, and her body swings to the side with momentum. It doesn't even take a fraction of a second for her to realize something is off, that her other hand slips off the wall, that she doesn't actually have a good grip on this one, that she's got too much momentum. She vaults off the top of the wall. She vaguely recognizes that she spins, that's a familiar movement, but there is no saving herself. Instead of landing, the ground meets her a second too late, it's disorienting and she's caught off guard. She bends her knees but doesn't lean backwards, and her knees slam into her chest as she lands. She falls onto the mat and lets out a whoosh of air that should've been a cry and her chest tightens in pain.

"Are you okay?" Mark kneels next to her. Lily gasps for air as she nods, but she's been winded from the fall. He picks up the front of her body and leans it against his side as he tries to guide her to take deep breaths, and it doesn't take long for a concerned staff member to appear in front of her. It's a painful minute, and Lily knows she should answer the people who ask if she's okay but she's just trying to remember how to breathe. She can't even enjoy the way Mark has her against his body because she's just trying to pull air into her lungs.

"I think I'm okay," Lily can finally breathe. Has she been clenching Mark's hand in hers the entire time? She lets go, and he moves his hand to her shoulder instead.

"Are you sure?" Mark rubs a small soothing circle into her skin. "Don't rush it."

"You should stay off the walls for at least another 10 minutes, and grab one of us if you feel anything wrong." The staff member inputs.

"I'm done for tonight," Lily tells them both. "Can you help me up?" Mark pulls her to her feet easily, and he helps her over to some of the seating at the edge of the mats.

"I'm so sorry about all this, I didn't think about you getting hurt. I should—"

"It's fine," Lily cuts him off, "I should have known better than to leap for it." She smiles as she sits down, but he's still frowning and hovering, so she moves over so he can sit next to her. Mark seems content to just fret over her for the rest of the night. She leans back into the seat and motions to the wall she fell off of.

"Can you show me how I should have done it?"

"Are you sure?" He runs his burning hand up and down her back. "I could just stay here, I don't mind."

"I'm sure," Lily leans into the touch, breathless in a new way. "I'm sure I'll like watching for a little bit, and then maybe we can grab some food?"

She shakes her hands out as he scales the wall again. He reaches the piece with ease after explaining where she went wrong, and then he lets go of the wall and lands gracefully. Lily points to a purple one that seems hard and he gives her a mock salute as he makes his way over. He starts this one by flattening himself to the wall, something Lily is now more than a little jealous of, and is able to use the back of his heel to pull himself upward. By the time he touches the top piece, two others are commending him and asking for advice.

"That's ridiculous," Lily shakes her head as he makes his way back to her, "what if your shoe falls off?"

"Then I'm in trouble," he laughs "but they are pretty snug." He sits next to her for a few minutes, and Lily debates trying one more climb as they talk. She clenches her hands, but they are sore, and as she turns them over, they are pink.

"I'm sorry to have ruined climbing for you." Mark stares at her hands so she shakes them out and nudges her shoulder with his. Electricity shoots through her skin on contact with his, and she doesn't move away.

"It was fun! In a few weeks or so, when I catch my breath. I'll come try again."

"We'll get you on a harness," he grins as he points to another section of the gym where the walls are higher. A few climbers make their way up the wall as the ropes they are tied to are pulled by partners.

"That looks more secure for sure!"

"Dinner?" He asks.

"Are you already done?" It's almost been an hour.

"Well, I think I have one more in me if you could record me?" Lily dusts her hands off on her shorts and then holds her hands out for his phone.

"It's for my Instagram," he hands her his phone, "I try to put up a couple posts a day, and I have a decent following, but I'm having trouble getting a really big following, which is what I need to get noticed."

He explains what he's looking for, and he walks up to a section of the wall covered in black holds and turns to her. She snaps a picture of him smiling at her and then starts a video when he gives her a thumbs up.

He jumps from the starting hold, grabbing onto the next two pieces and lightly swinging on them. The climb is a show of athleticism that has Lily biting her lip. Goosebumps break out across her skin as she can't help but to imagine his hands sliding over her skin and pulling on her the way he touches the pieces. Then he uses a heel hook and Lily huffs. His foot slides off and Lily yelps. He doesn't fall though. Mark swings his body again to get a better heel hook, and after using it to pull himself up there's only a few more moves before he reaches the top. He hangs from it with one hand as he turns to give her a smile and thumbs up. Lily blushes at the sight. Then he lets go, all grin, and falls out of frame as he lands on the mat.

Lily laughs as she walks up towards him. "No wonder you're not famous," she hands him back his phone so he can watch the video, "but you gained a new follower. What's your username?" As she scrolls through his Instagram, she's blessed and cursed all at once. It's full of workouts, sports, and random pictures showing off his physique. She is going to spend a bit of time scrolling through it in the near future, maybe with Tala and a glass of wine, or in the middle of the night with a good vibe. There's a video of him doing pushups while a girl is sitting on his back, and another of him, shirtless, doing pull-ups at the beach. She's suddenly, irrationally, jealous.

"Hungry?" Mark sits next to her and takes off his shoes.

"Ravenous." She double taps a picture of him flagging in the sunset in nothing but boy shorts.

"What are you in the mood for?" He smirks as she finally looks back up to him.

She licks her lips as she follows a drop of sweat that falls off of his forehead. She's hungry for him. She wants to take his cock into her mouth and suck out every last drop until he's a stuttering mess. She wants to run her fingers through his sweaty hair as she pulls him closer to her pussy so he can get his fill of dinner. Better yet, she wants him to throw her legs over his shoulders as he puts his athletic skills to use and pounds her pussy until all she can see are stars.

"I can think of something." She practically purrs.

***

"This is amazing," Lily takes a bite of her boneless wings. In front of her, Mark digs into his chicken sandwich.

She picks up a fry and points it at him. "Seriously, we'll have to come here every time we go climbing." She gives a light moan of appreciation as she takes another bite.

"Anything to make you moan," He winks and she blushes under his gaze. Lily doesn't pull her fry back right away, and his lips brush her fingers as he takes it from her. He locks eyes with her as he does and the heat of his gaze makes Lily squeeze her thighs together, and her nipples poke against her bra.

"Thanks for tonight," Lily picks up another fry but decides to eat it herself instead of offering it to him. "After all the chaos going on at work, I needed a break."

"What's going on at work?"

Lily sighs before giving a brief, and censored, version of the events since the static fire.

"And no one has any ideas?"

"Everyone has ideas, it's that none of them are holding up to any kind of scrutiny."

"When would you need to know by?"

"Yesterday," Lily huffs before biting a fry. "Seriously, we are on a day by day basis here."

"I'm sure you've told the team to hurry up, but what about your customer, did you tell them to hold on?" Mark steals a fry from her plate and it shouldn't be cute, but it is.

"Not really, the project manager meets with them about things like that without us, but we are certainly feeling the pressure."

"I always have to tell my clients to be patient to get the results they want, but I don't know if that's something you can do."

"Maybe I should try pointing that out again. It would be nice to let the team breathe a little." She lets out a long sigh and Mark chuckles. "Enough about me though. You're trying to get sponsored by sports brands?"

"Yeah, no luck so far though."

"What's the game plan?"

Mark details his slow start but steady growth, and how he's purposely making content in a certain way to increase his chances.

"Well, if you don't mind me saying. I took a quick glance at everything, and it's all just fitness based. There's a thousand people doing the same thing. I wonder what your personal spin could be."

"I hadn't thought about it like that."

"Like what?"

Mark gestures to himself. "Having a personal spin. I figured if I was all athletics and a blank canvas, they could make me who they wanted."

"I think they'd rather see you as you are, with the right following."

He pulls out his phone so they can look over the most recent videos together, and then he puts it down as he watches the recent climbing one. "I'm sorry about the fall."

Lily waves her hand. "It happens. I was just caught off guard. If I hadn't been winded everything would have been fine. At least I didn't fall onto ice from that high when I'm skating." She winces, "besides, you're going to fall when I take you skating, so no need to feel guilty."

"Now she's out for revenge," he poses dramatically, "and I'm so young."

Lily does her best impression of an evil laugh, and they dissolve into giggles over their food.

"I had a lot of fun," Lily says after she regains her composure. If this were a date, she'd certainly be looking forward to a second. It's not, because he doesn't date vanilla people. This is just a friendly hangout, and she is following her friend on Instagram, and she is going to go home and use her friend as inspiration. Friends.

"Good, I'd hate to lose my videographer as soon as I got her." He's joking, but even his jokes contain a level of heat that send her thoughts to the bedroom and all the ways she wants to put him to use. Lily shoves a whole piece of chicken into her mouth to avoid the thoughts of what she'd like to record from coming out of her mouth. Mark starts laughing again.

"Well, you'll have to take videos of me when we go skating then." Lily leaned in. Afterwards, I'll take you to this burrito place I really like."

"Good. I need more active friends." He bites down into his sandwich, and Lily's both happy and disappointed that he's using the word after staring at her like he wants to devour her.

"I'm going to post a video of you falling on your pretty little ass." She threatens him with a fry.

"You think it's pretty?"

Chapter 7

"I just want to fuck the daylights out of this guy," Lily whines to Tala as she slides the phone over to show a video of Mark doing pushups with a woman sitting on his back. It's Friday night, the week has sucked, and she just needs wine and whine time. "He's just so sexy, and he's got a bit of a joker in him. I just know I'd be laughing the whole time."

"Which is the best sex." Tala scrolls down a few pictures of him in the gym doing squats and double taps one. She's sure Tala is going to follow him on Instagram as well, if for no other reason than to write #bubblebutt on all his pictures. "I have to admit; I'd never looked at him that way. He's always in these big sweaters and blankets by the time I see him; like a sated puppy."

"A tired dog is a happy dog." Lily says automatically, thinking of all the dog training shows she used to watch. Tala bursts out laughing.

"I dare you to say that to him." She wipes imaginary tears from her eyes. "Right after sex."

Lily grabs a glass and goes to her fridge to pull out some wine. Tala grabs a cider and opens the can as Lily pours. "Yeah, sure, if I can ever get that far."

"Okay, he's a hot guy, but he's still a guy. I'm sure if you invited him over and answered the door naked he'd get the hint. Or you could wait until you both are at the club; a swinger club, if you need reminding, and ask him if he wants to grab a room with you. You did already jerk him off that time."

"Right, but we're kind of friends now and I don't want to make things awkward." Lily takes a big gulp. "I still want to take him ice skating, and we talked about climbing again, and I want to know if he likes my favorite burrito place like I like his BBQ spot."

"Oh?" Tala teases.

"Oh," Lily repeats, "*Oh*, I like him." She chugs her wine and sets it down on the table as she groans out. "I like him? You know better than that Liliana!"

Tala refills her glass. "Is that a problem?"

"He doesn't date vanilla."

Tala snickers. "Chocolate."

"Shut up!" Lily laughs. "Seriously, though," Lily takes the phone back to see another photo of Mark. "He's already said that he won't date without kink, so friends with benefits is the best I can hope for." It wouldn't be terrible, but the end of it could be.

"Come on," Tala huffs, "You are totally a domme in the making."

"Yeah, right." Lily scoffs.

"You went to a kink club with a sub, jerked him off in the middle of the dungeon, and made him beg you to come." Lily blushes as Tala smirks.

"I didn't tell you all that!"

"No, but I heard, because you did it in front of a dozen people."

"Ay Dios Mio," Lily puts her red face in her hands. "I don't know what came over me. I wasn't even drunk, I just…"

"And David left you because you kept telling him what to do, right? Inside and out—"

"Low blow." Lily scowls. Tala winces and lifts her hands in surrender.

"I'm just saying for someone who thinks you're not kinky, you sure do a lot of kinky shit."

"What?"

"Okay, let's look at the facts. You went to a swinging club on the fly," Lily narrows her eyes but says nothing as Tala begins to count on her fingers. "You certainly were watching all the good juicy bits of public sex without squirming. You went to a munch and didn't get freaked out. You then went back to the club, without me, and jerked Mark off in front of other people while he was blindfolded and bound." Tala shakes her head, "Now you've since decided you like the guy and want to date him but you are too vanilla?"

"Well, when you put it like that," Lily pouts.

"You may not be super kinky, but you are certainly not vanilla."

"Okay, so what if I'm a little kinky? I mean maybe just the tiniest bit, but I have no idea where to start, or what to do, or who to ask. All I know is I'm not doing the shit that they are. No one is setting me on fire or beating me with a cane, so I'm not kinky."

Tala holds up her hands in surrender. Lily sighs and Tala finishes her drink before speaking again. "So, you realize kink is a spectrum like sexuality, right?"

"I mean, I guess so." Lily takes a long drink.

"Feel free to say no, but I think we should set you up online. Not to do anything, just to perv around and see if anything catches your interest."

"Alright," Lily gives in, "let's set me up."

"Finish your drink up, I'm getting us another round for this."

With a new cup of wine, Lily pulls up her laptop, and Tala signs into her account. It seems to be a standard social media account, if you excuse all the naked images that people use as their profile pictures. Tala lets her click around for a bit, and she explores some of the tabs with growing levels of interest.

"I guess I should make a profile." Lily might have said no if she had any less alcohol in her. Tala laughs as she fetches another cider.

"Get it, girl!"

"So, how's Aleeyah?" Lily tries and fails to come up with unique usernames.

"She's amazing!" Tala exclaims. "She's just so perfect. She's passionate and driven, without letting it become her whole life. I just like that in a woman. Like I know that at the end of the long work day she's excited to come home to me."

"Home?" Lily knows how Tala can get, and she can't help herself from digging just a little bit.

"No. I mean. I know what you're thinking," Tala points an accusing finger at her. "I'm not trying to get too serious too fast, or rent a U-Haul," she uses air quotes. "I just know we've got a good thing going, and I want to keep it going."

"Hey, no judgement, right?"

"Right."

"So, go on," Lily prompts after a moment of silence and another couple of failed usernames. Lily frowns at the screen as she searches for anything else she would be okay going by.

"Okay, so she's a vet, which also means she would be down for getting a pet or two down the road as well, and then we can always be sure they are healthy because she'll be able to check on them."

"Okay, so house and pets. What about your dates? Are you having fun?"

"Loads." Tala winks. "We have been to the movies, and dinner, and ice cream dates. She even came over to my apartment during her period for some ice cream and cuddles. Which is next level, right? That's got to mean that this means something more than just sex and fun for her too. We were just sitting together but she was cuddling up and she would just look at me like I was special, you know?" Tala crosses her arms at Lily's teasing grin. "What?"

"Nothing."

"Say it!" Tala demands.

"Fine! I was thinking that, for someone who has a lot of sex and relationships, you sure are sounding like a teenager right about now. Do you want to tell me about holding her hand?" Lily sticks her tongue out and Tala gives a mock shout of offense.

"Okay, I know how it sounds, but I'm just happy." Tala sighs and Lily dissolves into giggles over it. Tala laughs at Lily's tipsy giggle and then shrugs. "Seriously, though, I just really like her."

"Good. That's what really counts. Just…" Lily looks away, then back. "Just be careful with your heart, okay?"

"I will, now give me that." Tala takes the laptop from Lily and snorts at her latest attempt at a username. "I've got it," she grins wickedly. She types in BabyDomme and before Lily can reach over to take it back, Tala pulls it out of reach.

"No," Lily warns, but she doesn't sound threatening.

"Yes," Tala clicks to the next step.

"Noooo!" Lily mock yells as she listens to Tala cackle. "You've ruined me. How can I now get thralls of men to beg at my feet for my affection?"

"Vanilla," Tala drawls sarcastically.

"Okay, so what do I do now, oh wise one."

"Now you send me a friend request and go explore."

Tala hands back the laptop with Mark's profile on the screen. Lily settles into the couch to look it over.

His profile picture is somewhat artfully taken for a male nude. At least it's not just a close up of a penis. He's leaning against something, and the shadows make his abs seem super defined. He's tugging his boxers down far enough that Lily wants to scroll down below where the picture cuts off. Lily clicks through the rest of his public photos. She'll come back to take a better look after Tala leaves. There are a couple of him in workout gear, from the neck down. How isn't he already a full time model? Then there are a couple of his cock.

Wow.

She's tempted to ask Tala to leave now. One of the pictures has a caption asking if anyone would be willing to cage his cock and the responses are a mix of men offering to cage him and dominate him, compliments from a variety of people, a few personal testaments to how wonderful said cock is, and some offering to play with it on local kink

76

night. She's tempted to throw her own name into the mix, but that's probably the alcohol talking.

There is a picture of a line of butt plugs in different colors, and an ask for which one he should try next. Lily doesn't think they'd fit in her pussy, let alone in anyone's ass. Lily clicks through a few more pictures of toys with disinterest before returning to his profile.

"He's a bisexual submissive seeking relationships, play partners, and friends." Lily reads the rest of his profile blurb and then sees the results of a BDSM test underneath it.

"They have tests for this?" Lily reads his percentage scores.

"You should take one." Tala advises as she sits on the couch next to Lily.

"Maybe later." Lily says absently as she continues to read. "It says he's a pain slut,"

"Nice, you'll certainly have fun with that."

"I will?" Lily looks over at a grinning Tala.

"You're in management, your job is causing people pain and giving them headaches." Tala says. Lily reaches over to grab a couch pillow to whack Tala with, and Tala laughs as she turns away. "See! You already got it!"

"We're going out again tomorrow. I'm taking him skating."

"Aww, look at you." Tala reaches up to pinch Lily's cheek. Lily pushes Tala onto the couch and she squeaks. "Ah! I'm being murdered."

Chapter 8

Lily takes a deep breath as she enters the rink. The cool air fills her lungs with happiness and she smiles as a few skaters make their way around the rink. Hopefully Mark gets here soon. She touches the plastic of the hockey guards as she walks towards the main desk. She blames work for the fact that she hasn't been here in years, but she could put more effort into it.

Lily buys a wristband at the main counter and finds an empty bench by the rink. She messages Mark to let him know she's here, and that if he's late, she's going on without him. It'll be his punishment. Instantly, the image of Mark's bruised ass comes to mind from his profile. Then the other images flash in her mind. She clears her throat. Should she message him something like that or would it be too much? Could she convey playfulness in the text as much as in person? They've mostly just messaged to set up hangouts.

Luckily for Lily, he texts her to tell her he's in the parking lot, and she doesn't have to find out.

Lily puts on her skates, the routine of checking her blade's edges and laces is ingrained in her. Lily slides on her skate guards and stands up to stretch. It won't be a hard skate, but she can almost hear her former coach's voice chastising her for even thinking of not stretching before heading on the ice. Hopefully it'll take her mind out of the gutter.

As she's in the middle of a leg stretch, Mark walks into the side entrance. She waves, but he doesn't see her as he makes his way across the building. When he spots her, his face lights up in a smile that has Lily waving so hard she almost smacks a nearby woman. He stops at the main desk for a minute, and she hugs him as soon as he's close enough to get her arms around him. She squeezes him, shivering at the way his nose and lips touch her neck, and neither of them let go as he pulls back. The stubble on his face might as well scratch her, for all the attention it draws. Her heart races as she looks up at him. Lily is tall enough with her skates on that their lips are almost level with each other, and the slightest push would have them kiss. She wants to lean just the slightest bit forward. It could be so easy.

"It's cold in here."

Lily steps back, smiling, and gestures to the ice. "I wonder why." She pretends to hum in thought, and he shakes his head as he sits next to her on the bench with his rentals. "Make sure to tie them nice and tight."

"You have nice skates." He bends down to tie his.

Lily looks down at her white boots. They are covered in rhinestones and tiny cuts, and her skate guards are bright pink. "I used to skate a lot."

"Feel free to keep stretching," he runs his eyes up and down her body. "I wouldn't want you to pull anything."

Lily grabs the boards in front of her and smirks as she arches her back and lifts her back leg up as straight as it goes. It's not nearly the vertical line of a needle she had once upon a time, but it's enough that she can see Mark staring at her as she leans forward. This is her chance to show off and impress him. They are in her domain.

For a brief moment, she allows herself to imagine what it would be like if he stood behind her and offered to help her stretch. For him to slide against her skin and push her leg the slightest bit, giving her a delicious stretch, like the stretch of a thick cock inside her pussy. Lily exhales harshly, leaving a condensation cloud on the plastic guard as she lowers her leg. She leans forward with the other leg and tries to shake the fantasy away.

"I didn't realize you were so flexible," Mark's voice is low and intimate, like he's asking her to spread her legs so he can get a better view.

"And not just on the ice." She boldly flirts back. This time, she reaches behind her to grab her leg and pull it closer. Her fingers brush her knee but don't get a good grip on it.

"Here, let me help." Mark's voice goes soft and seductive like he's in a porn of her own making. She nods, not trusting her voice, and his hot fingers push on her shin just enough for her to grab it herself. She pulls the leg closer, enjoying the stretch, but Mark doesn't move from his spot behind her. She can't feel his breath on her neck, but his hands are warm even through her clothes, and goosebumps rise up to meet him. She's never had dirty thoughts about these stretches before, as they usually were with other girls and burned in a different way, but now she can't help but to think of the ways he could move closer into her space and touch her body. Move those hot hands over her breasts as he pulls her flush to him and kisses her neck. She can't think of a good way to say she's looked at his naked pictures and loved them.

Without speaking, she switches her legs to lift the other, and he shifts the slightest bit to help her reach her leg again. The heat from his fingers linger on her skin against the chilled air of the ice rink, and Lily loses herself in the thick tension between them. She's sorry when she has to put her leg down to finish her stretch. As she turns to face him, he's still in her space, and his breath is warm on her lips. Their eyes lock and for the first time, Lily is sure that he wants to kiss her. Her skin tingles at the thought. She takes a quick peek at the pinkness of his lips and then smirks.

"You haven't put your skates on yet, have you?" She closes the space between them the tiniest bit and she hopes it sounds more like 'you should come over to my house and take all of your clothes off.'

"I got distracted." He's looking down at her lips, and she hopes he means yes.

"That sucks for you," she steps around him. "I'm going to have to go out on the ice alone then."

He grabs her hand. "No way, I'm going to fall on my ass if you leave me alone."

"I thought I'd already agreed to record that for your many fans." She smiles and he shakes his head.

"One more minute," he sits and pulls on his other skate. He takes two, as the second his skates are on, he pulls out his phone to record another video. This time, it's not just one of the actions, but of Mark. His smile shines as he looks into the camera and introduces himself. Lily waves in the background as Mark tells his followers he's trying out ice skating today. She's spent a lot of time on his profile, but he's never greeted the audience in his videos. She hopes people interact more with it now.

Lily steps onto the ice and skates forward with ease. She turns to Mark, who is gripping the boards for dear life. He slowly places a foot on the ice, and his body tightens; he lifts the foot back up. "You have to step on the ice." She holds her feet in a T. She means to be encouraging, but the giggle slips out of her.

"I know, I'm going, I just—" he puts one foot on the ice and then hugs the board tighter as he tries to get the other on the ice. His eyes are wide in panic, and Lily takes pity on him.

"Hey, you'll be fine," Lily skates towards him, holding her hands out for him to grab. He takes one of her hands, but his other is locked tight around the board. Lily chuckles and waits for a few seconds. "Let go, I've got you." She encourages.

It takes Mark another minute, one Lily will never let him live down, before he finally grabs her other hand. Lily starts moving backwards slowly to take him with her.

"I didn't realize you'd never been skating before."

"I said you'd have to teach me," he defends. His smile fades as it forms. "I'm just nervous about falling. The ice is a lot harder than a mat."

"You are going to fall, but you'll be fine." Lily guides him through some of the basic movements, and after a couple of laps, Mark is comfortable enough that she skates next to him, though he doesn't let go of her hand. Every few steps, he loses his balance and wobbles, using her for balance.

"Well, this is romantic." He jokes.

"You are making my fingers go numb." Lily teases.

"Well, I'm not letting go. We're in the middle of nowhere!" His eyes are wide and panic is etched into the way his lips pull down and his eyebrows shoot up. Lily can't help the giggle that erupts from her at the sight.

"We are three feet from the boards."

Around the fifth lap, Mark lets go of Lily's hand, claiming that he's got it. He takes three steps and falls forward and yelps. He laughs as he rolls over, so he's probably alright.

"How was that?" Lily stops in front of him.

"Not so bad." Mark gets to his hands and knees.

"As much as I like you down there…" Lily starts. Mark bites his lip as he looks up at her, and she really, *really*, likes that. It makes his eyes look bigger and cuter and makes her want to grab his chin and make him look up at her. "I think you should learn how to get up." Lily goes down her own knees and then demonstrates how to get up. "Now that you've had your first fall, ice skating won't seem as scary."

Surely enough, the Mark that rises from the floor is not the timid Mark that gripped the boards, but a determined athlete. He takes a breath to steady himself before starting to skate forward again at a faster pace. Lily skates in front of him a bit, so he can watch her form, and then turns so that she can check his. He is a little too eager to move faster after rounding his first corner and Lily tries to hide her smile when he falls again. He gives her a thumbs up from the ice before moving to stand up.

"Having fun?" Lily asks in front of him. He huffs as he gets to his knees.

"I'm liking the view." His voice takes on a husky tone as he looks up at her. Lily moves backwards a bit before doing a small spin. "You could go around a couple times if you want," he pushes off of his knee to stand up, "I don't want to hold you up."

That's an image that burns her insides. He could probably lift her so easily, and so long. She's never had sex with someone who could hold her up the whole time. He could hold her against a wall, or just in the air. He's still looking at her, his expression morphing into a sly smirk, like he can read her mind. "Sure." Suddenly, she's breathless. "Watch this." She winks, and then she turns and sprints ahead of him so he can't see the red blush that is probably burning down her shoulders. She passes a few people before spreading her arms and skating backwards. She grins as she moves into some nicer looking footwork before sliding to a stop right in front of him as he finishes standing up. The sly look on his face and whatever he's about to say get lost to terror as he wobbles. Lily grabs his arms to steady him.

"Give me your phone." Lily holds her hand out for it, though she wouldn't be opposed to checking his pockets for it. "I promised I'd record you."

"This'll be embarrassing," he hands over his phone before turning on a model's smile.

"Hey everyone," he grins into the camera, skating forward as Lily skates backwards, "skating is going amazing." He winks and speeds up, and Lily lets him pass her before stopping the video. Lily starts another as she turns to follow Mark. He speeds up further, letting out a whoop before an 'oh no'.

"Lily, how do I stop?" The panic in his voice has her speeding to him, but there is no time to explain, and she gets a perfect video of him trying to turn, falling to the ice, and slamming into the boards as she races towards him. She kneels in front of him as he sits next to the boards, and he groans as he leans forward to put his head on her shoulder.

"Are you in pain?" She looks him up and down, but he seems fine. His limbs are aligned and he's not bleeding. "Did you hit your head?"

"The only thing hurt is my pride." He mutters into her neck and her hands move across his shoulders and down his arms in frantic concern. "Please tell me you didn't catch that on video."

"I'd hate to lie to you." Lily giggles, relief filling her at his question. Mark groans into her neck. "Come on, let's get you up." One of the skaters working slows to a stop next to them, but Mark waves him away sheepishly.

"I think we have to stop having sports days," Lily muses as they take a slow lap, hand in hand, around the rink.

Mark shakes his head as he chuckles. "We seem to keep getting hurt, you mean?"

"I think next time should just be dinner and a movie or something with a low risk of injury."

He winks. "You are just trying to get into my apartment."

"Obviously." She quips back. "Before you know it, I'll be crashing on your couch every weekend."

"Nonsense, you'd have to sleep in the bed. I'd never hear the end of it if you ever told my mom I let you sleep on the couch."

"Fair warning." Lily keeps her tone light and friendly, even though her thoughts sink into the gutter. "I'm a cuddler."

"It's a date."

She's not sure if he's joking or not, and she can't bring herself to ask.

Mark tries to skate on his own again after a few minutes, and Lily turns to him as she skates backwards. He tries the two-foot turn as well and falls again. This time, his exhaustion is evident as he moves to stand up. He's clearly pushing himself here, and she doesn't want him to end today on a bad note. Lily waits for him to get up, and then suggests calling it a day. Mark nods and gingerly makes his way to the boards.

"Your feet must be killing you."

"I think they went numb twenty minutes ago," Mark leans on the boards, "but I did promise to take a video of you today."

"Oh no, I'd feel bad showing off after you fell so much. I'd hate to put you down."

Mark lets out a small whine as he looks up at her. "Please?"

"Okay, okay." Lily gives in. "Then we get some burritos. Anything you want to see?"

"Can you do a spin?"

Lily looks over the rink to see the center ice is open. She turns back to him with a nod and then waits for him to pull his phone out. "Which one?"

Mark twirls his finger. "Do one of the ones where you look like a T."

"Sure, give me a countdown for the video." Lily smiles and waves at the camera as he counts her in. "Hi Mark's followers! My name's Lily," she introduces herself with a smile she hopes is dazzling. Will Mark watch this back? "I'm going to show you some actual ice skating!" She winks as Mark makes a pained sound. She turns before pushing off to skate around the rink before making her way to the center of the rink to start her basic camel spin.

Initially, she hoped to do a camel into a sit spin, but she doesn't have quite enough speed in her spin to make enough rotations. Mark isn't going to notice, and hopefully he's just impressed that she can spin in the first place. She switches her positioning to turn it into an illusion spin before coming out of it. She dramatically turns to the camera and stops, throwing her arms to the side. After a second, she makes her way back over to him.

"I've been hustled, you're a pro."

"Not even close! I still remember some things. Now let's get you off the ice."

He follows her off the ice and collapses on the bench. He dramatically sighs in relief as he takes off his skates. Lily walks them over to the rental return as he welcomes feelings back into his toes. As she takes her skates off and wipes them down, Mark shakes out his legs and switches to his sneakers.

"You've given me my first sore bottom," he leans over the bench, rubbing his side.

"Your first?" Lily smiles, already imagining bringing him back to the rink. "Want me to give you another one?"

Mark's face reddens as he looks back at her, and the full implications of her words sink in. Lily's mind drifts to the image of Mark on the cross and Derrick sliding the flat leather of the riding crop down the swell of his ass. She thinks of the red crop in her hands. She doesn't take it back, even after the silence stretches.

"Yes." Mark eyes lower to the ground like he's telling her something important. Lily's heart pounds as she steps closer to him, and her whole body comes alive as she tips his chin up the slightest bit and leans forward.

He closes the distance between them with a soft sound and the shock of it sets her whole body alight. Soft lips firmly press against hers with a sweet, delicious give as she presses against his. They are cool, which contrasts against the heat of his body as she steps closer. It's like she's never been kissed before, with the way her hand grabs at his side and her heart pounds a chorus of *more, more* from her toes to her nipples. His lips part for her tongue and she barely has a taste of him before she remembers where she is and wrenches herself back.

Lily smooths invisible wrinkles on his shirt, "If you ask nicely enough for it…" she trails off, enjoying the slow smile that spreads on his face. "I'll bring you skating again."

<u>Chapter 9</u>

Derrick is out of town, but he told me I need to make myself useful. He suggested I find someone to serve.

Lily licks her lips at the memory of their kiss over the weekend. She hadn't dared to take another for fear of losing herself, but Mark's given her another opportunity here. At least, he is if she's reading this right. Her calves tingle with the memory of his hands as he helped her stretch. It's been four days, but the warmth of his hands linger as if it had only been seconds.

What kind of service are you offering?

Whatever you want. He replies immediately. There is only one task that comes to mind at the moment, and it involves him sinking to his knees in front of her and spreading her out against her table. She tries to let her confidence build into a form of dominance she could send over text. He likes to be dominated, and it's obvious that he wants her, but the truth is he wants to be dominated *by* her.

Oh come now, there must be some service you can recommend.

Well, I am hungry, and I can make us dinner. From there, maybe watch a movie? It's a nice low risk activity.

He sends a winky face next, and Lily bites her lips as she sees it. She wants to bite his. Dinner and a movie sounds like a good plan, and maybe him being here will lead to those heated moments going further.

And after?

I give good cuddles too.

Lily's heart speeds as she reads her message as her pussy clenches in anticipation. She decides to take a risk.

I think you missed a step in there.

***

In the time it takes him to arrive at her house, Lily tidies the living room, washes her clothes, cleans her bedroom, and makes her bed. She changes into a tank top and booty shorts to make sure, in case her text messages didn't, that she's interested in more than dinner.

Mark shows up at her door in a black T-shirt that barely stretches over the muscles of his chest and dark blue jeans. His face lights up in a smile as she opens the door. He's holding a bag of groceries and a skillet so she gestures in the direction of the kitchen as she grabs the bag from him.

"I hope you didn't get hurt getting those." She teases.

Mark somberly shakes his head. "I had to fight tooth and nail for this." He pulls a single rose out of the bag and hands it to her.

"Aww." Lily takes it, trying to make light of it, but as he turns away, she holds it up to her nose to sniff it. He winks.

Mark pulls vegetables and a fresh steak out of the bag. Lily spots garlic, grits, peppers and onions as she walks by to fill a cup of water to put the rose in.

"I hope you can cook, because that looks amazing already."

"Well, we'll see how good I am." He puts some butter in the skillet as he turns the flame on at the stove, already comfortable in her kitchen. "I have to make up for that disaster of a skating day where you spun circles around me."

"Hey, don't worry," she nudges his shoulder. "I was planning to skate circles around you anyway."

She catches the moment his eyes drop down to her lips. They tingle in memory, and she licks them.

"Can I help?" Lily asks and Mark smiles at her.

"If you want to, but I don't mind. I happen to like cooking a lot." He adds herbs and butter to the skillet to season the steak and the room fills with the smell of rosemary. Lily grabs an onion to wash it and Mark throws some more butter in the pan as she starts to cut the onion. The sizzle of the steak draws her attention to the skillet.

"This smells great, I can't wait to eat!"

"I just wish I remembered to bring some wine. This would be great with a glass of red." Lily laughs and pulls out two bottles from a cabinet near the fridge.

"I always have wine in the house, would either of these work?"

"Either of those would be great." He flips the steak. "I just can't have more than a glass if I'm going to drive home." He says, casually, like he doesn't know that it causes her heart to race and her skin to tingle.

If… it's such a small word with a big impact. That means there is a chance he thinks he'd stay the night. He mentioned giving good cuddles, but she had kind of taken it as a joke, especially since he didn't directly respond to her last message. Could he mean it? That he'd be willing to spend the night cooking for her and then spending some time in bed as well. What would it be like, waking up next to him?

Mark fries up the vegetables while the steak is resting, and Lily pours the wine for them. The food smells so good that Lily's mouth waters, and she is practically desperate for it when he finally starts slicing the steak.

"This is the chef's cut." He cuts one of the edges in half. He lifts the fork to Lily's lips. "Tell me what you think."

She can't tell him what she really thinks, because that involves leaving this meal on the counter and heading straight to dessert. "Yes, chef." She isn't prepared for the flavor of the steak. She moans, hand flying up to cover her mouth. He grins. "Mark, that's amazing!" Lily exclaims, still chewing on the piece, wanting to savor every juicy bit of it. It's like every steak she's ever had in a restaurant was garbage.

"It is, isn't it?" He uses that same fork to eat the other half. He cuts another in half, and he doesn't even have to ask. Lily pauses with her lips around the fork and looks up at a smiling Mark. He stares at her lips as she

89

pulls back, and this piece is half fat. She chews on it slowly, cherishing the flavor, and shaking her head.

"Are you a chef? For real, this is an amazing steak. I cannot believe this right now."

"I like to cook, and it gives me control of what goes in my body."

Lily is too far gone in the taste of the steak to make the lewd joke that comment deserves, so she nods instead. Does he plan to cut every bite in half and feed it to her? She won't complain. He splits the meal into two portions on the plates in front of them before giving Lily a slight bow.

"Dinner is served."

"Let's set the table," she clinks their wine glasses together as they move to the dinner table.

"How's your day been?" Mark's foot nudges hers beneath the table.

"Well, it's much better now, but it kind of sucked this morning."

Mark gestures for her to continue talking, so she does. "They might be canceling my program." Lily frowns.

"Ah, so the team couldn't come up with any ideas to save it?"

"Nothing that will actually work. I hate not being able to come up with the answer, I just don't know enough about the design to try and fix it."

"Well, that's what the team is for right? Just trust them to figure it out." Trust. There's that damn term again.

"I do trust them," Lily defends, "but I don't think that they fully understand all the constraints right now. The cost is blowing up, the schedule is messing up, and it only works if we save the technical."

"Sure, but one person can't do it all."

"I wish." Lily swirls her wine in her cup. "I just want to help and I can't, not with this. In fact, I bet I'm doing a lot of not helping by harping about the schedule and cost while they are trying to work."

"I'm sure no one is holding it against you."

"I hope not, but I know I'm shifting into micromanagement, and I keep having to try and hold myself back from doing it."

Mark doesn't respond to that, so Lily changes the topic. "How's your Instagram?"

Mark's face brightens before breaking out in a smile. "Got a bunch of new followers. One even went back to like pictures from two years ago."

"I'm just helping your numbers." The heat in her cheeks betrays her smooth words, and Mark swirls the wine in his cup.

"You did help. It's doing really good actually, showing more of my personality. I'm getting more engagement already, and it's only been a few days." He pulls up his phone to play his most recent video and he finishes his wine as he shows her the comments.

"You should have another glass." Lily reaches for the wine bottle, hoping he hears her invitation to stay the night. Mark's lips twitch as he puts his phone down.

"Not if I'm driving." His heated gaze sets her body aglow as he moves his glass towards the bottle.

"Have another glass." She purrs and she knows he understands by the way he leans forward and the way his gaze shifts down to her lips. He lifts the glass to the bottle, but stares at her like he'd rather throw her on the table than finish his last few bites. Lily's heart speeds at the thought of what's coming next.

***

"Dinner was amazing," Lily loads up the dishwasher. She takes a breath, heart pounding, but she decides to take a chance "but if I'm being honest, that's not all I was hoping for today."

"If I'm being honest," Mark comes up behind her, "that's not all I was offering." He puts his hands on her hips and she leans back into his warm hard body. He lowers his lips to kiss her neck as his thumbs slip under her shirt. His lips on her neck feel like fire and her mouth falls open as she lets out a sigh. "I believe I mentioned cuddles too."

"I think you missed a step." Lily murmurs as the smell of wine, steak, and Mark fills her with need.

"Is that so?"

Lily closes her eyes but she doesn't answer. Mark peppers kisses up to her ear and with her eyes closed, every kiss lingers after he leaves. His hands are warm against her hips, and Lily moves her hips back to press against his erection. Desire turns her into a trembling mess. Another deep breath and she shudders. She needs to know what he tastes like, and so she turns to kiss him. One hand reaches up to go around his neck and pull him closer and the other finds his cock.

The first time this happened, he was a whimpering mess, and Lily is surprised by just how much she wants that to happen again. The second time, they were limited by being in public. This time, he takes a step forward, trapping her between him and the counter. He nibbles on her lip as his cock twitches in her hand.

"Miss it already?" He rolls his hips into hers.

"I miss you begging me to come," Lily blurts out, almost gasping at her own boldness. Mark inhales sharply before his hands tighten around her hips. He lifts her to sit on the counter as he pulls back from her kiss. His warm hands settle on her bare thighs, a sharp contrast to the cold counter. His eyes burn.

"Fuck, Lily, I would lo—"

She cuts off his statement with a searing kiss, but he groans into her lips in a way that tells her that he doesn't really mind. Lily wraps her legs around his waist and pulls on the back of his neck to pull him even closer to her. She yanks on his hair to turn him slightly, and instead of surrendering into the kiss, Mark pulls her tighter to him with one hand on her hip and the other on her knee.

She hasn't grinded like this since high school, but it's just as fun as she remembers it to be. He rolls his hips forward, sliding his cock against her pussy and the thin layers of fabric do nothing to protect her from the sensation. She moans out as she leans back, and he lifts her shirt over her head. She pulls his shirt off next, and his skin is hot against her chest. She can hardly believe that this is happening, but she's so happy she won't be breaking out her vibrator tonight. There's almost too much to take in at once. She pants as he continues the rocking motion as a promise of what's to come.

"What do you want from me?" His hands squeeze her breasts, and his hips continue to tease. His thumbs graze over her nipples.

"At the very least," Lily pants, "you owe me from last time."

"Do you want me to return the favor?" He gently tugs on her hair. "Hand in your hair, tongue in your mouth, fingers in your pussy, making a mess of you in the best way."

"Mark," she moans, "please." Lily can't bear how much she wants him to eat her out right now. She helps him scoot off her shorts, and he pulls her to the edge of the counter. He spreads her legs, but she stops him before he can start to finger her in the kitchen. She wants him in her bedroom if she's only going to be able to get him once. If there is another time, maybe. She desperately wants there to be another time already. He steps back as she jumps off and she clears her throat.

"I'm going to go get in bed, and you'd better be naked by the time you join me there." She gives him another scorching kiss before nipping at his lips and pulling away to the sound of his groan. He's so vocal, and it reverberates in her core in a way she didn't know she liked. It takes everything in her to walk away and not giggle, and he unbuckles his belt behind her.

She sits on her bed with her legs spread as she looks to the doorway. Which pose would be sexiest for him to walk into? Could she cause him to moan just by the sight of her? She glides her own finger along the edge of her labia to find she's helplessly wet already. She hears Mark washing his hands and opening a bag, and in a few seconds he is standing in her doorway; a condom in his hands and a smile on his face.

He's easily the most handsome man she's ever seen in person, and she's a little embarrassed to be thinking that as he stands in her doorway naked. She moves her eyes from his face to take in his broad shoulders, the results of his daily fitness regimen evident in his broad shoulders and the sleek, defined muscles of his chest. What would it be like to see him there; with his muscles on display as they flexed and rippled? What would his sweat taste like as she kissed it off his neck? She could trail her kisses down to his nipples and—His pecs jump and Lily laughs and looks back up to his face.

"Thought I lost you for a second." He turns sideways and grabs his arm into what must be a bodybuilder pose. "But I'm happy to let you keep looking." He winks with a devilish smolder.

Lily rakes her eyes down his body. "I thought I lost you out there."

"I was just making sure I'm prepared." He tosses the condom onto the bed next to her as he crawls up the bed to kiss her again. Lily leans back, taking him with her. She reaches down to stroke his cock, but he pulls away before she can start to stroke it.

"That's right, I owe you an orgasm, don't I?"

"You don't have to." Lily offers him an out even as he begins to kiss along her neck, getting lower with each kiss.

"Believe me, I want to." He sucks her nipple into his mouth and flicks his tongue against it. He pinches the other and then licks a trail between them. "When I heard you tell me no at The Playhouse, I wanted nothing more than to be freed so I could kneel in front of you and ask you properly." He sucks on the other nipple as his fingers gently trace the curve underneath her breasts.

"Mark," Lily moans.

"You can tell me what you like if you want, but I also love figuring it out." He squeezes her hips slightly as he kisses around her belly button. He's teasing. She shivers under him.

"I like everything you are doing right now." Lily pants as his kisses get lower and lower. "Is this how you usually thank people for orgasms?" He hums his yes into the line where her thigh meets her crotch.

"It's how I ask for them too, sometimes." He lightly nips at her thigh, and Lily spreads her legs further for him.

"Don't just tease me, Mark," she whines.

"I won't." He slips his finger between her labia, moving up and down her slick folds before retreating. He licks his finger, staring at Lily, and she trembles as he groans. "Better than dinner."

94

Lily wants to smirk. She wants to say 'dessert usually is', but her words and her thoughts float away as he pushes her thighs up and open, and begins to lick her in earnest. She moans out wantonly as her hands clench the bed sheets and closes her eyes as she presses her pussy into his face. Fuck, she's so glad she finally gets to throw her legs over his shoulders. It's even hotter than she imagined.

"Fuck!" She shouts when she can finally get enough air. "Oh, Mark..." He sucks on her clit before licking again, and Lily moans. "Oh yeah." She breathes as he lowers her leg to shift his angle and he slides a finger into her. "Yes," she encourages.

Mark climbs up her body slowly as he adds a second finger and continues to slowly thrust them in and out of her clenching pussy. He curls his fingers, and Lily whimpers as he uses his other hand to pull on her hair as he lays it on the bed. He shifts his body and hand, and there are stars behind Lily's eyes as he uses two fingers to pump her and his thumb to rub circles on her clit. She gasps. He's found her g-spot. Their eyes connect, and he smirks, concentrating his efforts there.

"What was it I owed you exactly," he asks conversationally, as if she could do anything but cling to him in the moment, moaning and riding the wave of her building orgasm and— "Ah yes, hand in your hair, tongue in your mouth, fingers in your pussy, making a mess of you."

He lowers his body to slowly and languidly kiss her, and Lily is over the crest. He swallows her moan as she jerks against him, and he continues to finger her as she clenches around him. She grinds against his hands as her orgasm washes over her and he doesn't stop kissing her until she slows her grinds down.

"Are you too sensitive or—" Mark laughs as Lily yanks his head back down to kiss her but she's too horny to feel embarrassed about it. His fingers move to continue to pump her in a steady rhythm, and she can't help but think of that glorious, neglected cock and how good it's going to feel when she finally gets it. She pulls his hair again as she pulls him closer, and his deep guttural moan in response causes her to clench around his fingers.

He pulls back from her lips. "Anything else I can do for you?"

"I can think of something." Lily's breath comes in short, hot bursts. Mark moves his hands away as Lily tugs on his arm, and he hisses when she reaches down to grab his cock. She strokes him lightly at first, squeezing and tugging on him until he is rolling his hips into her. His eyes close and his mouth falls open in a sigh and Lily uses her other hand to bring him down to kiss her.

"Is this all you wanted," she checks in a few seconds later, "or did you want to put that condom on and fuck me?"

Mark nods. "If you want it too, I would love to give you this cock."

Lily lets go of his cock as she gives him a slower kiss. "Hurry up then."

Mark fumbles for the condom and Lily settles into her pillows as he slides it on. Lily spreads her legs again and smiles as he lines up his cock and rubs it along her lips, teasing her and using her cum to slick him up.

Lily groans out her approval as he slides in a few inches. Their lips meet in a searing kiss as Mark begins to rock into her gently. Lily is surprised at the gentleness. She moans into Mark's kisses as he slowly sinks in further. Once he's fully in, she impatiently shifts her hips to grind on his cock.

Mark nibbles on her lips as he increases his pace, making the bed creak in protest, and Lily lets go of his mouth in order to let out a large moan. His cock stretches her pussy deliciously and she gasps as his hips meet hers. She grabs at his shoulders, daggering her fingers into his skin as Mark moves his lips to her chin and then to her neck. He bites gently and sucks and Lily lets out a small noise as he shifts and lights her insides on fire.

"Fuck me!" She shouts, loud enough that her neighbors might hear. "Mark, harder."

"Like this?" He groans and he complies instantly, sucking on her neck harder as his hips snap into hers, and Lily lets out another moan.

"Yes, just like that." She curses. Mark continues to fuck her and he groans into her neck. Her whole body clenches around him as she gets closer and closer and he lets out a pained sound she can barely hear over her own loud moans as she comes on his cock. He doesn't stop thrusting, but he does slow down and take a deep breath.

"You feel like you don't want to let me go," he mumbles into her neck. "So fucking tight when you come."

Lily should be a little flattered, maybe, and she should probably respond to that, but all she can really think of is how amazing that was, and how long it's been since she had an orgasm around a real cock, and that she wants another one. She wants to keep him here all week. Her legs wrap around his waist. "Make me come again," Lily bites his ear. He shudders as she tugs on his lobe.

"Yes," he moans into her as he moves his knees forward, shifting from missionary into a new position. He picks up her legs a bit and then thrusts again and Lily curses in ecstasy.

She comes twice more before he shows any signs of being near the edge. She has the abstract thought that maybe he's not good at quickies, but she can't dwell on any thoughts for long, not with the way her insides are on fire.

"Oh god, Lily," He pants, slowing down his thrusts so that he can speak, "Please, can I come?" It should be weird that he always asks. She didn't ask him to before. She clenches around him and he lets out a breath. She should just say yes.

"What if I said no?"

He whimpers. "Please don't say no." Mark begs. Lily doesn't answer, enjoying the tortured look on his face, even as he keeps up the slow and steady thrusting she likes. "I'd stop, of course I would. I'd plead and beg for it but I'd listen. I'm good, I swear."

Lily wants to pull his hair again, but he's out of reach. She wants to kiss him, but she doubts he's that flexible. Next time. She wants to make him beg, but she doesn't feel brave enough to demand it.

"Please let me come."

"Come," she orders. The power feels like fire in her veins.

"Thank you," he pants as his hips jerk. The next thrust is harder, and the one after that sends stars dancing behind her eyelids. His hands tighten against her as his hips stutter, and he lets out a low long groan that she hopes to never forget. He shallowly thrusts as he comes and when Lily opens her eyes his are locked onto hers.

"I'll be back in a second." He promises as he slips out of her and Lily's empty. She stares at the ceiling, remembering how to breath, as he tosses the condom in the bin by her bed and then flops down on the bed next to her.

"That was amazing," Lily curls into his side. His arm wraps around her body and pulls her closer. Her whole body is soft and languid, and she traces the ridges of his muscles as he catches his breath.

"It was, thanks for letting me come over."

"So do you get assignments a lot? Any way I could sign up in advance?" Lily pushes herself up slightly, and Mark turns into her to kiss her waiting lips.

"You could always just invite me over." He mumbles into her lips.

"I'll have to remember that." Lily pulls back, and his eyes are bright as they look up at her. "Do you want to keep seeing each other?" Her thoughts begin to race as soon as the words leave her lips. Does that sound too much like dating? If he's not open to dating someone who isn't a domme then there really is only one option for right now. Before he can turn her down she blurts "as friends. Friends with benefits?"

She liked when he went to his knees for her, when he begged her to come, when he moaned into her mouth at the rink. She certainly enjoyed everything that happened tonight, and she just wants more. She can't imagine hurting him the way Derrick did, but there's so many other fun things they can do together.

"I'd love to." His other hand comes to rest on her hip, and she's happy, she is, but she's disappointed as well. "Just something fun and casual."

"Is it like that with Derrick too?" Lily can't help but ask. Mark shrugs under her.

"Pretty much. If I was dating, I'd need a dominant closer in age, and honestly, I'd prefer a girlfriend."

The buzz in her head is probably from all the orgasms, but this new information threatens to scramble her remaining thoughts. He does want a girlfriend, and maybe that could be her. She'd have to be his domme. "I mean, what are you, like fifty?"

He laughs as he rolls them, so he's on top of her and captures her lips again. "I'm twenty-five." He eventually gets out in between breaths.

"Twenty-six." Their kisses make her want to do anything but sleep, and her core aches for more. It could be minutes or hours for all the thoughts she's able to have. As their kisses turn slow and languid, she lets her hands run over the muscles of his back and hips and back up to settle on his biceps.

"I've got an extra towel, if you need to shower."

"I really must stink." He flops on her chest playfully and Lily giggles. She runs her hand through damp hair, and he snuggles into her chest. He moves his weight to his side and kisses the side of her breast gently.

"You haven't told me much about your modeling," Lily murmurs as she listens to his steady breathing.

"What do you want to know?" He yawns. His arms come up to rest against her sides. It's warm and comforting. His breath tickles her skin, and goosebumps race across her chest and harden her nipples.

"I don't know. Is there anything exciting coming up?"

"I just send my portfolio in most of the time and hope for a call back. It's not the best strategy, but it's alright for now."

"I wonder if you should—" Lily yawns. "Get an agent."

"Don't tell me what to do." Mark sticks his tongue out.

It's a joke, but that doesn't stop the thought from racing up her spine and forcing her to straighten her shoulders and bite her lips. He does what she tells him to. He asks her for permission to come. Her hand stops. What else could she make him do? The silence stretches just a second too long, and Mark's playful expression falls off of his face as he looks up at her. His beautiful bright eyes search her face. She doesn't know what he sees in them, but he pauses. She should say something. Joke back. Flirt. Anything.

"Do you, uh, want me to tell you what to do?" Lily finally asks. He probably can't even hear her, with the way her voice has gone soft and high in her nerves.

"No, no, no, I would never force you into doing anything you're not comfortable with." He waves his hands as if to dispel the idea, apologetic and kind. Lily doesn't respond. He seems to come to a different conclusion a second later. "Unless you want to?"

"Maybe?" Lily's voice is practically a squeak, and she clears her throat as heat rushes to her cheeks and she looks away. "I mean, if I wanted to, where, uh, how would I start?"

<u>Chapter 10</u>

This should be awkward in some way or form, but she's not going to be the one to make it that way. Mark is only wearing boxers, and he's leaning over the table in his dining room. There are a few toys next to him, and he's got his face propped up with his hands. They've been standing here for some time already, and she can tell Derrick is trying not to get impatient with her questions.

"You're sure?" Lily asks. Derrick nods. Has she already failed to not make it awkward?

"Yes," Mark doesn't bother to hide his eagerness as he wiggles his hips. "Green as grass."

"And if he says red for any reason, stop whatever you're doing," Derrick adds.

"Right." Lily nods. "The safe word."

"The safe word stops anything; any play, any teasing, any CNC."

"CNC?"

"Consensual non consent," Derrick pauses.

"Basically it's me saying I want it all, even what I don't want." Mark explains. "Like if I want a really tough spanking, or like really rough sex, where saying no might be my instinct, but I want it to continue."

"Don't play around with it though. Not for a long time. You still have to figure out your basics." Derrick says.

"Got it! And speaking of basics," she gestures to Mark's ass. It's been twenty minutes of just talking about things, so she doesn't want to hold them up any further. Derrick mentioned not having a long time when he got here, and she's wasting it on nonsense.

"He's been asking for some impact for a while, and I figured it was a good opportunity to teach. Just start small." Derrick gives Mark's ass a gentle slap as a demonstration.

"Okay," Lily tries. Her hesitation slows her hand so that it merely taps his ass and she can almost hear him laughing at her. She tries again, but she can't bring herself to hit him harder. What if she actually hurts him?

"It's fine if this isn't something you like," Derrick starts but Lily shakes her head.

"I think I'll like it. I just, can't," she tries again and it is another glancing blow.

"You can hit me harder than that." Mark comments as he shifts his hips from side to side. "I barely feel it." He continues as Lily pauses. "It's okay, I want you to." He encourages. Lily takes a breath to steel herself, and then slaps his ass hard enough to make a sound. Mark laughs softly. "At least try," he pushes his ass back.

Lily flushes and slaps him harder, happy to see him react to that. Her hand stings a little from it. "Is that better?"

"You want to try again?" Mark laughs.

"Stop being a brat." Derrick swats his ass hard and Mark laughs again as he finally puts his head down. "I'm trying to teach her."

"Teach away." Mark wiggles his ass. Lily smacks him again for good measure, and she almost laughs. She wants her marks to be as bright as Derrick's were, and she wants to make him moan for her from it. The thought surprises her and stills her hand.

Derrick goes over the areas she should spank to warm up and how to know when the sub gets needy. Lily asks way more questions than the situation warrants, but her nerves get the best of her. When Mark rolls his hips against the table, Derrick gives him a hard spank of finality before instructing Lily to grab the crop. As Lily lifts it up, she's reminded of the red crop in the dungeon. She likes the way the crop sits in her hand, or rather the way it makes her stand straighter and gives her confidence. It's not as intimidating as the one with a lot of tails or a whip, it looks more fun than the cane, and the leather is cool in her hands.

"Sir." Mark sounds desperate and needy. He squirms on the table. The languid way he lays on the table makes her want to reach out and touch him, and the low whine he lets out shoots from her toes to her nipples. Derrick ignores him for now.

"Turn around." Derrick takes the crop from her. "I'm going to use this on you so you know what it feels like." She does. A second later sharp pain blossoms on her ass cheek. Her arousal dies as she yelps.

"Ouch! That hurts!" She covers her ass and turns back to him. Derrick then slaps Mark with the crop, making a louder, sharper, sound. Mark moans out.

"That's the point."

"Sir," Mark whines, and Derrick places a hand on Mark's hip.

"Stay put and shut up, this isn't for you, it's for her."

"Be a good boy for us," Lily coos, and Mark nods as he places his palms on the table.

Derrick lightly hits his forearm with the crop. "You should have an idea of how much force you need to cause levels of pain, that way you don't hurt someone more than you want to. Try lightly hitting yourself before hitting someone else."

Lily's ass throbs. It's more in memory than actual pain. Derrick hands her the crop and she waves it around a bit to get used to it. She starts with a few light taps on her forearm, and then a harder one that has her pulling her arm back and wincing.

"Hit him here, lightly," Derrick instructs as he moves his fingers across Mark's muscular ass. Lily takes a deep breath.

"Okay, I can do that. Are you ready Mark?"

"Please," He responds, and Lily gives him a light tap with it. "Harder," he whines, "I barely felt that one." Lily hits him again, the crop making a dull thud, but Mark only pushes his hips backwards. He whines again, a low breathy sound, and Lily's fingers tighten around the crop.

"Mark." Derrick scolds, and Mark sighs and slumps back into his position.

"Fine," Mark pouts, "but I want a proper spanking before you leave today."

"Maybe," Derrick rubs Mark's ass as he talks to Lily next, "you can give him a few more, space it out in these areas. You can alternate between hits and gentle nudges, or touches. Be careful to switch sensations every once in a while, so it is still new for the bottom."

Lily nods. "Got it."

"Go for it." Derrick instructs.

Lily thwacks the crop against him, hearing a nice thud. Mark sighs into the table and seems to relax. "Yes," he breathes, "thank you."

"Don't thank me yet," Lily swings again. "I'm just getting started."

"Good." Derrick comments, "you're learning."

They spend another few minutes with the riding crop, and then alternate to spankings. Lily reaches for the crop again, deciding she likes it better, and Derrick pulls out a flogger. He is interrupted by his phone going off. Derrick checks it, and then puts the flogger on the table.

"It's been an hour already?" Mark asks, still whiny and needy.

"Yes." He turns to Lily, "Sometimes he gets to come at the end of spankings," Derrick holds his hand out for the crop, "but most of the time he doesn't."

"Oh, okay," Lily hands it over, "are we done?"

"I have to run to the doctor with Michi."

"Sir!" Mark squirms. "What about my spanking?" Mark stands and Derrick smiles at Mark.

"But you've been such a good boy," Derrick coos, but it comes across as mocking to Lily. "Why would I spank you for that?" Mark huffs as he leans against the counter and he sweeps his arm across the table, knocking the flogger off of it. Derrick's eyes narrow as his hand tightens on the bag.

Mark stands straight, seemingly growing taller, and all signs of the languid mess he was on the table are gone.

"Pick it up."

"Pick what up?" Mark crosses his arms, juts his sharp chin to the side. Lily glances between them. Derrick sighs.

"Mark. I don't have time for this. You'll get your spanking later, okay? I need to go." Mark picks up the flogger, face tight with anger, and puts it on the table in front of Lily before turning around and walking out of the room.

"Is he okay?" Lily asks after she hears the door slam.

"He'll be fine." Derrick walks over to the other side of the table to pick the flogger up. "Sometimes he just gets in these moods. I don't really put up with it, but he likes the whole brat aspect and sometimes I just have to beat it out of him."

"Okay?" Lily comments, looking down the hall and making the decision to stay for a while. "Good luck with Michi."

"Thanks."

"Mark," Lily calls out as she makes her way down the hall to his room. "Are you okay?"

"Go away," he pouts as he lies on the bed with his head in his pillow and Lily can't help but smile.

"Do you really want me to leave?"

"No." He admits. She sits on the edge of the bed, and he maneuvers so that his head is in her lap. His warm breath on her legs threaten to consume her thoughts with lust, but she has to focus. His hair looks so soft.

"Is this an aftercare thing? Like did Derrick just do a bad thing?" She asks.

"No," he huffs, "and Michi's been having lots of doctor's appointments lately, so I'm not surprised, it's just frustrating because I need a spanking." Lily wishes she could offer him one, but that wouldn't help either of them.

"Is Michi okay?"

Ally Marr

"Not really," Mark admits, and Lily runs her fingers through his hair. It's soft and silky and he nuzzles into her legs. "She's really been trying to get pregnant, but it's not going well."

"Oh that sucks." Lily's not sure what else to say.

"He's been so distracted lately, and I don't want to come between them, but I'm feeling needy." He speaks in low tones and sighs. Lily hums as he continues. "I'll message him about it, and I'm sure he'll make time for a maintenance beating, but I was hoping to take the edge off today."

"Sorry I can't help."

"I didn't expect you to," Mark waves her off, "you're so new at this and we don't have a dynamic, so it's fine."

Lily nods but can't help feeling disappointed by the interaction. Derrick mentioned something about regular beatings too. "Did you say maintenance beating?" As in a real beating? Something that could seriously hurt him?

"You should come next weekend." Mark suddenly sits up. His face is inches from hers and she has a view into the endless dark brown of his eyes. She'd go anywhere if he'd just ask. "You'll get a demonstration." Mark smiles and Lily should just lean forward and bite his pink lips. "It'll be more for you to learn too."

"Since you asked so nicely," she teases. She leans forward to kiss him, but he flops backwards onto his bed with a groan and the moment is lost.

Chapter 11

She barely makes it in time to see his scene, but she still manages to snag a good seat to watch it. Mark is already up there. Lily crosses her legs from her spot by the door as the rest of the room fills up. She's not surprised to see more people than normal in the dungeon, since it's kink night and Mark is part of the show, but she is shocked at just how many people there are. It's standing room only now. Ronnie is sitting in the far corner, acting as a second DM in the dungeon today. Lily returns her attention to the men standing by the center of the room in front of the Saint Andrew's cross.

"He might ask to stop," Derrick continues. "He'll probably beg for it. He'll certainly cry."

"Do you consent to this now?" Thorn asks.

"Yes." Mark nods. "I consent to the CNC play for tonight. I understand there will be impact and sensation play, and probably a lot of humiliation." Mark shakes his head as Derrick shrugs. "We will use the color code, as per DM rules, but my safe word is gimbal in case I don't think to say red."

"Thank you," Thorn says, "and I'm sure you both already know, but we are only allowing CNC today for vetted Doms since it is Kink night."

"Thank you, Thorn."

Mark smiles at the other two before taking a drink of his water. He stretches and has a few more quick words with Derrick before beginning to strip; more methodical than performative. Mark strips down to his boxers but doesn't get fully naked. Lily hoped he would, but she knows she's in for a spectacle either way. He is gorgeous to look at, and she tries to commit him to memory. Lily traces the gentle lines of his abs with her eyes, wanting to trace them with her finger and tongue. His V cut disappears into his boxers, and it's almost more enticing to not see him in all of his glory.

Mark turns to face the Saint Andrew's cross, and his arms are cuffed to the top. Derrick picks up a riding crop first, the same crop Lily used on Mark a few days ago, and he slides the flat leather from the swell of his ass to the top of his shoulders. He moves it across Mark's shoulders and all the way down to the bottom of Mark's calves. Mark leans into the touch, curving his back to try and get more contact.

"I haven't even started yet, and you already seem desperate." Derrick shakes his head. Mark lays his palms flat against the wood as he looks over his shoulder.

"I thought you liked that." Mark retorts. Instead of an answer, Derrick snaps his wrist and the crop strikes Mark's ass cheek. Lily doesn't flinch at the sound this time, but she does wish she could see the red marks start to appear. Mark lets out a shuddering breath and looks forward again. Derrick continues his strikes.

"I wonder if I can make you cry today."

"I'd like to see that," Mark taunts as Derrick hits him again. How can Mark talk while getting hit? She can only imagine how she'd flinch and sob and demand to be released. Her ass throbs in memory of the quick swat Derrick gave her before.

"Where are we?" Derrick asks, "How are you feeling now?"

"Green." Mark wiggles his ass. "We've barely started, Sir."

Derrick seems to take that as a cue and delivers a bunch of strikes in rapid succession. Mark moans out. Lily watches him squirm with rapt attention. "Is that enough for you?"

"No, Sir." Mark arches his back, as if offering himself up for more. How far is this going to go? "Don't you have more for me?"

"I do." Derrick leaves a pink mark behind on his shoulders. "I have enough to make you cry. When you beg me to stop, I won't." Derrick threatens. He continues to strike Mark and Lily leans forward in her seat as the pattern continues. Talking and then hitting. Could she make him beg one day? What would he beg her for that she had the power to give him? Could she ever say no? She mouths the word. Mark starts panting. His eyes are closed, his head is upturned, and she envisions standing in front of him, grabbing his chin to make him open his eyes and look at her. Mark lets out a cry as Derrick hits him again, and Derrick laughs at him. There is a flash of a smile on Mark's face after he lets out a deep breath.

"If that's all it takes to make you cry, then this will be a short session."

"Oh, are you already tired?" Mark laughs and the blows Derrick gives him next are much harder. There is something different about today. Mark's demeanor is completely different from the last time he was spanked: he was whiny and needy and thankful before, now he seems to be defiant and snarky. Is this part of the scene?

"Such a brat." Derrick spanks Mark's ass and Lily's hums to herself in realization. This is the bratty behavior at his apartment, that Derrick said he'd beat out of him—that Mark said he needed beat out of him. Mark leans forward and sticks his ass out, and Derrick spanks it again. "When I'm done, you won't be able to sit down."

"Then we should probably start soon, right?" Mark pants out. Derrick responds by dropping the crop. He walks over to the table to pick up the paddle.

"Okay, then. Remember this?"

"Should I?" Mark snarks and Derrick huffs. "Fuck!" Mark exclaims at first contact. Derrick pulls it back and hits him again. "Have we started now?" He asks, casually, as if he doesn't really care.

Mark presses against the cross, tense and coiled. "You tell me."

"Are you still green?" Derrick asks.

The tension melts off Mark. "Yes, Sir."

"Good." Derrick starts to hit him with the paddle. Lily glances at Ronnie and Thorn, but they are both watching the scene before them. Neither of them look concerned. Even as Mark begins to cry out for longer periods of time. Tears race down his cheeks. Surely he's had enough? He's not smiling anymore. Lily bites her lip as he shudders against the restraints. Derrick has to know he's crying.

"Color?" Derrick places the flogger on the table.

"Green." Mark sobs out.

Derrick lifts a cane from the table next, and gently taps it against what must be the bruised skin of Mark's ass. Mark shudders and starts crying. Derrick still keeps up the light taps. "I told you, didn't I," Derrick taunts. "That I would make you cry tonight."

"Yes, Sir." Mark whimpers.

"It's a shame you need these regular beatings to remember your place." Derrick scolds. Mark doesn't respond. Derrick rakes his fingers across the fabric of his boxers and Mark groans out, but there's not even a hint of arousal in the pain. He shakes as Derrick repeats the motion.

"Do you remember the second part?" Derrick's voice is deceptively tender. "I said you would beg me to stop." Derrick squeezes a cheek and Mark cries out again. "I said I wouldn't." Derrick steps back after another moment, lifts the cane, and hits Mark's thigh hard enough to bruise. Lily winces. Mark rises onto the tips of his toes, and Derrick repeats the motion. Mark doesn't beg, and Lily is strangely proud. She would have broken and begged a long time ago.

Still, it's enough, isn't it? Mark squirms away from the cane, but Derrick doesn't stop. Lily flinches at a hard thwack and then looks to the DMs. She's new, and she doesn't know what's normal, but this can't be okay. Can it?

When he's done with the cane, Derrick goes into his bag to pull out a short flogger that's made out of metal chains instead of leather strips. It's just like the one Mark didn't want her to ask about. The woman in front of her winces. Mark said he didn't like that tool. Derrick should know that.

She should do it. Just stand and say something. She can make him stop. Isn't this what Mark wants? Isn't this CNC? She flinches at the next blow. Nothing about Mark looks happy right now. Nothing about this seems like something she wants to be a part of.

Lily glances at the door, but there are so many people between her and it that she doesn't get up. Mark cries out again and Lily turns to see Derrick trail the metal down his back. It must be a new sharper pain, because Mark writhes against the cross and his restraints. A second later he breaks.

"Sir!" Mark calls out. "Not this!" Derrick pulls it back. Ronnie and Thorn look more alert, but neither move to intercept the pair. Lily wants to stand and cradle him in her arms, to throw herself between them and stop this.

"Are you safewording?" Derrick asks and Mark shakes his head even as he cries into the cross. Lily is sure he is safewording. Look at the state of him! He takes a shuddering breath. Maybe he forgot the words.

"Asshole." Mark grunts. "You're such an asshole."

"That doesn't sound like a safeword." Derrick tightens his grip on the handle.

"No," Mark groans, "I am not safewording."

Lily stops breathing. Is this part of being the perfect sub? Does Mark even want this? Is part of the consensual non consent so consuming that it seems like Mark couldn't want a single part of this? Mark knows what to say to end this, so he must want some part of it. Lily lets out a deep breath. He must.

"Green, we're green."

"Then I'm not stopping." Derrick brings the tool to brush against Mark's lower back. Mark jerks against the wood, and it rattles in the room. He cries out as his body tries to move away from Derrick's tool. Lily looks away and closes her eyes. They are warm and her breaths come faster and faster. Not a minute later, Mark tries again.

"No more, please, no, stop." Mark begs. It sounds like he jerks against the restraints. "Please, Sir."

"No," Derrick voice takes on a hard and firm tone. Mark whimpers, "I do enjoy finally hearing you beg. You should continue to do it."

Mark does, continuously, and Lily opens her eyes to watch. "Fuck you." Mark jerks against the wood again.

"No." Derrick responds, calm and still firm. Firm enough that Lily's chest tightens like she's done something wrong. "You don't deserve an orgasm today." Mark shudders. He begins to weep, openly and without shame, and Lily suppresses the urge to stand and flee the room. It's like a dam has been broken, the way the tears leave him and he sags against the cross. Neither one of them says anything else as Mark cries and Derrick continues to hit him. Mark weeps through the rest of the scene and it almost makes Lily sick. She doesn't know how the scene ends, she can't pay attention to whatever Derrick is saying. She just sees Mark. She just listens to his sobs. He doesn't stop as Derrick puts his tools on the table, doesn't stop crying when he's unbound from the cross. He doesn't stop as Michi leads Mark from the room with a ginger touch. The room clears out and Lily follows the crowd in a daze until she gets to the hallway with the couches and collapses on one.

Lily tries to process what she's seen so that she doesn't fret over Mark when he comes out to see her. What in the world happened? Derrick just—and Mark—and no one stopped them. Mark never safeworded. He wanted that. If she were to believe his words from before, he *needed* this. People here have a different definition of normal, and she likes that, but this? It's frightening. Is that the evolution of the fun she had learning with the crop? Is there no in between? She can't do that. It's not learning or growing, she'll never be able to hurt someone like that.

Instead of Mark approaching her on the couch, it's Derrick. He doesn't explain where Mark is, and she doesn't ask. She can only imagine the aftercare after a scene that intense takes a long time. She needs a long time. Even if she wanted to say something, her voice seems to be lost in the tension in her stomach.

"How'd you enjoy the scene?" He sits on the other side of the couch, where she'd expected Mark to flop into with his giant blanket. He's quieter than he was a few moments ago. His voice is reserved and almost soft. It's deceptive. Lily doesn't respond for a few seconds, looking down the hall and then down to her hands. Could her hands hurt the way his did?

"It was way more intense than the first one." Lily finally speaks.

"Yes. He really was hurting in there today." Derrick stares at his hands and swallows.

"He, um, likes that?" Lily's hesitant to ask because she has no idea what she'll say if Derrick says no.

"Yes," Derrick shakes his head. "We talk about all of our scenes beforehand. He knew about most of this before it happened. He said he needed it, especially after I had to leave him last time." Lily pats his shoulder, trying to be comforting, trying to be comforted. Is this the top drop Michi mentioned?

"I've got some questions on CNC but I think I'll save them for later."

"Thanks," he pinches the bridge of his nose. "It was intense for both of us." Derrick stands. "I think we both need some more aftercare. I'll come find you later."

Lily nods. When he leaves, she makes her way towards the main room, grabs some chips, and sits on one of the couches. She greets a few familiar faces, but she's not up for much conversation. She keeps thinking back to the dungeon and what just happened. Ultimately, she doesn't see a future in which she could ever do that to him, and that means that there isn't a future for them.

It's disappointing, but there is no other conclusion she can see. She thought that she could do this softly, or slowly, but if that's the end goal there's nothing she can do. If Mark was upset with Derrick for not getting this before, if that's truly why he threw the flogger off the table and pouted in his room, then he'll be doing that a lot with her.

"He's looking for a domme," Derrick says from behind her. It's only been a few minutes, and there's no way he was able to find someone to help him. "He's always looking for dommes."

She turns to look at him, but he's looking at the dance floor. "He gets these ideas in his head about how the girls he likes could grow into dominants and then he lets himself get hurt."

"He told me about his ex."

"About one of them, maybe." Derrick doesn't move from his spot, so she shifts to face him.

"I like you, but I don't want him to get hurt."

"I don't want to hurt him." That's the real problem here. He wants to be hurt.

"You might, if this continues."

Lily should feel happy to hear that Mark might like her, but she's incredulous. No one would mistake her for a domme. Especially Mark, who apparently likes being beaten by his dom. "He can't possibly think I can do some of the things he likes." She gestures to the dungeon. "I could barely watch. There's no way he could see me being his domme."

"He likes a lot of things," Derrick insists. "Gentle things you'd start with."

Derrick must mean it to be a warning, but she really doesn't believe him. "Like what?" She's incredulous.

"Like worship, or pet play, or service." He answers, but doesn't elaborate. Lily waits a moment, and he releases the tension in his body with a sigh before turning away.

"You're just trying to protect him." Which is absurd given what she just saw. He makes his way around the couch and sits next to her on the edge of it. "I get that—"

"I am. I'm concerned."

"I don't think you have to be. I like him, but I know he is very kink focused, and I wouldn't propose anything serious with him unless I'd be willing to go all in." She doesn't say it, but the truth is she can't go all in. Derrick nods, but Lily gets the impression he is more defeated than satisfied.

"I look out for him. I'm trying to keep him safe."

Lily recognizes guilt in the way his shoulders are slumped and his hands rub each other. He's been acting differently since the beating. Michi must still be with Mark. "If I can ask, how'd you find out about all of the things he likes?" Lily changes the topic, "like the service and stuff, I can't imagine that came up in casual conversation."

He doesn't answer at first, scanning the small crowd on the main floor. "You'd learn about this stuff when you negotiate. You take feelings and embarrassment out of the equation and lay it all out on the table so that you can be on the same page."

"It seems weird to have to negotiate in a relationship." It's also weird to beat your partner.

"My wife and I are trying to have a baby, but I'm not very fertile." Derrick says, and Lily shifts in her seat. "That's why I had to leave the other day, to take her to the doctor."

"I'm sorry to hear that," she responds, moving to sit up straight. She is saved from having to figure out what to say next as he continues.

"Now we have to explore other options and negotiate there. It's the same." He leans back on the couch. "There is negotiating at every stage of a relationship: kinky or not. It's when you decide who takes out the trash, or walks the dog, or cooks dinner. There is trust in every relationship. A kinky relationship just takes that all to the next level."

After a moment he continues. "There is more of a chance for people to get hurt, or overstep boundaries, so there has to be more steps to make sure you're on the same page. You can't just use someone because you want to, you have to make sure you've earned it."

"Right." Lily nods. "That makes sense."

"And that's why in the dungeon, you see the D types asking the s types for their status. It's our job to make sure that our subs are okay, that we don't give them more than they can take." Derrick brings the conversation back to Mark.

"Mark was green," Lily says, mostly to remind herself. "He gave you the go ahead. Multiple times." She wouldn't go so far as to say he wanted it, but she can tell Derrick needs some comfort. "Where is he now?"

"He's with Michi. He," Derrick pauses, "he—he didn't want me touching him."

"Okay, and he's safe with Michi?" Lily can't blame Mark.

"He is; she's going to help him with aftercare."

"Is anyone here to help you?"

Derrick shakes his head. His leg starts bouncing. "Michi usually helps."

"Can I help?"

"I don't know. I think Michi will be good to Mark."

"You," Lily clarifies. "Is there anything I can do to help you?"

Derrick pauses, like he's not sure how to respond. Lily waits, but Derrick stares at his hands without answering for long enough that it's awkward again. She almost stands, wanting to search the area to see if Mark and Michi are finished, but she doesn't want to make him feel worse by leaving. "Michi usually holds me." His voice is so low Lily almost loses it under the music. "She tells me I'm not a bad person."

"You're not a bad person." Lily says, immediately. "You never were a bad person. I haven't known you that long and even I can tell that." She takes a chance, grabbing his hand in hers. "It's okay."

Derrick squeezes her hand. "Is it? Michi doesn't let me do that to her, because it hurts her. I just—Mark—he." Derrick whispers.

"He wanted that." Lily's voice is equally quiet. There's not much comfort she can offer him here.

"He did. He does. He's just, he's such a brat, and this helps with the—usually it's fine. But today he didn't—he didn't want me to touch him," He sighs out and Lily looks around the room for help. When none comes, she taps her hands against her legs.

"And you can ask him about that later, but I think it was as intense for him as it was for you."

Derrick lets out a sigh, and they sit in silence until Mark arrives.

"Can you take me home?"

Mark looks tired. His eyes are red and swollen from crying.

"I can do that." Derrick stands. "Whatever you need, I can—"

"I meant Lily," Mark corrects softly, pulling the blanket further around himself.

"Of course," Lily turns in her seat to fully face him. "Did you want to go now?"

Mark shakes his head. "Derrick and I need to talk for a little bit, and then we can go if that's okay?"

"Of course, I'm going to load up on free chips while I wait," she smiles, but he only nods as he turns to walk into an open bedroom. Derrick follows Mark, immediately asking questions as he does.

By the time Mark comes out to meet her, he's alone. Other than asking if he's ready to go, there isn't much to say until they are already in her car heading to his apartment.

"I kind of had a freak out in there, sorry." Mark looks out the window. His voice is hoarse but soft.

"Do you want to talk about it? Is it the maintenance thing?"

"Maybe?" He sighs, and his eyes shine with fresh tears. "I just have this nagging feeling lately that he doesn't want me." He stops talking and Lily waits until he continues. "It's kind of stupid, because we are just impact play partners really, and there's no sex, so we've been up front about this the whole time."

"But?"

"But I've asked him to collar me, to kind of be more than a one off, and he's not interested. He's not interested in me being a brat. He's not interested in me, I'm just the pretty boy he gets to spank every once in a while." Mark slumps against the chair, looking out into the night through his window, and Lily can't get a read on him.

"You are more than a pretty boy, and he'd be a fool not to see it." Lily pauses, and decides to make a quick stop before dropping him off home. "But you're not really in a relationship from what I've seen."

"We're not."

Lily taps the steering wheel with her finger. "So, if you don't mind me asking, why does the collar mean so much to you?"

"It means I'm not just a toy." Mark closes his eyes, leaning his head back. Tears slip down his cheeks. A toy, like the flogger he shoved off the table before. Is that what he thinks of himself? "That they aren't just going to throw me away if I stop working right."

"You're not a toy to me," she puts her hand on his and he smiles, "and I don't think you are just a toy to Derrick either." He turns his hand over so it can hold hers. "He was really worried about you today."

"Thanks." Mark tails off.

"It's so stupid," Mark starts again a minute later, shaking his head "because we set the rules, and it's me that's just pushing him and I'm clearly pushing him too far. I know we're not a couple, but I am tired of just being half of myself with everyone and then hating myself for it."

"I'm sorry." Lily soothes, but he just starts crying in earnest.

Words begin to pour out of him. "That's why she left me, and now Sir's going to leave me, and I know I'm just too much—"

"Mark." Lily squeezes his hand harder. He squeezes back as he uses his other hand to wipe his tears.

"I'm just too much." He repeats, continuing to ramble. His voice is still low and soft, but there is an edge to it. "I know this. I just find someone I care about and I want to do everything for them and I always want to be with them. I want to make their meals and I want to have their attention and I need their affection. It always becomes too much. I see people pulling away and then I get worse and Derrick is pulling away and it should be fine. He wants a kid, and I won't fit anymore, but I can't stop."

"I'm too much too," Lily confesses, and he quiets to listen to her. "but you're never too much for the right one, at least that's what my mom says."

"Kelsey wasn't into kink at all when I met her, and I thought I could change that. When I brought it up, she was freaked out, and I could see her pulling away. Instead of giving her space and trying to talk more about it, I got desperate for her affection. I wanted her to tell me she wasn't going to leave me after all the years we had, but she couldn't. She left me soon after, and I can't be sure it was the kink that drove her out."

"I'm sorry." Lily's voice is hollow. Wouldn't she end up doing the same thing, if Derrick was right?

"*I'm* sorry," he emphasizes. "I'm just having a moment," he looks away from her. "I'll be okay."

"You can't change people though, no matter how much you want to or how much you like them." Lily sighs out. "I was in a long-term relationship before. His name was David. Everything was perfect, or so I thought. I was giggling with Tala about rings and trying to figure out if a wedding on the east or west coast would be better. I wanted the proposal and the wedding to be this big story, and I started doing more than dropping hints. I was trying to control everything about it." Lily takes a breath before continuing. "More than the wedding though, I was trying to drop hints about houses in the right school zone and who's health insurance was better. I was worried about life insurance. It turned me into too much. Here I was, trying to plan everything about our future life together, and he hadn't even thought about a ring."

Lily takes a chance, and kisses the back of his hand before speaking next. "So I get it. If you need a moment, take two, we can just drive around if you want, or we could find a nice spot and stare at the stars."

"I'd like that," he wipes his face. "Thanks for, uh, for listening." He sighs out in relief.

"You too." Lily sits in silence with him for the next few minutes. Lily didn't think the perfect sub routine was real, but she didn't realize how much it hurt Mark. He probably doesn't want to wallow in this any longer.

"Now," she pulls into the drive through, "what's your favorite type of milkshake?"

"Vanilla," he grins as she playfully groans.

"Vanilla? Not even strawberry or something?" She jokes, glad to be able to lighten the mood, even if just a little.

"Let me guess, you're chocolate."

"Obviously, and we'll need fries to dip in them."

"You're gross." He laughs, and it's such a relief to hear.

His apartment is only a few more minutes away, and Lily walks him in to be sure that he's safe in bed before she leaves. He's not drunk, but there is something vulnerable in the raw way he is open right now that makes her want to be sure he's okay. He's quiet as they exit the car, and he's moving as if he's in a daze.

"Key," Lily holds her hand out when they get to the door. "Shoes," she reminds him as they walk in. "Sit," she moves to the couch. When Mark finishes his milkshake she takes it from him to throw out with her own. It doesn't feel different from taking care of someone who is drunk. She brings him a glass of water and tells him it's time to go to bed and he nods slowly. He winces when he stands.

"Do you need any pain killers?"

"Michi gave me some already," Mark shakes his head. "I just need to get some sleep." He doesn't move from the couch, so Lily offers her hand to help him up and she brings him to his bedroom. He doesn't seem very talkative anymore.

"Well, I guess I'd better go." She doesn't want to, but she can't invite herself over. She turns to leave but his hand catches hers. He sits up and looks at their hands, but he doesn't speak right away. She rubs her thumb along his hand and waits for him.

"Can you stay?" His voice is hoarse from crying and raw with emotion, "if it's not too much."

"It's not too much." Lily steps closer so he can hug her.

Chapter 12

"Derrick is having a breeding party next Saturday. He said I could invite you if you wanted to keep me company there." Mark turns to face her in bed in the morning. Lily blinks the sleep out of her eyes and yawns. Is he still going to keep seeing Derrick after last night? They were surely breaking up, weren't they? She won't bring it up before he does but he must see the question in her eyes because he gestures to her.

"A breeding party?" Lily asks instead. Mark yawns.

"Michi is trying to get pregnant and it looks like Derrick is having trouble," Mark frowns, "so the thought is that they are going to have a party with a bunch of men that kind of look like him. Hopefully she'll get pregnant from one of them."

"That's kind of sweet." It's also kind of weird. "Do the men ever find out who it was?"

"No, they like the idea of it, but I don't think any of them actually want kids." Mark shrugs. "The whole point is for Derrick and Michi to have a kid anyway, so it's easier if they don't care."

"And they all look similar so you wouldn't really be able to tell."

"Exactly."

"So, uh, what would I be doing there?"

"Nothing to do with the party," Mark quickly clarifies, waving his hand back and forth. "I'm there to provide everyone with water and do cleanup and just help out. They won't need me the whole time, so Derrick said I could invite you to keep me company."

"Oh, okay?"

"I think he said puppy sit to be honest," Mark blushes, "but either way." Lily shakes her head.

"I'd be happy to puppy sit." She gives him a little scratch under the chin playfully, and he smiles so bright that she is sure that if he actually had a tail, it would be wagging. "Should I bring a movie?"

"I don't want to make too much noise, so I was thinking of bringing a board game and you and I can play. I'd have to disappear when they summon me of course, but otherwise I'd just be hanging out for a few hours, so I can make lunch to bring for you."

"I'll never turn down your food." Lily murmurs.

"If that's all it takes to keep you around, I'm a lucky guy."

Maybe she's luckier.

***

Next Saturday, Lily texts Mark after arriving at Derrick's house. It's a big house in the suburbs. She sits in her car as she waits for his message, and a few minutes later he asks her to come through the side door.

Mark opens the door as she approaches it and smiles at her. He is dressed in a mockery of a suit. It must be made to be the male equivalent of a French maid outfit, but Lily cannot find it in her to complain or poke fun at him. She can't even find it in her to speak. The black cotton vest in the shape of an X barely makes it to his belly button at the longer points along the sides. The middle dip shows off the curve of his pecs, and there are white lines to indicate a seam and buttons. He is wearing a bowtie collar, white cuffs on his wrists, and black mesh underwear with a thick white band that is only solid at the crotch.

"Are you coming in?" He must know he looks like sex on legs at the moment. He shifts, drawing Lily's eyes to the shine on his chest that must be from body oil.

"Am I overdressed?" Lily tries to be seductive but it comes out breathless.

"You could undress, if you'd like." He looks her up and down slowly, and his gaze is heavy enough it's like physical touch. He motions again for her to come in, and she finally does.

"Have they started yet?"

"No," he shakes his head, "but everyone's had a drink and conversation to loosen up a little, and Sir just sent me away from the bedroom I was preparing. I imagine they'll start soon, and then I should be more free to hang out with you."

"Where is the boy?" A man asks loudly, and Mark rushes from her side to another room.

"The boy is here, sir. How may I be of assistance?" Mark's voice carries down the hall. Lily doesn't want to walk in where she isn't supposed to, so she stays in her spot by the door.

"We need the lube from the other bedroom."

"Right away, Sir!"

Lily waits at the door for another few minutes, until Mark pops his head back into the hall. "You didn't have to wait here; everyone knows you're coming."

Lily follows him down the hall into a large living room. The back of his shorts are mesh too, and that's just beautiful. "This place is huge." Lily runs her fingers along a soft couch. Mark nods.

Mark pulls a bag out from under the table and slides her a container of food. "I never asked you which games you wanted to play so I brought a few."

Laughter spills into the hall from another room. They sit on the carpet together and look through the games until Lily picks up her favorite. Lily glances down the hall as a bed starts squeaking; heavy breathing and moans floating down the hall. Goosebumps erupt across her arms. Maybe they should move to a quieter part of the house, but Mark probably needs to be in earshot in order to serve them as required. They set up the board together, but Lily's eyes keep drifting down the hall as louder sounds fill the air. Do they take turns? Is it a free for all?

"Is it weird?" Mark asks. "Are you okay with it?"

"No." Lily shifts on the couch, crossing her arms and leaning back. "It's not too weird, and I am okay." A bit more than okay, if she's being honest with herself. "Let's play."

Mark is called to bring towels over. They could have done the towel and lube prep work before starting, but having Mark wait hand and foot on them is kind of the point. Lily certainly would come up with an excuse to keep calling him back over if she could too.

"It's a little weird, to be honest." Lily says, a few turns into the game, as she places a few cards down to buy a piece.

"What is?" Mark rolls the dice and picks up new cards. In the background Michi lets out another loud moan, and Lily shifts in her seat. Mark's eyes narrow onto her shifting hips and then look up into her face.

"Playing a board game while they are having a gang bang." There is another groan, and squeal, and Lily swallows as she rubs her arms and looks down the hall.

"We don't have to play a game," he hands her the dice as his voice dips down so low it scrapes on the gravel beneath the house. His fingers glide across her hand and grab it. "If you want, you could sit on the couch and I could go down on you right now, and you could listen to them while I did." Lily bites her lip.

Lily can't deny that she's wet and ready. Michi's scream echoes within her. She could be screaming too. She squeezes her legs shut, and her clit sends a shiver up her spine in retaliation.

"You'd have to leave if they called you." Lily rolls the dice, trying to pretend she isn't very interested. They pick up cards and Lily passes the dice over to Mark.

"I'd come straight back to you." He murmurs. "You'd have a couple orgasms at least." He puts the dice and his cards down. "What do you say?"

"Roll the dice."

Mark does, but he doesn't look at the result. Lily doesn't either. She lets out a breath at the increasing noise and clenches her fists. She really wants to reach down and touch herself. Mark glances at her skirt hungrily, and it would be so easy to just lift her skirt up, spread her legs and tell him to get started. Another moan hardens her nipples.

Lily stands. Mark rises to his knees. Lily reaches for her panties, but a voice yells, "butler boy!" from down the hall. Lily jerks as she glances in that direction. She's doused, and she lowers her hands and looks back to see Mark in front of her. He looks torn and doesn't move right away. "Boy!" The voice calls again. Mark sends her an apologetic look as he rushes off. Lily flops down into the couch and sighs. When Mark comes back, she shakes her head to his curious look.

"Let's just play," she sighs.

Disappointment fills his eyes, but she doesn't comment on it. He might ask questions, and she doesn't have answers. What's so different between now and five minutes ago? She can't shake the thought of what if, and she can't quench the desire she has for him to sink to his knees and lift her skirt. To stop temptation from overriding common sense, she opens the grilled chicken and vegetables he brought for her, but all she can taste is a missed opportunity.

Over the next few hours they pull him away from her over and over again, but he returns with big smiles; radiating happiness. She doesn't exactly regret not taking him up on his offer, but in a small way she does.

"I'm just about done for today, so we can head out whenever." Mark walks back to her, backpack in hand. "I just have to change."

Lily takes him in again, hoping she'll get to see him don this outfit again in the future. Mark has a cocky smile on his face as she blushes. "You should come over for dinner." Lily steps into his space.

Mark's smile grows as he meets her eyes. "I should?"

There's only a few inches between their lips. Lily bites hers. Marks eyes fall to her lips. Does he want to bite them? She leans in, and her breasts press against his warm and firm chest. "I'm going to order pizza, and you'd be doing me a huge favor by making sure I don't eat a whole pie by myself."

The hunger in his eyes dilates his pupils. His smile turns feral. His clenches his backpack strap in his hand. "Is that so?"

"Unless you have plans."

Mark shakes his head. "Nothing I couldn't heartlessly abandon for you."

"Good." She finally closes the distance, pulling him into a quick kiss. He grunts into her lips and deepens the kiss.

"I'll be back in a minute," he pulls back, "don't miss me too much."

"I'll try."

Chapter 13

"This is amazing." Mark moans around a mouthful of pizza. "I wish I could eat pizza more often."

"You should."

"Not if I want to keep a six pack." Mark shakes his head. Lily frowns, but she knows where he's coming from. There's no way she would have broken her ice skating diet before. "I mean I can eat pizza. I can eat anything, it's all about moderation and self-control. When it comes to pizza, I don't have any."

"It's the pizza monster." She laughs, and Mark takes a huge bite out of his slice with a playful growl. Lily is full after a few slices and Mark decimates the rest of it with ease. Lily washes her hands as Mark eats the last slice.

Mark looks lost in thought but doesn't speak until he's thrown the pizza box away and washed his hands. "I want to try something different today."

"What do you want to try?" Lily walks up to him, wrapping her arms around his waist. She looks up when he turns to her. A new position? A toy? He takes a small side-step out of her arms. "Mark?"

"I don't just want to have sex today."

Their eyes meet as he slowly kneels in front of her. Lily takes a startled half step back, but Mark gently places his hands on the outside of

127

her thighs, fingers slipping under her skirt, and she stops. He lowers his eyes and leans his head into her leg.

"Mark," she whispers, unsure of what to say or think.

"Let me worship you," he whispers into her thighs "please." He begs so beautifully. He should stay there forever. "I'd be such a good boy for you."

She reaches her hand down and runs her fingers through his hair, the same way she desired the very first time he kneeled for her. This time, he is there under her own power. He hums. "Would you?" she whispers, scared a loud word could break the moment.

"Yes." His hands move in slow small circles on her thighs, and she gently guides his head back, meeting his hopeful gaze, and his. "If that's what you want. If this is where you want me." He stops talking, and she enjoys the moment of having him beneath her and looking up to her. She can make him do almost anything. She's seen him serve others. She'd had him to herself when Derrick sent him. But what does she want?

Ultimately, she wants this for herself.

"I don't want this because you're mad at Derrick."

"It's not that." Mark shakes his head, and he lowers his hands to lay by her ankles. "I want this because I want you." He presses his cheek to her thigh. "You have no idea how much." He shudders. "How desperately I want you."

"You do?" She breathes.

"I'd stay right here as long as you want me to, only because you want me to."

He is giving her power, and it's almost too much for her in its sincerity. Does she deserve it? Derrick said Mark would make her a domme and build her up in his head until she had no choice but to disappoint him. She struggles to cause him pain, and it's clear he desperately needs that.

"I'm not a domme."

Mark doesn't seem deterred. "Maybe not, but look at all the power you already have over me." His smooth cheek glides across her thigh as he nuzzles into it. "Look at what you do to me. I'm already so hard for you, just at the thought that you might use me."

Just like Derrick said. Lily steps back, out of his embrace. This time he doesn't reach for her. He just looks up at her, waiting.

"I don't deserve this yet." Lily takes another step back and motions for him to get up as she sits on the couch. It's too soon. "I don't deserve your trust."

"You don't have to know everything before you start exploring." Mark reassures as he sits next to her, but all Lily can envision is the beating at the Playhouse. She could never do that.

"I can't do the things I've seen them do to you."

"You don't have to."

"I do want to explore some of this with you, but there are so many things that could go wrong."

"It's okay to be unsure, and I won't pressure you into anything." Mark assures her. She nods. "And you'd have a safeword too if we ever did anything, so you could always safeword if it got to be too much for you."

"I'll have to think about it." But in the space he gives her, she builds the courage to speak again. "Let's…let's negotiate." She hesitates. "Let's talk about what you like."

He smiles widely. Maybe negotiating a potential D/s relationship is worth more than a night of worship. "Yeah." His voice is husky in her ears, "I can do that."

"I'm not interested in a perfect sub. You said that before, that you were a perfect sub and I don't want that. Not when it means that you'll do things you don't like because you think I'd like them, or that I would expect them of you."

"Right." Mark sounds relieved. "Okay, you're right."

"I'm nowhere close to a perfect domme," she continues, "and there's things I won't be able to do for you. I'm just me. So just be you."

"Okay."

"So," Lily fidgets after a few seconds of silence, "who are you?" Mark laughs and shifts on the couch to face her.

"I'm Mark." He starts. "I'm a bratty sub. Who are you?"

"I'm Lily, and I'm a baby domme." She chuckles.

"Do you know what you might like?" He asks. "Any ideas as to hard and soft limits?"

"Kind of?" Lily purses her lips as she gestures uselessly with her hands.

Mark gets up off the couch to fetch his laptop from his bag. "The internet has a bunch of tools for this, so let's find one." Mark sits next to her on the couch and lifts his arm for Lily to come under. He pulls up a kinky quiz.

"I've used cock rings before," Lily opens as she reads the first question. "My last boyfriend had a bit of trouble staying hard, so I bought him some. I didn't consider them kinky before."

"I don't have a strong opinion of them either way. I'd wear one if you wanted me to, but I don't already own any. Did your ex like them?"

"No, and he didn't like that I bought them either. Which was stupid, because it helped, but it was a pride thing for him."

Mark clicks the *Interested* button. Another picture pops up. "Well, I like being humiliated a little now and then." Mark taps the bottom of the laptop. "Not in terms of cross dressing, but in terms of calling me dirty or desperate or a slut or things like that."

"You dirty, desperate, slut." Lily shakes her head and Mark playfully rolls his eyes. He clicks *Interested.* The new picture on the screen is very clearly anal sex, and it's a line she isn't going to cross. "Not my ass."

"How about mine?"

Lily purses her lips. "Like with a dildo?"

"Or a strap on," he smiles, "that's really fun."

"Well, maybe?" Lily takes Mark in. Had he? Could she? It's a world she's not sure wants to explore. The next question pops up and it's much easier. "I'm a no on watersports."

Mark shakes his head at the next one. "Scat is a hard no for me."

"No pictures." Lily insists.

"Fisting is a no."

"How would—okay." Lily looks down at her hand. It's not even a big hand… "Yeah, No." There are a few more intense kinks that pop up next, including blood and electric play and torture? Mark warns that she shouldn't attempt any of them for a while. He clicks *No* on a few in a row.

"I do like cucking." Mark hums as a picture of a threesome pops up.

"Threesomes?"

"No," he points to the woman on screen. "See how she's having sex with this man and the other is mostly watching? Cucking is when you have sex with someone that's not your partner."

"And you like that?" Lily can't imagine wanting to share past lovers that way. The idea seems ridiculous given every cheating story she's ever heard or seen.

"I do. I love seeing my partner sated after being with someone else. What about you?"

"I don't know." It's probably a no. "What do you like about it?"

"Well, I like to watch. Especially if I'm being degraded at the same time, or if I'm bound and not allowed to touch. There's lots of opportunities there."

"You don't want to join at all?"

"Sometimes I do. Sometimes I just want to see how far they go, in someone else's hands. A different style, or a different cock, or multiple cocks, or a woman, or even a pair. I want to see my partner completely taken apart in pleasure, especially if it's in ways I can't treasure them normally." He pauses. "Then, after all of that, I want them to come back to me, to choose me."

"That's a nice thought," Lily admits.

Mark rubs his chin, looking away. "I would kiss your bruises, but I could never put them there. I wouldn't ever want to gag you or deny you anything. If you need that, I'd let you go have that, so long as you always come home to me."

"Sounds like polyamory…" Lily trails off, not sure if she wants to know. The dominant thing is hard enough, if he's poly too she may have to stop him now. She can't share, not if they were serious. The very idea causes pain to radiate from her chest.

"No." Mark's voice picks up an edge of fierceness as he turns back to her. "I would have to be the only one you loved. I would have to be number one. I can share your body, but I refuse to share your heart." It's a bit of a contradiction, but a lot of this is. The excitement seems to come from that contradiction. The pleasure of pain and the control in submission.

The next picture is a bound and gagged woman with tears running down her face. Her makeup is ruined. "I like bondage."

"Me too." Lily agrees. "Either way."

"I don't like tying other people up, but I love cuffs and ropes, especially when paired with impact and orgasm denial."

"Do you like the little, um, cages?"

He licks his lips. "I love forced chastity and giving someone else control of my orgasms."

What would happen if she had complete control of all his orgasms? Would he get as needy for them as he does spankings? Would he do anything to get out of it? She could keep the key in her purse, or put it on a necklace; a constant reminder to both of them that she is in control.

"Do you do orgasm control with Derrick?"

"No, we don't really do stuff like that. It's mostly impact and sometimes service stuff or a bit of pet play."

"Pet play?"

"It's kind of like role play, but a bit more than that," Mark explains. "It's a different headspace that I go into where I'm just wanting different things."

"Is there a specific animal or is this like a…." Lily waves her hands to try and convey her thought process, but Mark answers anyway.

"Puppy, I like being a puppy. I like getting head scratches and belly rubs and I like being told I'm a good boy."

"Anything else?"

"I have a tail I like to wear," he confesses. "I haven't worn it in a while, but I used to like it."

"Well, that sounds a little weird to me to be honest, but not something I'd go so far as to throw a limit on. I guess we'll see if the mood ever comes up and I'm around?"

"I'll get extra cuddly." He winks and she leans over to click the *Interested* button.

"No." They say, almost in unison, at the question about waterboarding.

Lily shivers as she reads the question about permanent markings. "Also no."

"Yes." Lily's nipples harden as soon as she sees the image of an ice cube melting on a woman's breast. She can imagine trailing an ice cube down Mark's chest, kissing where the water pools in the divots of his muscles. Maybe he'd shiver as she swirled them around his nipples. She could take his beautiful cock out of her mouth and place an ice cube between his cock and his balls, causing him to soften before her as she takes his orgasm from him. Her body tingles in anticipation, and her pussy clenches around nothing.

Mark clicks the *Yes* button. How much does he truly like to serve? She has a growing desire to widen her legs and tell him to eat her out, but it's not just that. She wants him to eat her out while she continues down this list. Maybe she could use him as a table while she does so. Maybe he'd stop for a second to answer her questions and she could guide his head back where it belongs when he's done. Fuck, that's perfection. Mark turns his head to look at her and has he been talking to her?

"Tell me." He smiles wolfishly at her. "What are you thinking about?"

"You," Lily admits. "I'm thinking about you on your knees in front of me. I'm thinking about using you as a table as I go through the rest of the list." Lily swallows. Mark quickly puts the laptop on the table in front of him. "I'm thinking that I'm wet at the idea of you eating me out while that happens."

"Lily—"

She cuts him off by kissing him. She throws her leg over him to climb into his lap. "We're not done," he playfully protests, but his hands wrap around her hips.

"I don't care," Lily lifts his jaw with her hand and kisses him. He moans into her mouth and grinds up into her. "Just kiss me for a bit," she mumbles into his lips. She moves her hands from his face to the couch behind him and slowly grinds into his hips.

"Yes, Mistress," he breathes as he kisses her again. It doesn't sound right, but it sounds nice, and she continues to grind into his hard cock as he kisses her jaw and neck, and moans as he softly bites her. She bites his neck and he bucks into her. She needs to get him into the bedroom and get those pants off so she can…

Negotiate.

That's what they set out to do. Mark said he wanted more than sex today, had to turn away from her to build up the courage to admit it. She wants to finish that with him. They can continue this later. Mark won't turn her away. Lily shifts from harsh kisses to soft ones. She slows her grinding and stops pulling on his hair. "Later." She's gentle as she pulls back. "Let's finish our worksheet, and get to this later."

Mark hums into her lips as he kisses her again. "Are you sure you're not into orgasm denial?" His breath in her ear sends her breath far away. Lily sits back onto his thighs.

"I never said that." She gives an exaggerated wink as she gets off his lap and sits next to him.

This time, as she moves into his side to cuddle, she lets her hand trace the outline of his cock in his pants. It twitches, and Mark shifts as he tries to widen his legs and maintain balance of the laptop. "Lily?"

Lily continues tracing his cock, detouring to squeeze his balls softly. "What's the next one, Mark?"

He whimpers. "Collars."

"Well, I know you like collars." Lily traces the skin of his cock's head through his pants. He twitches.

"I do." He pants. "You?"

"I like them. I really like the day collars that you'd wear all the time." Lily hums. Mark groans. "I just like the idea of having a visual symbol of the relationship, or even just for playing with."

"Good to know." His voice drops down into husky territory. "I love play collars, and I can't wait for a real one."

Could she make him come by squirming in his lap and talking about collars? What if she reached up and wrapped her hand around his neck? Would he like soft feathery touches? Would he want more?

"Once, Sir put a play collar on me." Mark runs his hand down his face. "I loved it so much, but part of me was like 'you know I want a real one, why would you tease me with this?' But he doesn't really get how it teases me."

"I think I get it." Lily turns into him and kisses up his neck until she reaches his ear. His cock jerks as he closes his eyes. She presses down on his cock and breathes in his ear as her face heats. "You want to be owned, and not just at play time."

"Yes." His voice is raw as he sinks further into the couch, like he's become boneless. His cock presses into her hand, hot and heavy and wanting. Lily eases up on his cock to click on the next question, and then frowns. "I don't think I like pain: giving or receiving."

Mark stills and the heat of the moment fades. He glances away before asking. "Is that a hard limit?" He drags the words out slowly.

"No?" Lily shifts on the couch. "I didn't really enjoy it when Derrick was teaching me, but I didn't hate it. I hated what I saw last time. I hate the idea of hurting you."

Mark is unnaturally still. "Even if I like it?" His voice is quiet.

"I guess that's the part that I don't get." Lily confesses. "There was no way you were happy at the party after Derrick beat you."

Mark shifts. "I was happy that he beat me. I wasn't *happy* at the party because of other reasons, but the beating helped a lot. I was feeling worse before it, but it helped me get out all of these pent up emotions I had in me. It was amazing to be able to let out a good cry, and then once I was done with that, I was able to center myself and have a conversation about what was bothering me. It got me out of my head and into the moment." His eyes meet hers, and they are pleading for common ground.

Lily swallows. "Well, I guess I do feel better sometimes after a good cry, but I usually have a headache too."

His smile dies before it fully forms. "I'm not immune to those."

"So what about it do you like?"

"Everything?" He sighs. "I realize that isn't very helpful." Mark pauses as Lily glances at the picture of the woman across on a man's lap getting spanked on her bare bottom. "I like the sensation, both of the hits, and then the warm throb after. I also like the anticipation, where I don't know where or how hard it will be. I like the attention I get when I'm getting hit, and the attention I get after. It turns me on, it is a way that I can submit, and it's a way that there can be non-permanent marks of ownership on me."

"So you really do like it; it's not something you just do for Derrick?"

"I'm way more into it than Derrick is." Mark's body language is still all wrong, and Lily wants to just say whatever he wants to hear, but she can't lie to him. That would just hurt them both. "It is more about levels of pain for you, or pain in general?"

Lily sags helplessly. "I don't know."

"So there is lighter impact, like what you and Derrick went over, and then there is some of the heavy stuff that Derrick and I did at the party, and then there is the super wild primal level, where they literally fight and punch and bite each other."

Lily's eyes widen to the point that Mark stops talking, and she hopes there aren't more levels than that. "I could never hurt you the way Derrick did." Lily confesses. "But I kind of liked what we did in the kitchen."

"So let's start small," he tries, "and go from there."

Lily doesn't know what to say to that. The next click brings them to a completion screen. "Worship wasn't on the list." That's what started this in the first place.

"Do you want me to show you?" This time, it's not teasing or seductive, but a general question, and it's because of that that Lily nods.

"I think so."

Mark places the laptop on the table, and then pushes the table back and to the side so he can kneel in front of her on the couch. Lily sits up straighter, moving back on the couch.

"Worship is different for different people, of course." He softly grabs her ankles. "Some people like worshiping different body parts, from kissing and licking feet…. He lifts her right foot to rest it on his shoulder, and places a kiss on it. Thankfully, she took her shoes off at the door, but maybe he'd kiss her foot straight out of a shoe as well. Is the stink a kink? "To massage." He places her other foot on his other shoulder. "To pussy worship."

"What's the difference between pussy worship and eating out?" Lily flexes her toes, pushing them a little further into his skin.

"It's not just eating out, for one. It includes things like smelling it, cleaning it after sex, or shaving it for you, it's about enjoying the whole experience as opposed to just trying to make you come."

Lily not sure about it. "Sounds interesting."

"Let me try then," Mark gives her ankle a small kiss, "and feel free to shove me back or tell me to stop if you don't like it."

"I can do that, and if you don't like it?"

"I'm going to love this." Mark's voice is heavy and full of promise. She'd try just about anything if it got him talking to her like this. "But I'll stop and let you know." Mark picks up her foot again, and lowers it into his lap to start giving it a little massage. "Some of this may feel weird or funny, but please give it a chance before telling me to stop."

Mark moves his fingers in small circular motion as Lily closes her eyes as she leans further into the couch. It starts as a gentle massage; and Lily lets out soft sigh. None of it is weird until Mark starts licking and kissing her ankles. She gives it a chance, as promised, and after he moves up her calf, her mind starts wandering to where else he could be kissing, and how much he must like her if he's doing this to her calf. Mark kisses the inside of her knee, which changes things, and she lets out a breath as he pushes her skirt upwards.

Lily shifts to the edge of the couch, anticipating what comes next, and in a minute she's rewarded as he plants a few kisses around her labia. It's a slow process, filled with savoring kisses and long licks instead of diving for her clit like she's used to. Still, her clit throbs at the attention she's not receiving.

Mark sucks on one of her labia and Lily squirms as he moves to the other. It's not bad, it's just a new sensation. He uses his nose to nuzzle between her labia to rub her clit, and Lily lets out a little sigh. Mark kisses around it, and then he gently traces his tongue around the edge of it. Lily is impatient, but also curious, and so she waits. Mark meets her eyes as sucks on her clit, and the heat in his eyes steals her breath.

"It's so pretty." He moves back and uses his fingers to move up and down her labia. "It smells so good." He takes a deep breath that causes Lily to furrow her brow. "And it tastes amazing." He uses his fingers to open her labia and then kisses her clit. "Have you ever squirted before?" He uses his tongue to lick up her entire vagina.

"No!" Lily's face burns as she brings her thighs closer together. She looks away and stammers, but Mark doesn't react to her embarrassment. He pushes against her thighs softly to open her back up to him, and Lily's face scorches as she gives in.

"Do you know if you can?" He starts licking her clit in earnest.

"No," Lily pants.

"I really want to find out." Despite the heat in his words, Mark's movements are deliberately slow, unhurried, as if he means to drive her mad. His tongue glides past her slick clit and down into her entrance, and slowly he slides his hot tongue into her pussy. It's a new, welcome sensation, and Lily heaves a shuddering breath as her skin flushes with heat. Mark's fingers graze against her clit and then gently circles it with the pad of his finger as his tongue fucks her. She whimpers, fingers clenching into the couch cushions as she shudders.

"There is one thing I'd like." He slides his fingers into her slowly. She clenches down on them, but he continues moving slowly.

Lily moans out. She needs *more*. "What is it?" Lily's desperate to keep him right where he is.

"I want you to sit on my face."

"What?" Lily breathes. Mark circles his tongue around her clit. He flicks it with his tongue and then sucks on it gently.

"Would you sit on my face? It feels really good, I promise."

"I… what?" Lily's brain is foggy with sensation. Her orgasm creeps up on her with insistence, and she can't imagine how crushing him under her will help with that. Mark lips twitch.

"You're right, how dare I ask for anything without giving you your first orgasm." Mark's fingers somehow go deeper in her pussy, rubbing along her insides in a way that curls her toes. Lily's response is lost as Mark laps at her clit. Lily jerks on the couch and then tangles her fingers in his hair as a low guttural groan escapes her. She pulls him closer, nearly crushing him against her hips as she moves them in time with his thrusts. He groans as she pulls on his hair and that's enough.

She curls herself around him, ensuring that he stays right where he is as she comes, and he continues to lick and finger her as her pussy clenches around his fingers. Her orgasm crackles across her skin like a firecracker and leaves her breathless as she leans back on the couch and releases him. He looks up at her with bright eyes and a grin.

"Now will you sit on my face? Please?"

"How does that work?" Lily's lungs are heaving, and Mark stands to offer her a hand up. He lies down on the carpet before beckoning her forward.

"Put a foot on either side of my head," he grins at the view of her as she does so, "and just lower yourself down until your pussy is in my mouth." Lily doesn't move. "It's probably easier to kneel and then position yourself."

"I'm going to crush you."

"You won't, I promise." He licks his lips, lips that glisten because of her, and Lily gently kneels. Mark's hands grab her hips to guide her down, but she pauses before sitting on him.

"You won't be able to talk. How would you safeword?"

Mark taps her thigh twice.

"Well, I won't be able to talk to you."

"How about one tap for yes, and two for stop?"

"Okay, that makes sense to me." Lily lets him guide her further down with his hands. He lowers her until she's almost fully seated on his face. His nose brushes up against her clit, and Mark sticks his tongue in her pussy again and Lily lets out a sigh of pleasure. His hands slide across her thighs to grab her ass and tug her closer. He shifts her and then laps at her clit again.

"This feels good." Lily moans out. "Are you okay?"

Mark taps her thigh once with his hand. "Fuck," her hips jerk. His hands tighten in her skin and help hold her in place. Pleasure shoots up her body, but she's too worried about suffocating him, or hurting him, that she can't focus on it.

Lily keeps asking Mark if he's good, and with each singular tap on her thigh, Lily slightly relaxes. She shifts into the position he wants, she closes her eyes as a jolt of pleasure shoots from her clit to her nipple, and she finally relaxes into it. She trails her hand up her stomach to her breasts and rolls the hard nub between her fingers. She can't stay still. Mark gives her a single tap after she jerks into him. He's okay.

"Fuck, Mark," Lily warns. "Just like that. Don't stop. I'm coming!" Mark doesn't stop, and Lily's orgasm crashes over her in waves. Lily lets out a deep breath as soon as she can breathe again. His arms tighten around her.

"Mark?" She asks, but he doesn't answer. He takes a deep breath, tickling her sensitive clit with it, and seems to relax. He doesn't release her. "Do you want me to return the favor?" She purrs.

"No." He closes his eyes to take a deep breath. "I just want to serve sometimes. You could just randomly open your legs and I'd be there unless you pushed me away and told me no."

"Anytime?"

"Just about."

"Well, next time, maybe I'll try setting up my own scene."

<u>Chapter 14</u>

"The project is being canceled at the end of the month." Their project manager opens. Lily can't help but gasp. She should have known this was coming. It's been weeks of failed attempts. How many more could she have expected the team to be able to get away with? Jeff sighs and rubs his eyes. "It's not an official communication, so don't stop working, I just want everyone to be prepared."

"Do you think there is a chance to prevent this?" How can she be prepared to give all of this up? She has to fight for it somehow.

"If we can get a working system, I think they would be open to the option, but I wouldn't get my hopes up."

"We have enough time to try the triple redundancy path, right?" Lily desperately hopes the answer is yes.

"Maybe with some mandatory overtime," Jeff grumbles. Lily grimaces. Any single setback and there is no hope they'll make it. Still, there is hope. The thought that there is nothing she can do to save the project gnaws at the back of her head. When she asks for the next step, Jeff shakes his head. "It's all up to them now. Let's hope this works."

She just wants one thing to go exactly as planned, so when Mark asks to come over on Thursday, she hatches a plan.

The planning manages to get her out of her own head, even if just for a few minutes at a time. She messages Mark about everything except her urge to hit things, because that's not a conversation she thinks they can have right now. She watches BDSM porn with rapt attention and takes notes. She practices her words and her tone. On Thursday, she dresses up for the part of the dominatrix with care; red painted nails, red lipstick, red lingerie with black lace, and tall black heels.

She moves the table to the counter and places a single dining room chair in the middle of the space and leaves her door unlocked so she can be in position as he enters her home. When he does, she smirks. He bites his lip as he looks her up and down, frozen in the doorway with the door half open.

"Close the door behind you and take off your shoes." She commands before he can speak. He closes it, slips off his shoes, and then looks to her for another command. "On your knees." Her confidence waivers. She doesn't have the right to treat him this way. This is exactly what he asked for. Her legs are crossed at her knee, and she fights not to bounce them in nervousness. She's spent all week thinking about this. She just needs to follow her plan.

Mark says nothing about her voice wavering, or her hands shaking at her sides, just goes to his knees at the door with a spark in his eyes that is almost teasing. She beckons him forward with her fingers, not trusting her voice, and he crawls towards her. She meets his eyes as he does, to try and read how she's doing, but her breath is caught at how handsome he is.

Realistically, they are just in her living room. It's part of the reason she's so nervous in the first place. There's no way she can recreate the feelings he experienced in the dark sensual club in her brightly lit carpeted living room. Yet, she's caught in his eyes and transported. It's like she's back at the munch where he kneeled to her for the first time. She's at the club listening to him beg to come. She's over by the couch as he asks to worship her. It doesn't matter where she is. What matters is where he is; on his knees before her. What matters is that he wants to be on his knees in front of her.

She tilts her head, leaning it on her hand as he shifts his gaze to the floor as he reaches her. Despite her initial hesitation and numerous conversations in the mirror, it's almost too easy to lift her foot, place it on his shoulder, and push down. His breath leaves him in one long sigh, and he yields to her will without protest.

"Good boy."

She moves her foot, letting the material of her shoe rub against Mark's cheek as she brings it closer. She's not expecting him to turn to it and nuzzle her foot, which means she hasn't given him permission to; which means bad. She taps her foot against his cheek, but she can't find the words to say bad, or no, or stop that doesn't make it sound like she's scolding a dog. Well, he said he likes puppy play. Maybe he wants to be scolded like a dog. Mark turns to the shoe and kisses it, and she jerks her ankle to push against his face harder, forcing his head to turn away. She sits straighter.

Well that's certainly crossed a line. He never said he liked being hit in the face. Shit. Surely he's about to stand up and curse her out. That was certainly not how she wanted this to go. Except, Mark has let out that gorgeous sigh again. Lily pauses, gauging Mark's reactions, and is surprised when he not only says nothing, but returns to gazing at her shoe. Now she's curious. She lifts it slightly, in offering, and he peppers kisses her shoe. Some kisses are fast and light, but others slow down, like he's savoring it. Lily is not sure what there is to savor: the taste of the shoe, the fact that it is a shoe, the fact that it is her shoe, or if this has to do with the worship. She's also not sure how to deal with the new knowledge she has, that she has this freedom over him. She can kick this giant man in the face and he'll kiss the shoe that did it. That's more arousing than it should be, honestly.

She lowers her heel to the carpet. Mark follows it. What now? She should probably praise him, he liked when Derrick did that. "That's a good boy," she repeats, hating that it sounds like she's praising a dog— that she can't get the idea of praising him like a dog out of her head, "you're such a beautiful boy. You're so good at that, kissing my shoes like I know you'd want to kiss the rest of me."

"Only if you'd let me, Mistress." It slips out of him naturally. How would the word taste in her own mouth? She doesn't try it yet.

"Why don't you take off your clothes for me, and show me that pretty body?"

Mark takes his shirt off to reveal his sculpted chest to her. He stands only to step out of his pants, and then resumes kneeling in front of her. One day, she'll ask him to do this slowly, instead of the methodical stripping she's seen before, but for now, she doesn't mind.

"Perfect." She traces the lines of his chest with her eyes. "You really are beautiful." He smiles at her. Is he told that a lot? He is a personal trainer, and he works and models with his body, but does he truly get enough compliments on it, or does he stand in the mirror looking for imperfections to tighten with deadlifts or squats? She really does want him to feel like enough; to know how striking he is. "My beautiful boy," she's both praising and claiming him, and his smile grows.

"Come here," she pats her thigh, opening her legs to him, and he settles in, looking up at her as his head rests where her hand was. God, she can't believe this. Here, in her lap, is a literal model, built enough to carry her on his shoulders for hours, waiting on her command. Somehow, with this powerhouse, she has all the power. He has given her all of the power.

BDSM is so much more than just sex, and Lily wants more than that, but she can only think of sex right now. She'll get better with time. "You said you were hungry earlier. I think I know what you've been craving."

He licks his lips in anticipation as he beams up at her and it is hard to not be weak; hard to do anything other than leap into his arms and beg him to fuck her. "Good boys get to taste treats, don't they?"

"They do. They do when they can; when they are allowed." Mark practically whimpers the last word and it breaks Lily's resolve to keep anything from him. She opens further and encourages him to have a taste, moaning when he practically dives into the chair to press kisses against her panties, right over her clit. She pulls his hair and pushes his head closer. She's not going to be able to take her underwear off at this rate. He licks at her underwear and her foot lifts from the floor, slipping out of her heel.

Heel.

Wait.

No. The whole point of wearing these heels was to step on him. Before she can get lost in the feeling of his lips through her underwear she pulls back on his head, hard. He lets out a breath and looks up at her with wide eyes and blown pupils. She releases his hair and uses her bare foot to push his shoulder backwards until he is laying on his back. She shoves her foot back into her heel and stands, staring down at him. She probably has to give a reason for that.

"I said a taste." She scolds. She crosses her arms with all of the playful contempt she can muster. Maybe it's too much. Regret starts to crawl up her spine. This is it. The moment he says enough and storms out.

"I'm sorry, Mistress. Please forgive me. Please give me another chance to serve you. Punish me please but don't send me away. I won't forget my place."

His place is beneath her.

"That's right." She starts, using his cue, taking tiny steps forward next to him. "It seems you forgot your place."

"I'm so sorry, Mistress." Mistress still tastes weird in her mouth, so she doesn't repeat it.

"Where is your place, boy?"

"Underneath you, Mistress."

"That's right." Lily could not have asked for a better opportunity, but she cannot bring herself to step on him in her heels. That probably hurts way more than it should. She's seen Mark take a beating, but she can't hurt him, not really. She will step on him though. She slips out of the heels and gently places her foot on the center of his chest. Mark lets out a strangled moan, a sound Lily has only drawn from men during oral before. "You have to take what I give you…" She's not sure how to finish the thought and lets the words trail off. Mark doesn't respond. His gaze is focused on her foot, and so she slowly applies more pressure until he

146

gasps beneath her. Honestly, she probably could stand on him without hurting him too much, but she's not taking that chance. She lowers the pressure, but keeps her foot there. "…And you have to give me what I want." Lily finally finishes, searching Mark's face for any sign of discomfort. Mark's lips are parted, his eyes are sparkling, and he looks so happy.

"Please," he starts and her heart sings at the arousal in it, "please tell me what you want. I live to serve."

She pushes her foot into him again before removing it completely. He stays on the ground as she stands next to him, panting and hard. "Carry me to the bedroom, gently." He stands, lifts her swiftly into a bridal carry, and walks her to the bedroom. She's weightless in his arms. Domme or not, she can't help the blush on her face as she leans into him to cuddle and pepper kisses on his neck.

At her various commands, he places her on the bed, undresses them both, and kneels between her legs. Her first orgasm comes to her easily underneath his tongue and fingers, and she demands a second in a breathless voice that probably doesn't count as dominant but she doesn't care. He grins as he obeys, claiming it to be his pleasure to serve with a genuineness that seems too good to be true. After her second, she gently pulls on his hair and tells him to stop.

He nuzzles her thigh and waits as she blinks at him. He's certainly obedient, because she's never been with someone who wouldn't have tried or asked to be in her at this point. She guides him to lie on his back on the bed, rolls a condom onto him, and slowly sinks onto him. Rocking slowly until she sits on him, filled. She curses, he groans, and she slowly starts a pace that lights her insides on fire.

"Can I touch you?" Mark asks.

Lily leans over to kiss him as she rocks on top of him, searching for her rhythm. "Only if you say please."

"Please," Mark begs. Lily grabs his hands and places them on her hips. He groans and thrusts his hips in time with her rocking. It builds, each thrust just a little deeper, a little rougher, until Lily's bouncing on top of him, her hips lifting and slamming down onto him roughly.

"More," she whimpers. Mark shifts, digging his heels into the mattress and lifting his hips, bucking up into Lily. She braces herself on his chest and matches him thrust for thrust.

It's not enough, or it's not what she wants. What she really wants is to be fucked in a way that leaves her sore, when her legs are angled back enough to let the thrusts sail into her in just the right way. She told herself she had to ride him today, that this way she'd be the dominant, but honestly, she doesn't want this. Her leg will cramp soon, her orgasms are leaving her weak, and she wants this man on top of her now.

His cock hits a spot with enough force that it disrupts her pace and she moans out embarrassingly loud. She just has to take it.

Lily slows to a stop, and Mark's hands rub circles into her sides. She captures his lips again. "I need this harder Mark." She whispers between kisses, letting him slip out of her. "I need you to give this to me as hard as I can take. Okay?"

"Yes, yes," Mark murmurs and he follows her as she switches their positions. She opens her legs for him and he settles over her and sinks back inside.

"Hard." Lily repeats, and Mark delivers instantly.

"Like this?" He snaps his hips.

"Yes!" She answers once, then repeats to have something to moan out. Mark lets out a controlled breath, and proceeds to pour every ounce of his strength into making sure she is sore and sated. At least, that's what it feels like, with every thrust sending the bed skirting along the floor in protest and filling her to the core. Her pussy clenches around him, but he doesn't change his relentless pace, and he launches her into a mind numbing orgasm.

She doesn't wait for him to ask this time. When his hips start to stutter against her clenching pussy she locks her legs around him. His eyes shoot open, and she locks hers with his.

"Come for me," she orders. "Give it to me."

Mark stumbles through a thank you as he shudders and jerks through his orgasm. She can't help but to lean forward and capture his lips in a sweet kiss. He leans his head into her shoulder, and she runs her hand through his hair.

"How was that?" Lily asks after he throws the condom out and crawls back into bed with her.

"Great," he kisses her collarbone. "Fantastic." He looks up at her, soft and wanting. "I couldn't have imagined anything better. And you? I could see you were unsure in the beginning."

"I was, but I think I got the hang of it."

He's wonderful. He's beautiful, and happy, and hers, and it's wonderful.

"Can I stay the night?" Mark murmurs into her skin as Lily kisses the top of his head.

"It's Thursday, I work tomorrow." Lily doesn't want to say no. She likes cuddling with him throughout the night. She snuggles into him a bit more. She could always kick him out in the morning, even though he wouldn't be able to get his morning run in before going to work.

"I won't make you late." He tries again. "I'll make you breakfast."

"I don't know…" Lily's already planning on giving in, but she smiles as he looks up at her pleadingly.

"Please?"

Lily tilts her chin up, pretending to think. "Okay, you can stay. Now, enough with the puppy dog eyes." Lily kisses his forehead, and his puppy dog eyes melt away as he tightens his arms around her and snuggles in.

"Thank you."

"Now tell me something about you I don't know yet."

Mark hums in thought. "Well, my favorite color is black… like when you go out at night and just stare up into infinity."

"and beyond," she yawns. "It's amazing how big space really is."

"Would you ever go?"

"To space? No. We're really not meant for it, so I'd rather stay nice and safe here."

"I would. It's risky, but the reward would be worth it."

She walks her fingers across his chest as it moves up and down with his breaths. "So you're a big risk taker."

"Maybe I am."

"I like certainty."

Eventually they break apart to get ready for bed and clean up. Lily has a spare towel and toothbrush that Mark gratefully uses and she leaves out some oversized clothes for him to wear. He flops onto her bed as she leaves to go shower.

"Just let me set my alarm." Lily settles into bed.

Mark turns to face her. "You never told me your favorite color."

"White, but not like paper." She puts her arm over his waist. "I like the white of fallen snow, when it covers the whole world in a layer of softness; the white of a freshly zambonied rink in the morning, when the day is still full of potential."

"You're full of potential." Mark gives her a soft kiss. He lets out a yawn and blinks away sleep.

"We don't have to talk if you are falling asleep." Lily uses a hushed tone, but Mark shakes his head.

"I'm good." He yawns again and Lily smiles at him.

"I promise I'll be here when you wake up."

"Good." The word escapes his lips half formed as he closes his eyes and snuggles closer to her.

"I didn't realize you were such a cuddle bug," Lily teases. Mark doesn't answer, already asleep. "Good night," she closes her eyes to join him.

<u>Chapter 15</u>

What are you doing tonight?

It's a nice simple text, one that is perfectly safe to send to Mark, but Lily's arms break out in goosebumps. She has a plan that only works if she doesn't lose her nerve along the way.

I don't have plans.

I'll be coming over then.

Okay!

That's the easy part. The next part takes her a minute to send because she keeps rereading it. Is it too much? Her heart beats in a nervous flutter as she reads the message again. He'd let her know if she crossed a line but she's not even sure there is a line. She hits send, closes her eyes, and takes a deep breath before opening her eyes to see that the message went through.

I saw your picture online about your different plugs, I want you wearing one by the time I come over. Which one is up to you.

The little bubbles come up, indicating that he is reading it. Lily bites her lip. He doesn't respond. She taps on the table in front of her. Too much? No. It couldn't be. Too much because it came from her? Her foot picks up a tremor as she waits. He might not answer before her meeting. He might not answer at all. She rocks back and forth in her chair. Her phone goes dark but she taps it again to light it back up. She can't have ruined this already. It's only been a minute. It doesn't mean anything. She lets out a deep breath as his next message comes through.

Lily, I love this, I do, but you've got me hard in the bathroom already. My client will be here in a few minutes. Can we talk about this later?

That's… a better response than she was expecting. Oh, it wasn't too much. He's already hard for her. He had to run to the bathroom. He *loves* it. Is he begging his erection to go down so he doesn't get fired? The thought of it causes her nipples to harden. There is a rush to the thought that she is at work too. She wants to see it. She wants to push a little more. Her desire overcomes her nerves at her next request, and a smile tugs at her lips as she sends it.

Send me a picture of that nice hard cock of yours. Then, to have mercy on him, she sends: *We can talk later.*

He sends her a picture, but she doesn't click on the notification yet. She has a meeting in five minutes, and she has to be on her game for it. If she gets to see his wonderful cock, she might have to make her own run to the bathroom and that won't end well for her. She's already eager at the thought of a picture.

Even the lack of progress can't dampen her mood. As the meeting stretches on, the temptation builds, like its own round of foreplay. Once she's finally alone she eagerly snatches her phone off the table. She slaps a hand over her mouth to stop herself from making an embarrassing sound.

It's not the up close dick pic in a bathroom stall she was expecting, but a shot she can imagine being on display at a porn shop. She tries to take in every detail. He moved to the shower, pulled his pants down out of frame, and bit his shirt to keep it up. Lily almost licks her lips at the sight of his glorious erection. It juts against his stomach and Mark's hand grips the base of it. She can practically feel it, hot and heavy, in her own. His muscled chest and abs just add to Lily's need to put her mouth on absolutely everything she can see.

There's a hint of a smirk on his lips, like he knows what this picture will do to her concentration. It's going to drive her wild until she can see him. She's still staring at his picture when he messages her again.

Done for the day!!! Do you want me a certain way when you get here?

What do you mean?

Naked or in an outfit? Kneeling or in a pose? In the bedroom with a blindfold on?

Is that safe?

Yeah. If you text me when you are outside, I can unlock my door then get set up, and you can walk in right after.

Yes, to all, but perhaps not right away. If he's posing like his picture when she walks in his door her plans will fly out the window and she'll end up on her knees taking his cock into her mouth before she even forms words to say hi. Not that that's a bad idea. Lily looks up to spot people gathering at the door for the next meeting and sighs. At least she'll see Mark at the end of the day. She just has to get through a few more hours.

Maybe next time! Nothing special today. I loved the picture.

Anytime.

She wants to test that; to text him on random days and times for pictures. Maybe she could tell him where to take them or what to wear when he takes them. Maybe she should take her own sexy pictures to send him as well. Lily can't stop her mind from wandering into that shower with him, but she doesn't text him again until she makes her way to her car after work.

Do you have ice?

Yes, and just so you know I'm hard again.

Lily kind of wants to ask for another picture, but she doesn't know if she can take it. She sits in her car and looks at the first one again. Did he will his cock to go down or did he jerk off before his client showed up? Was he distracted all day like she was? She takes out her script from earlier and takes a deep breath as she unfolds the paper.

Are you home?

Yes.

She calls.

"I hear scenes are supposed to be negotiated ahead of time. So let me ask: Do you want me to be mean to you?" She asks as soon as he picks up. He takes a sharp breath but doesn't respond. That's probably for the best, as she's written down exactly what she wants to say, and she doesn't have his responses in her script. "Do you want me to tie you down so you can't move; so you can't squirm or writhe when it gets to be too much?"

"Yes," he groans. "I want that. I want all of that."

"Do you want me to edge you all night; edge you until it hurts and then ruin every orgasm you have until you cry so prettily for me?" The need in her own voice is thick and heavy.

"Please," He breathes. She's glad he can't see the way she's clenching the paper in her hands. "Yes, *please.*"

He looked so put together in the picture he sent her. So confident and sure of himself and she wants to make him beg. She wants to turn him into a mess. She clears her throat and straightens her shoulders.

"Good. I'm going to need you to pick one of your nice little butt plugs and get that in before I get to your house. Can you do that for me?"

"Yes, I can do that."

"Are you hard?"

"I am already so hard," he confesses.

"Grab it for me."

He moans into the phone. Lily can almost feel it tickling the hair over her ears. Is he grabbing the base like the picture? Did he wrap his whole hand around his cock? "Squeeze it gently," she orders, and he starts to pant. He's so desperate for her when she's like this. "Now let it go. You won't be touching it anymore tonight. Am I understood?"

"Yes, yes, I understand," he's already breathless. "I won't touch myself anymore."

"Good boy. I'll be there in 15 minutes." She hangs up before he can respond and then she lets out a deep breath.

She puts on the playlist Tala helped her make over the weekend titled 'Fuck the boy up' and starts driving to his house. She channels her inner domme with every drum beat and bass chord. She arrives with her backpack, her nerves, and the sounds of female rock anthems in the back of her head. She knows what she wants. She's here to take it.

He opens the door with a smug grin. "Nice to see you here."

Lily can't say anything at all. She can barely hear him over the blood rushing in her ears. She steps directly into his space and leans up to capture his lips in a rough kiss. He gasps and returns her kiss as he grabs her waist. The one spot where his skin touches hers is electric. His soft lips return every hungry kiss with a happy murmur she's not sure she's meant to understand. She bites his lip and his fingers squeeze her hips tighter.

"Hands behind your back," she pulls back slightly. He follows her lips, eyes opening as she moves a little further out of reach. His shoulders seem to grow wider as he moves his hands, and this angle shows off the cut of his biceps. Lily reaches out to grab his bicep lightly, and then leans in for a softer kiss.

"Do you want to do this in the hallway?" He asks with smoldering eyes. As long as they see Mark, see what she does to him, she doesn't think she'd mind the neighbors watching at all.

"I do," Lily pushes him into his apartment. She steps inside and closes the door behind her. Mark doesn't move from his spot and he leaves his hands behind his back, "but I also want you all to myself."

"I'm yours." He is. He is for now.

"Then kneel."

He goes down slowly, looking up at her with an easy smile. She reaches out to run her fingers through his hair. He leans into her hand, closing his eyes and letting out a soft sigh.

"Stay here," Lily locks the door and walks over to the couch to empty her backpack out. The towels and scarves should go in the bedroom, her change of clothes can stay in the bag, and the blindfold… well the blindfold is for now.

It's not really a blindfold, honestly. She bites her lip and turns it over in her hand. It's a black eye mask and it's not exactly tight. She'd probably get the same results just telling him to close his eyes. Her heart starts to race in her chest.

"I'm going to go into the bedroom and set up," Lily grabs the towels and scarves.

"Okay, I already cracked some ice for you. It's in a bag in the freezer. I doubt it'll come up, but no impact today. I've got a potential underwear gig coming up."

"When will you know?" She puts the ice in a bowl slowly.

"Maybe in a week and a half."

"Good luck." Towels go on the bed. The scarves on the pillow. There really isn't much else to set up. She stalls just a moment, taking a few deep breaths.

"Alright," she makes her way back to him. "I think I'm ready for you."

"You have me." His eyes are closed. Lily cups his face in her hands and he opens his eyes to look up at her. His facial expression is so open, so soft, so pretty. She can't imagine anyone looking at him and wanting to hit him.

"So ice, edging, and a potential ruined orgasm," Lily moves her thumb to catch on his lips. Goosebumps crawl up her arm as he turns to kiss her hand. He sounded eager on the phone, but she wants to double check before starting. He looks up at her and smiles.

"Yes, please."

"Okay, stand up for me." Lily orders, and he stands slowly, keeping his hands behind his back. Lily trails a path from his neck to his chest with her fingers and his breath hitches as her thumb brushes across his nipples through his shirt. Her own harden in response. She slips her thumb under his shirt to stroke his skin.

"I really liked your picture." She's almost lightheaded with desire. "It's the best dick picture I've ever gotten. I want to keep it forever."

"I'm glad you liked it," he leans forward, and Lily meets him in a kiss. "I'd send you one whenever you wanted it." He murmurs as he pulls back.

"Don't give me that kind of power," Lily tries to laugh, but it comes out as a whisper.

"You already have it." That's quite the declaration, but it rings hollow. Lily looks up into his eyes as she bites her lips. He doesn't say anything else, but he maintains eye contact with her. Her heart beats against her chest as her fingers shake. His eyes are brighter than she's ever seen them, like she could find him in the darkness.

"Get naked for me, and don't rush it."

"Do you want a strip show? I could put some music on," Mark grins. Lily puts her hand on his chest and he stops talking.

"Maybe next time." She certainly will have him do that another time. She's wet just thinking about it. Today however is not about sex, and the full Magic Mark performance is a sure way to make her ovaries explode.

"Promise." He winks. "I'll sit you in a chair and everything."

He walks to the bedroom before starting to strip. He pulls his shirt up again to bite it, and then trails his fingers down his abs to draw her eyes to his v cut. Lily swallows, thinking back on that picture, and has to force herself not to squirm. He pulls the waistband of his shorts down slowly then lets it fall to the floor. His dark blue boxer briefs do very little to hide his erection and Lily wants to cup it and squeeze it and make him moan in her hands. The only thing that stills her hand is that she wants to watch him unwrap himself like a present for her more than she wants to touch him. He pulls his shirt over his head next and his smirk is on full display as he tugs the briefs down inch by inch until she can see all of him. He steps out of his briefs and then he leans back and flexes for her.

He's even better in person. Almost too much; like she'll shatter this illusion if she reaches out to touch him. Her brain scrambles in a hazy lust. She licks her lips, and she wants to lick him everywhere.

"Do you have the butt plug in?" She blurts. So much for tact.

She might not understand his fascination with it, but she appreciates the way his fascination has him flushing as he leans over the bed to show her. She doesn't see it though, what she sees is the array of colorful bruises that litter his ass. Her eyebrows furrow as she reaches out to touch them. She stops her hand before it makes contact. Bruises *hurt*. They hurt to touch, they hurt to get. He's got dozens of smaller dark bruises against the general yellowing of healing. She's only been bruised like this a few times, after learning ice skating jumps. She'd never ask for them. How could she give them?

"Lily?" Mark wiggles his hips slightly. She places her hand on his ass and he stills.

"Does it still hurt?"

"The plug?" Confusion coats his words.

"No," she's unsure of how to approach the subject. Her fingers trace the outline of a small bruise and Mark nods.

"They're bruises, so not really. If you push on them it'll hurt, but I kind of like that too."

Lily traces another dark spot. How long ago were these put there? How much force did it take? Is this really what he needs?

She can't dwell on that, not right now. She moves her hand towards the plug. It's a smooth black material and Lily is more curious than anything. It's the same material as her dildo, probably. He lets out a small moan as Lily runs her finger along it, pushing it in slightly.

"Is it one of the bigger ones?" Some of the ones in that picture were comically huge. She can't help but to sate her curiosity and pushes on it some more. He lets out a mewling sound as she does so. He shakes his head and she releases it. He shifts his knees to give her better access and she gently tugs on the plug.

"It's a small one." He lets out another mewl as she slightly pulls it out. She lets it go, and lets out a small huff of laughter as Mark's ass sucks it back in. She looks over his ass again and frowns. Unbidden, she reaches over and kisses the dark spot by the top of his ass. "Lily," he whines, but he doesn't ask for anything, and Lily can't stand to look at his bruises any longer.

"On your back," her voice is sharper than she intends, but he rolls over without complaint. His cock stands proud, and Lily hopes it's from the plug and not the bruise. She sits next to him on the bed and grabs the scarf. "Is this okay?"

He gives her his hand. "Of course it is. I trust you."

With the soft scarf in her hand, she loops it through the headboard and around his wrist. She pulls it taut but not tight. He would be able to pull himself free if he tried. He doesn't resist her movements, not even instinctually. He lets his arm hang once she releases it and gives her the other one when she reaches for it.

She leans over to kiss him once he's bound. A deep kiss that sets her tongue on fire and lights her up with an electric feeling all the way down to her toes. The sounds she makes are desperate and insatiable, but she can't stop. If only she could kiss him forever. She only pulls back slightly as the headboard rattles. Lily glances from his restrained hands to his pink cheeks and a smile slowly spreads over her face.

"If you break these, there'll be trouble." Lily warns. Mark doesn't say anything as the soft pink darkens on his cheeks. He said he liked to be embarrassed and talked down to. "Do you understand me?"

"Yes. I do."

"I'm guessing you've done ice play before," Lily reaches for the ice bowl by the bed.

"Not really, maybe once or twice."

Lily takes an ice cube into her mouth and lets it melt. The cold hardens her nipples, and Mark's eyes narrow in on the hard buds. Lily takes the ice cube out and leans over him, kissing him again.

This time, his tongue is searing hot in her mouth, leaving scorch marks of sensation as they kiss. She takes the small piece of ice in her hand and places it on his chest. He hisses in her mouth. Lily moves the ice cube from the center of his chest to circle a nipple.

"Oh," he gasps.

Lily traces the ice cube with open mouth kisses and Mark squirms slightly on the bed. "You're so responsive." She grabs another ice cube and repeats the treatment on his other nipple.

He arches. "It's so cold."

"You must be a summer person."

He was also cold in the ice rink. Does that make this better or worse for him that he doesn't like the cold? "I am."

The ice cube slips from Lily's hand to land on the bed. "I forgot the towels," she murmurs as she turns from him to grab one. "Up." He arches off the bed so she can slide the towel under him and while he's up she takes the opportunity to push slightly on the butt plug again. He lets out a pant.

"Down." She traces the outline of his pecs with the ice cube, down the line of his sternum to the checkerboard of his abs. She leans over him, following the icy liquid with her hot breath. Mark skin retreats from her as he sucks in a startled breath. She traces her cold fingers along his side as she leaves hot, open mouthed kisses on his chest as he trembles beneath her. He doesn't speak, but moans a symphony of mewls, happy sounds, and whimpers.

She slides down his chest, moves the ice bowl to the foot of the bed, and takes his half hard cock in her mouth. He lets out a strangled moan and the headboard rattles again. Wetness rushes between her thighs. The headboards would rattle even more as he slammed into her. He grows in her mouth until he returns to his full length. She licks his tip and then takes him in again as he shudders. Is he already close? Her hand is too cold to stroke him, so she places the warmer one between her thighs to bring it back up to body temperature.

"Lily," he begs, "please, oh that feels so good."

"Remember, you aren't going to come until I say so."

"Yes, *yes,* of course," he throws his head to the side and his whole chest concaves with his deep breath. "Lily." His voice breaks on her name, and it sends a warm tingle straight to her clit.

Lily switches from a blow job to a hand job. Her hand glides up and down his shaft, and she rubs her thumb over the head. "I was thinking about our negotiation the other day." Mark hisses at the change.

"What were you thinking about?" Mark gets out in between pants. His fists clench as he lets out another whimper.

"I like watching, I like listening, and I'm wondering if I'd like putting on a show." Lily squeezes harder for a few strokes before licking the tip.

Mark groans and his hips buck under her fingers. His cock pulses in her hands and Lily's pussy clenches. Focus. This is not about fucking him!

"With me?" Mark pants. "Would you put on a show with me?"

"I wouldn't do it with anyone else."

"Please," he begs. Lily slows her hand as he repeats the word until it loses meaning. She squeezes tighter; curls her hand around the tip to tease him. "Please let me come. Please." He's desperate and jerking, but he'll be worse by the end of the night. That's the plan, at least. She doesn't know if he can get hard after going soft, but now's the time to find out.

"No." She takes the ice cube and places it between his thigh and groin. He jerks again and the headboard rattles as he pulls.

"Fuck," he lands against the bed with a whoosh, but his other leg props his hips up. Lily gently pushes his raised hip so he lowers it. When he does, Lily moves the ice cube to the other side of his groin. His cock sags and Lily takes the tip into her mouth again. Mark hisses out and his foot slips out from under him.

He grows hard again and Lily's insides light up. The *possibilities.* This time, she brings him to the edge quickly. Jerking him in her hand and sucking and licking the head of his cock. It takes almost no time at all for him to start squirming on the bed again, for his mewls and pants to start to form words. He begs to come with desperation that shouldn't be that sexy. He promises to eat her out until his tongue falls off, to be her footrest or her chair for days, to fuck her in just the way she likes. *Anything* she'd like if she would just let him tip over the edge. Lily takes her hand off his cock completely and he lets out a broken sob.

"I'm not interested in having an orgasm. I want to ruin yours." Her voice doesn't betray the way her heart is pounding a beat straight to her clit, how she's heaving with him, and how she is desperate to take him up on all of his offers.

"Ruin?" He sobs. "Please no." He repeats no until it becomes a drumbeat. He begs even as he squirms on the bed and comes off of the edge. It's easy to keep him here now, and so she reaches out a finger to trace one of the larger veins on his cock. She moves up and down slowly.

"Lily," he whines.

"You know, I was browsing online and I read that most s types have a name they like." Lily uses two fingers now, and he shudders anew. "Some like Baby Boy, some like Pet, some like Kitten, some like Honey…" She's already picked his, but she'll be able to see if she got it right. His eyes scrunch together as his mouth falls open, "so what do you think, Puppy?"

Jackpot. His whole body jerks. The headboard rattles again and his eyes shoot open. He doesn't say anything at first, but his chest is heaving. Lily hums as if she's thinking.

"Yes, please, that's me. I'm Puppy. Please, Lily, please."

"Please what, Puppy?" She teases and Mark whines.

"Please let me come, please, I'll do anything. Please let," he pauses and Lily slows her strokes, "please let Puppy come."

"Aww, you know I wasn't going to give you a real orgasm today."

He continues to beg and plead and Lily is determined to ignore him until he finally says what she wants to hear. "Please ruin my orgasm. Do anything you want to me, Lily, only release me. Please." His voice cracks.

"Oh, you poor thing, I was going to ruin it anyway, but now that it's your idea…" Lily teases as she wraps her hand around his cock and tugs once, twice. "Come," she releases him and Mark grunts. His cock twitches, looking for sensation as he gasps. The cum starts to dribble out of his cock as he whimpers and groans on the bed.

"You knocked over the bowl," Lily picks it up.

"I'll clean it later. Come kiss me, please, Lily."

She gives him smaller softer kisses as she undoes the scarves. "I thought you would have pulled these undone towards the end."

"Would have been easy," he murmurs as he turns into her, putting his head in her lap, "but you said not to."

"Mmm, good boy," she pats his head.

He shakes his head. "Puppy. You said I was Puppy." His voice is softer now, almost sleepy, and Lily smiles as she continues to pat his head.

"Good Puppy," she amends and he hums. It fills her with warmth and happiness and she's glad for all the risks she took today.

"We have to get you cleaned up."

Mark's hands wrap around her waist. "A few more minutes, please."

"Okay," Lily runs her fingers through his hair, clearing a few tangles, and even the soft breath on her belly doesn't turn her on. It's not about sex today, not for her. This is somehow more. Mark doesn't pull back from her for a few moments, and her heart clenches when he sheepishly looks up at her.

"Let's get you cleaned up," she wipes him down with a warm towel and checks his arms for marks—there aren't any. She even takes the plug out, and it squelches with lube as it pops out of him. He gives her a searing kiss when she declares him ready for the shower, and Lily can't help but to smile stupidly wide as the bathroom door closes and the enormity of the night settles in her bones.

She cleans up the mess in the bedroom as Mark showers. The wet spot on the bed from the melted ice will have to air dry, but the rest of it is simple to clean up. She washes her hands in the kitchen sink and sits on the couch to wait for him.

Mark comes out in just shorts, and he leans over to kiss Lily as soon as he sees her. He sits on the couch and pulls her on top of him. Lily lets out a squeal at the manhandling but settles on his lap as she pokes his nose.

"I'll see you at the Playhouse on Friday, right?"

Mark slides his thumbs under her shirt as he nods.

"I'll give you a real orgasm there." Lily promises.

"I suppose that means you don't want me coming until then?" He leans forward for a kiss. Would he really wait just because she wants him to?

"I don't want you to come until I tell you to." Lily murmurs. "No masturbating either."

Mark hums. "That'll be hard," he nibbles on her neck, "especially after tonight."

"Isn't that the point?"

<u>Chapter 16</u>

"You look like a new woman," Nick waves as she walks down the hallway at The Playhouse. He gives her a hug and kisses her cheek with an exaggerated "Mwah!". He's in a short skirt, tank top, and knee high boots. "Give me the good gossip, darling. It feeds my soul!" Well, the gossip is all based on the way Mark squirmed in bed as she edged him, how he yanked on the restraints with restraint, and how she hasn't been able to stop thinking about it all week. It's in the way she's practicing saying puppy so that it seems more natural. "It must be good gossip; your face is turning into a cherry tomato."

"Well, it's not like *hot* gossip. I've just started being kinkier." Lily's face grows warmer. "I liked it."

"Details!" Nick demands. He pulls her to some of the couches and sits down with an expectant glance.

"It was just ice play and some edging." Lily sits next to him. It's not a huge deal, maybe it was for her, but it's not here.

"With Mark?" Nick asks. Lily doesn't say anything, but Nick grins. "Oh girl. First of all, great start. Second of all, look at the hulk of a man you have right now, beat the boy up. Or you could totally test him out in ways that skinny boys wouldn't be good for. Sit on his back and make him do pushups or something. You could make him carry you around all day."

"No, I couldn't make him do that," Lily starts, but Nick raises a single perfectly shaped eyebrow and she caves. "I do love being carried."

"I bet a nice strong hunk like Mark could also fuck you in some interesting positions."

Lily is going to combust. She coughs out as she waves her hands and Nick bursts out into laughter.

"Looks like I'm missing all the fun," Mark walks into the room. His smile is sweet but his eyes never leaves hers. Those eyes would bore into her in all the positions Nick mentioned: against a wall, against *nothing*. Could he eat her out in the air? Lily can't possibly flush anymore, but she turns away all the same. Nick cackles. "I hope you're talking about me." Mark walks over to the couch and sits on the floor in front of her. How much did he hear?

"Lily's not giving me nearly enough information. How's the new relationship going?" Nick asks.

Lily doesn't answer, can't answer, not with the way her heart is pounding. Relationship? They aren't in one, but she wants to be. She's not a domme yet, but she wants to be that too.

"Lily's keeping my orgasms already." Mark leans against her leg, caging it with his arm and chest. Nick waggles his brow. Is that acceptance? Is Mark sidestepping the question or is he admitting a relationship? Lily's head spins with questions.

"I bet you liked that."

Mark rubs his cheek against Lily's thigh, and Lily pats his head absentmindedly. Her composure comes back to her at his happy hum.

"You know I do," Mark says to Nick. He looks up at Lily, "and I think I've been promised an orgasm today."

"Now, is that any way to ask for it?" Lily teases. Mark rises to his knees and places a hand on each of her knees. His eyes burn and her throat dries. She parts her legs slightly, but not enough to let him in. He might actually take it as an invitation to eat her out in front of everyone and that's a couple steps further than she wants to go in with an audience.

"Of course not," Mark places an open mouthed kiss on the inside of her knee. Lily looks up from Mark and her eyes dart around the room to look at the people nearby. Some are looking, some are walking by, and some don't look like they care. Even one person is too much for her to let him go higher than her knee. Nick is sitting right here. Nerves settle in her stomach like lead. She doesn't move.

"Oh, don't mind me." Nick winks, crossing his legs. Lily catches the shine on the buckle of his heel. Mark could go lower, right? It wouldn't be so weird if it was her foot. It would still be a little odd, but she was thinking about putting on a show. It was so much easier to think about it while she was jerking Mark off, but here and now? Lily lifts her leg and gives him her foot. They can start there, and Lily will see where the night takes her. Mark kisses under her knee and then places a few open mouth kisses on her calf as he works his way down to her foot.

She focuses on Mark and ignores the people around them. He runs his fingers down her calf slowly, and it sends tingles skittering up her legs. He lifts her leg to his lips again and then scoots backwards so he can reach lower. Lily lets out a breath his pink tongue peeks out from between his lips to lick her. It's so much easier to tune everyone out now. He takes her heel off and places it to the side.

What if she did focus on them? That's part of putting on a show, part of public play. All of them would be too much, but Nick is sitting right there. She could talk to Nick, but she can't pretend Mark isn't there. Maybe she could talk about Mark. Would that turn him on? It would be objectifying, maybe even humiliating.

"You know, Nick," Lily shifts slightly so she can face him. "I was thinking that the walls by the couches upstairs look pretty sturdy."

"They sure do." Nick muses, and Lily hopes he knows what she's trying to do, hopes he's on board. "If you moved one of the couches over you could even have enough room for a couple people to find out how tough they are."

"If only I could find a man to help me out with that, you know?" Lily hums like she's thinking about who can help her. Mark's hands still on her leg for a second, but he doesn't say anything or stop. In fact, the reverence in the way Mark's kissing the inside of her ankle while she's ignoring him somehow makes it all the more special.

"It's so hard to find strong men like that." Nick agrees. Mark puts her shoe back on and Lily lifts her other leg. Anyone looking can tell she's practically panting at this. Her face is flushed and her nipples are hard. Is Mark hard on the floor? She can't look. Nick waves his hand around. "The acoustics are great up there. Anyone in the main room can hear you screaming." He goes on to detail some of the more interesting events he's been able to hear.

"That does sound promising." That's a good way to see how much she likes public play. That's a step further than this without having to show her naked body to everyone. Could Mark make her scream? Would everyone hear it and know he submitted to her? The need to find out rushes over her.

Lily pulls her foot out of Mark's grasp and places it back into her shoe. She stands and meets Mark's eyes as she pulls down on her shirt. She breaks eye contact. "If you'll excuse us, I think I am interested in that wall."

"My pleasure," Nick laughs as Lily starts walking away, "enjoy the acoustics."

"Heel," she calls over her shoulders, and Mark scrambles to his feet to chase her. He catches up to her easily and she grabs his hand to lead him to the stairs. She hasn't been up there since her tour, but there are only two spots with couches and the good wall must be the one by the stairs.

"I wish I had a leash, Puppy, then I could really drag you around." Lily leads him upstairs.

Mark squeezes her hand. "I'd wear it, if you asked." He says, like it's important for her to know.

"Good to know," she gives him a quick kiss before pulling him towards the stairs.

At the top of the stairs Mark lets go of her hand to shove one of the couches over away from the wall that she talked to Nick about. It slides all the way to the railing. Her throat dries at his display of strength. Is he showing off because of her earlier conversation? She kind of wants to bring it up. He turns to her and steps into her space as she stands where the couch once was.

Lily trails her hands over his biceps, "I've been thinking, that a big strong man such as yourself…"

"Yes?" He interrupts. His breath is hot against her face.

Lily licks her lips. "…could certainly hold me against this wall and fuck me."

"I could, if that's what you want." His eyes are molten embers that threaten to consume her. He takes a step forward and cages her to the wall with his hands. Lily's back hits the wall. He looks wild, with wide eyes and dilated pupils, like she's the only thing holding him back from ravishing her. "But are you sure you want to have sex right here?"

"Well, it's not completely visible." Lily laces her fingers behind his neck. She doesn't want to stop him. Her blood pumps with adrenaline and desire to see what her public stunt has turned Mark into, because it's clearly done wonders to his sex drive. Or is the fact that he hasn't been able to come since she ruined his orgasm before? Is this what she does to him? Is this some combination of public worship and orgasm control?

"From down there they'll still be able to see me kiss your neck," he kisses her neck, a hot open mouth kiss that she lets out a soft moan at. His breath tickles her ear. "They'd be able to see me touching you," he moves his hands to her waist and squeezes her. His fingers slip under her shirt and leave goosebumps in their wake.

"What else?"

"They'd be able to hear you scream."

She wants him closer. She wants him to pick her up and crush her to the wall. She wants to know how long he can fuck her against this wall before his arms start to quiver. "If you *can* make me scream." She challenges.

"I will." He promises. He pulls her up effortlessly. His skin is hot against hers as he places more open mouth kisses on her neck.

"Mark," Lily moans out. He gently scrapes his teeth against her neck and she pants. "You can bite me," she offers. He nips at her neck. She moans and he licks her ear.

"Can I fuck you?" His hot breath causes her neck to break out in goosebumps. "You said you wanted to test this wall. I intend to fuck you through it if you'll let me."

He probably can't. He's strong and built and works out every day but he's not actually going to drill her into the wall, right? Lily wants him to try anyway. He would have thrown the couch off the balcony if the railing wasn't there. He's so strong.

"Fuck me, Mark. Right against this wall. If you can make me scream, I want everyone to hear it."

"Fuck," he groans out, and then he captures her lips in a kiss. It's harder and more insistent than normal. His whole body rolls against her as he slides his tongue into her mouth. She tilts her head for better access and tries to roll her body into his. She's weightless and it's amazing. She kisses him like that, desperate and wanting, until her pussy lips glide against themselves with how wet she is.

"Put me down," she pants. Mark moves from her lips to her neck and Lily lets out a strangled sound as he nips at her neck again. "Put me down," she repeats. He pulls back to look at her, and at the dazed look in his eyes she gives him a soft short peck on the lips. "Down." He lowers her until her feet touch the ground, and she reaches for his shirt. He helps her pull it off before moving to undo his jeans.

"How naked do you want to be?"

Lily is about to be completely naked before she catches sight of a couple on the far couches staring. She's not going to stop, but maybe she'll leave her bra on. She takes off her shirt but she can't make out too much from this distance. "Lily?" Concern creeps into his voice. She shifts to look at him, standing in all his naked glory; unabashed, unafraid. She wants to be that brave too. No matter what anyone thinks of her, she's the one who has Mark. She unclips her bra and drops it to the floor before pulling down her own pants.

"You're beautiful," he kisses her again.

Lily moans into his mouth and only pulls back to say one word. "Condom."

"Okay," he pulls away from her and bends over to reach into the pocket of his discarded jeans.

He locks eyes with her as he slides it on, and the fire in his eyes consumes her. She wants to lick him from head to toe, she wants to parade his naked body to the world to show off, she wants to take his cock into her mouth, her hands, her pussy. She wants, she wants, she *wants*.

She takes.

"Up." She commands with all the confidence she has. She takes his mouth as he crashes into her. He's as desperate as she is. She takes his cock as he lines it up to her entrance. He's hard and pulsing and so hot. Everything is fire. She takes his hips as she wraps her legs around him. Then, she takes a breath. "Make me scream." She bites his lip. He almost growls into her mouth with his sharp exhale and his hips drive into hers with a force he hadn't given her yet. She curses as he threatens to dislodge her.

"As you command," his hands tighten on her hips and he thrusts in again.

She's being punished in the best way. His pace is unrelenting and she has to stop kissing him so she can breathe in between the moans and whines. His hands are so tight that they hurt, her back scratches against the wall, and he nips at her neck. It hurts just enough to feel good, and she doesn't want him to stop until that makes sense. She lets out another loud moan as she comes around his cock and can feel him smiling into her skin.

"Good?" he slows his thrusts to slam her harder. Her pussy doesn't want to let him go but is powerless to stop his assault. She scratches his back as her lungs fight for air. Her eyes close as the sensations build and build.

"Yes." A tingling runs up her spine. "Yes!" She yells. "Mark!" If they really can hear her, everyone will be able to know the mess he's made of her. She wants them to know. She wants them to see. She opens her eyes and looks at the couple from before. They are playing. They are watching.

They're fucking gorgeous. She looks better, especially wrapped around Mark's muscular back. Fuck. *Fuck.* Mark speeds up again, and she'd throw her head back if it wouldn't hit concrete. She's louder now, almost challenging anyone listening to say something. As if she could reach across the city and show Derrick how much Mark does for her. A fresh round of goosebumps erupts on her skin as her second orgasm approaches.

She screams as she comes around his cock again. It's long and loud and would be embarrassing anywhere else. Here, it's like a claim; her claim on Mark. She hasn't heard anyone scream the way she just did right now. If the acoustics are that good, everyone has just shared in her pleasure. Mark slows down and his thrusts grow softer. Lily leans back against the wall as he looks up at her with a coy smile on his face.

"That sounded like such a lovely scream."

Lily opens her mouth to reply but he gives her another punishing thrust and Lily just moans again as she scrambles for purchase on his shoulders. Anything other than being a writhing mess on his cock.

"Ah, it was. A great one." Her pussy is still clenched around him so tight she's surprised he can move at all.

"Will you give me one then? Will you let me come, just like this, in front of everyone?"

"Puppy's being so aggressive," Lily barely manages to get out as she fights to get her breath back, but Mark only growls and nips at her lips.

"Maybe I am." He thrusts into her harder now, and Lily is glad she doesn't have to hang on. "You are the one that wanted me to mount you in front of everyone. Claiming me in public like a pair of animals. You commanded me to *heel*. I want you to howl for me again."

"I might," she confesses as her insides clamp down. Her pussy is on fire, and she leans over to kiss him again.

"Might howl, or might let me come?"

Lily can't focus enough to do anything but mewl. "Yes," she moans.

His hips jerk as he lets out a moan, and then he pants out in her ear. "Will you let me come, Lily? Can I come, Mistress? Will you release me, darling?"

"Mark." Lily groans, digging her fingers into his back. He's scrambling her brains with his cock.

"Do you want my orgasm now, Mistress? Have I been a good boy? Does Puppy get to come?" His voice is too close to cocky for this to truly be begging but right now Lily doesn't care.

"Come for me, come for me now." She finds his ear and bites it as his hips stutter. "I want to swallow your cock in my pussy and never let go."

"Fuck," he curses as he crushes her body against the wall. Lily lets out all the air in her lungs as Mark jerks as he comes.

After, he nuzzles her head as he pulls her off the wall. His arms don't quiver at all as he kisses her again. When he lets her down, Lily whines at the loss of his cock.

"I'll be right back," he gives her a quick kiss and he pulls the condom off. Lily watches him go and then shifts to the other couple still in the throes of fucking. She's kind of dizzy. She kind of wants to do it again.

"It's a shame we don't have a wall like that at my house." Lily breathes. She's still trying to catch her breath as he returns to her. He's not even winded. His cock and part of his abs are glistening from her, but she's not embarrassed. It's like ownership in a way she can't describe. He picks up his jeans to fish out a tissue and she's only a little disappointed to be wiped away.

"I don't need a wall." Mark kisses her forehead. His voice somehow drops lower. "Next time, I could just lift you up and slam you on my cock. We can check out the acoustics in your living room. I think I like you screaming."

"Next time." That's so promising. Would he ever tire holding her? When *is* the next time she can see him? "Actually," she sighs and leans over to pick up her own clothes. "I won't be able to hang out much this week, but I'll see you here next Friday."

He grabs her shoulder and spins her, and his mouth swallows her words as he pushes her back against the wall. "I don't know if I can go that long without seeing you."

She bites his lip as she pulls his head back by his hair. His moan is strangled, and power flood her veins. "Don't tell me my Puppy's got separation anxiety."

Chapter 17

"That is wild! I can't believe you had semi-public sex." Tala grins from her spot at the foot of the bed. "My little baby domme almost pulled off her first exhibition!"

"Tala, be serious!"

"I am serious." Tala sticks her tongue out. "This is chocolate we're talking about."

Lily groans.

"Okay, okay, we can be serious."

"I need help." Lily mumbles into her pillow.

"Well, if you want this guy, you've got to go get him."

"I want this guy." Lily sits up and lowers the pillow. She hugs it.

"So what's in your way?"

"Well, I'm not a domme, he already has a dom, and I'm not sure if he even wants me in the first place. I think he does. He sure acts like he does, but I don't know, maybe he turns that charm onto everyone he sleeps with." Lily crushes the pillow. "He likes to sleep around, and I don't know how I'd feel about having an open relationship. What if there is something he absolutely needs that I wouldn't be able to do or handle? He got beat before, Tala, beat to the point of bruises and cuts and he was sobbing and I can't do that to him."

"Well, you guys are friends." Tala points out. "So that's in your favor. You guys already know you like each other enough to date."

"Right."

"And the open relationship is just a conversation you need to have with him."

"I don't know if he'd leave it for me."

Tala doesn't respond to that, and Lily sighs, "if we dated, I'd have to ask him to stop, or at least stop for right now."

"Which you can totally do, most people expect monogamy when they start dating."

"True."

"So are you going to ask him out?"

Lily groans. In the past month and a half, they've been climbing, they've eaten lots of food together, they've been skating, and they've had a fair amount of sex.

"We've been kind of dating, to be honest." Lily looks up to the ceiling, but it doesn't have any answers for her. "Neither of us made it official, but the skating and the climbing, and the dinners. It's kind of dating"

"It is, and he's all over you when you are together. It has to be more than friendship to him too."

Lily just squeezes her pillow tighter as the silence drags on. "But is it a relationship? If I ask him before I'm a domme, he might just pull back entirely."

"So how do you become a domme?" Tala crosses her arms. "I've seen a bunch, but I've never heard of a metric for it. If you say you're a domme, then you're a domme."

"I think there is more to it than that. The dominants I see always have this confidence. I don't know if I'll just wake up one day and have that. They know how to do the ties and how to use the crops and floggers." Lily frowns. "It's like they all went to school to learn this stuff."

"I think The Playhouse has classes." Tala muses. "I know they have rope classes, maybe they have the other classes there. You could study to be a domme there and then make your move."

"Classes?" Lily questions. "Haven't I spent enough time in school?"

Tala barks a laugh, which sends Lily into giggles. Lily sighs and starts fiddling with the pillow. "I should look into them."

"At least the subject matter is more interesting and Mark could help you study."

"I have something to show you." Lily grabs a plastic bag from her bedroom. After Mark left The Playhouse last night, she stopped in the dungeon. Tala pulls out the red leather riding crop. It may have been an impulse purchase, but maybe it was a long time coming.

Tala claps her hands together once. "Kinky!"

"Tala!"

"But this is proof, isn't it? That you are serious about this."

"I should talk to Derrick about this, again." Lily grabs the crop. She gently swings it to hit her hand, and something about it is just right. "He's Mark's dom now, so he has to know about learning how to do the things Mark likes."

***

"Thanks for coming, Derrick." Lily takes her seat across from him, smoothing her sweaty hands on her pants. His long sleeves are rolled up and his thumb nail works at the plastic laminating the menu.

"Sure, thanks for inviting me." Derrick taps the menu. "I've been craving sushi recently."

"How's Michi?"

"Sick, actually." He frowns. "She's had a fever for a few days, but today it got worse. I would have stayed home but she practically kicked me out."

"I'm sorry to hear that."

They talk, but Lily can't bring up what she wants to talk about until food is delivered and the waitress turns away. Lily takes a deep breath. "I wanted to ask you about being a dominant."

"So ask." Derrick digs into his food.

"Well, I'm curious about some of the events I've witnessed in the dungeon. I want to try some of them, but I have no idea where to start. I wouldn't know what to buy or how to practice. I heard that there were classes, but I don't know where to start."

"Okay. So, what's your question?"

Lily purses her lips. "Are there classes at The Playhouse?"

"Yes."

"What do they teach? Can anyone take them?"

"Members can take them, so you are free to take any of the classes. There are classes on rope tying, an introduction to impact play, and rotating extras like the basics of wax play or fire play." Impact play. That's really what she's looking for. That's what she has to learn.

"Would I find that online?"

"Yes. You could ask the DMs when you go to parties." Derrick pauses as the waitress stops by to ask how the food is. "I teach a rope class on Sunday afternoons."

"I'd be interested in that." Lily smiles.

"Thorn teaches the basics of impact play on Thursdays."

"That's what I'm hoping for, to be honest. I know Mark really likes that, and I'm not there yet, so I wanted to learn more about it. I'm not sure if I'll like it or not, but I figured it wouldn't hurt to try."

Across from her, Derrick straightens and frowns. He lowers his chopsticks to the table and carefully dabs his mouth with his napkin. Has she said something wrong? She thought he'd be pleased that she was trying to learn how to be a better kinkster and to be safer with Mark.

"You should learn for yourself, not for someone else." He finally warns.

"I would be learning it for me, because I'm curious about what he likes."

"Mark is not your sub." Derrick voice takes on a possessive tint. Has she misread their relationship? Mark doesn't think they are anything other than playmates, which now sounds completely juvenile.

"I'm not trying to take him from you," she soothes. Maybe coming to Derrick was a bad idea. She does want Mark, and that would mean taking him away, and she really should have thought this through before deciding to have this conversation.

"I'm not worried about that. You couldn't." Derrick takes a deep breath and seems to backtrack. "Okay. I know you've had fun the couple of times you've played with him." Derrick doesn't know about all of the other times. He doesn't know Mark asked to worship her and that they had their own negotiations. "I'm glad that seems to have awoken your inner domme. I am." He lets the waitress refill his water before he continues. "That doesn't mean you get to be Mark's domme."

"Right."

"Mark likes a lot of things, things that can be unsafe if done with a new domme."

"Which is why I mentioned the classes."

"You can't just take a class or two and expect to know enough for that kind of play."

"Well of course not, I'd have to practice." She sighs. He doesn't speak for a moment and she eats a piece of her king roll.

"I warned you." He crosses his arms, and it's the same tone he scolded Mark with, the same tone he used when he beat Mark and turned him into a crying mess.

"Mark says you guys are just play partners," Lily retorts, and Derrick doesn't seem to have any response to that. "He said he'd asked you to collar him, to be something more than that, and you refused." Derrick eyes narrow and his palms flatten against the table, but he doesn't disagree. "Mark wants more than to just play with someone. I want to be more than friends or play partners with Mark. I want to learn how to be a domme, or a better domme, or a trained domme because I want to be Mark's domme. I want to be his girlfriend. I want to…" Lily trails off and looks away.

"I came to you," Lily dips her roll into the sauce more carefully than needed. "Because you've been a mentor to me. You've shown me the ropes and taught me a lot and I thought that I could learn more from you."

"I'm sorry if I came off aggressive. Please understand I want what's best for Mark. I have no doubt that you like him and care for him, but that doesn't mean that you are a good choice for his domme. And you aren't the first to treat him as some sort of prize for joining the lifestyle."

"He's not a prize," Lily bristles, sitting up straighter and clenching her chopsticks, "and he's not a toy for you to give me! I didn't call you to ask for him."

"Of course not, but I'm looking out for him. I'll always look out for him, and right now, you are not a good choice." Derrick stops to take a drink of water. "It's not your fault, but you're either not going to do what he needs, or you'll be unsafe about it. You need to take classes, you need to figure out what you need and want. You can't pretend to be a domme just because you like him. He needs more than a tourist who's going to leave once the kink isn't shiny anymore. He deserves more than that." He pulls out his wallet, "and if you're not willing to give him more than that. I'm going to cut you out of his life completely."

"You can't do that." Maybe he can.

He tosses money on the table. "Don't make me."

"Don't leave."

"I don't think I need to stay. I've had this conversation before, and I know how it ends."

"Derrick!"

"He's a pretty man, and he gets lots of women who think they'll boss him around a little and he'll love them for it. When you all get bored or when the kink becomes too real, you leave him shattered and I'm the one who picks up the pieces. You've been on the scene for weeks, and you can't even hit him. You think that's what he wants?"

The silence drags on, but she doesn't have a response. That can't be what Mark wants. Something on her face must stop Derrick because he pauses.

"I don't think that's what he wants, and it's not what I want either." Lily smooths her napkin on the table to have something to do with her hands. "I want to be able to give him what he needs, hence the classes. I'm not trying to rush anything."

"I look forward to you proving me wrong, until then forgive my skepticism."

"Fine."

He shakes his head as he bids her goodbye and walks out of the restaurant. She needs to talk to Mark.

<u>Chapter 18</u>

Her lipstick and lingerie are bright red. Her mini skirt and high heels are black. She blows herself a kiss as she winks in the mirror and then she brushes her hair back over her shoulder. She hopes people stare. She hopes Mark stares. It'll make it a lot easier to ask him out and confess that she wants to be something.

"You got this." She smooths down her skirt and steps out of the bathroom. A man winks at her as he walks by and her confidence skyrockets. This will catch his attention.

Except his attention is clearly elsewhere. Her stomach drops as she rounds the corner and spots him in the big bedroom. Her throat closes. He knelt at her feet, he'd asked to worship her, and now he's using those lips to service others. Her stomach twists at the sight. Mark going to his knees for her isn't special. Of course it wasn't special. Mark has Derrick. Mark was always playing with others. It's one thing to know it and another to see it. Seeing it hurts.

She startles at a loud moan from the tangle of limbs on the bed. She wanted everyone to hear how Mark made her scream, but now he's making them moan. It's like an answer to her; another, bolder claim. He's their puppy now.

She moves her arms over her breasts to cover them, but she can't tear her eyes away from him. There are five of them in a mess on the bed.

Mark moves from one to the other without hesitation, and he's so focused that he doesn't notice her in the doorway. She tries to focus her gaze, to somehow stare hard enough to make him aware of it. Any second now he'd lift his gaze to meet her eyes and notice her. He could wink and invite her in, or leave to ravish her. Would she even join if he asked? It doesn't matter. He doesn't notice her.

She glances at the other voyeurs in the room and finds them completely engaged in the action. She's the odd one out here, and maybe she's always been. Maybe Derrick is right. She can't bear to watch anymore. Lily takes a step back and then flees. She keeps herself covered as she retreats into the long hallway and starts heading towards the lockers where her backpack is waiting. Her eyes are hot, but she won't cry. She could just leave. She didn't tell anyone she was coming and it's not like she'll be missed. It honestly may have been a relief to Mark to not have to babysit her again.

"Are you okay?" It's Derrick. He's standing with his wife. Oh great. Would he gloat?

"I'm fine," Lily lies quickly, "but I might head out soon."

"Oh, don't do that." Derrick doesn't sound like he's holding their earlier conversation against her, but he has to know. He has to be able to see the distress on her face. He has to know he was right. "It's early. You look great. Mark is around here somewhere, and there's lots of other people you could play with. I could even help you out if you want. Or you can come sit with Michi and I. We brought snacks."

"No, but thank you." Lily blinks away her tears before they can fall and Michi reaches out to grab her shoulder.

"I'll catch up honey," Michi locks eyes with Derrick and he turns away and enters the room where Mark is. "Are you sure you're okay?"

Lily brushes at her cheeks to catch the errant tears. "I'm okay."

"Listen, if something isn't fun anymore you have to say something," Michi runs her hands up and down Lily's arms and then pushes her hair over her shoulders, "but you're young and here to have some fun so go find some fun, and if you need anything, you can come to me, okay?"

Lily gives Michi a small smile. Michi gives her a reassuring squeeze and follows Derrick. If Mark is out there having fun, she should be too, right? Lily tries to walk back in with confidence but pauses at the sounds of an enthusiastic paddling in the dungeon. She leans against the wall outside to listen and scrunches her eyes shut. Is that the only way to keep him?

When Derrick hit Mark, the impact reverberated in the room. People held their breaths, squirmed in their seats, and couldn't take their eyes off the pair. Mark sighed, moaned, and cried under Derrick's blows, and that's what he wants. To him, the pain is pleasure, it's euphoric. He enjoys a spanking the same way he enjoys a blowjob, and he'd need her to provide him with both before he would offer himself in submission. He wants to be taken apart at the seams and put together. He's a *pain slut.* A woman moans, ecstatic with pain. What did she think he would have said to her? If this is what he needs, then she is never going to be enough for him.

She walks to the doorway and stares at the pair in the dungeon. The worst part is it seems like he likes her as much as she likes him. The way he looks at her is the way she wants him to, but there's no future for them like this. They'll break each other's hearts because she won't be able to break him in. Lily's gaze lingers on a bruising mark on the woman's leg before she moves on to the wall of display toys. Her gaze settles on the spot her red crop used to sit before she shakes her head and backs out of the dungeon.

The dance floor is filled with people line dancing as she walks in. Lily's only seen people dancing on the floor once or twice before, but today they are all laughing along and dancing together. That's what she's used to from clubs. That's where she belongs. "Fuck it." She remembers the moves. "Let's find some fun."

Lily walks to the center of the space and laughs at the absurdity of dancing in her underwear with a bunch of strangers in their underwear. She hops around and another laugh escapes her. Someone else laughs behind her, and Lily turns her head to see Amos.

"Nice to see you again," Amos greets over the music. He's not in his underwear, just a plain T shirt, jeans, and boots. "Are you here with anyone?"

"Nice to see you, too." She hasn't seen him since the first time she was here. She was so frazzled on the couch with Nick. Look at her now. Lily shakes her head as everyone turns so he's beside her. "No, it's just me. I was looking for someone, but he appears to be occupied."

"Well, I'm here with a friend, but she's occupied too." Something about the gravelly tone of his voice slides over Lily in a delicious way. She came here for Mark, but if he doesn't owe her anything then she doesn't owe him anything. She could be intimate with another stranger today, or multiple strangers. She's at a swingers' club. He said he liked when his partners slept with other people.

The next time they turn, she takes half a step back so that she's in his space, and he steps in and wraps his arm around her. This song isn't meant to be danced to this way, but as Amos' large hand settles on her waist she leans back so she's pressed against his chest and she doesn't care how it's meant to be danced to.

"Are you looking to play today?"

Screw Mark. She came to have fun, and she will. "I am." She blushes, and after a few more words, she lets him lead her away to a bedroom. She squeezes her hand in his and spots a few people watching them walk through the main room, including Nick who gives them a thumbs up. Are they looking at her in her revealing outfit, noticing her in the way Mark hasn't?

"How's this room?" Amos asks and she smiles up at him.

"It's good." She doesn't look at the room at all, and she fists his shirt to pull him in to kiss her in the doorway. He's rough against her lips and it takes her breath away. She wraps her other arm around him and deepens it.

"Anything you really like?" He mumbles as he nips at her neck. His hands slide down her sides to cup her ass and pull her closer to him.

"I'm kind of new at this," she confesses, "so we can play it by ear."

184

"Okay," he kisses her again, and she only notices the crowd when she steps into the room. "Now let's get you out of these clothes."

"I'm closing the door," Lily pulls back slightly and nudges him into the room. She turns to the door and spots Mark watching her with hungry eyes. His hair is a mess and he's in nothing but shorts as his chest heaves. Did he see them dance too? Is he jealous? Is he turned on? Does this hurt him? Spite has her smiling at him as she winks.

Amos pins her to the door and captures her mouth in a searing kiss. He holds her arms to the door above her head as he bites her lip and pulls her flush against his body. Lily moans out and he moves to kiss down her neck and bite her gently. Everything about Amos screams rough sex and Lily's head spins as he squeezes her hands and bites her neck harder. If she screams, Mark might hear her.

"Marks?" His voice rakes against her skin.

"What?" Lily's breathless. Oh, he means leaving marks and nothing to do with Mark. "No."

"I was hoping you'd say yes." His smile is slanted and his eyes roam over her. Somehow, she feels like prey. He mouths at her shoulders and neck, but doesn't give her any hickeys. "Do you like being spanked?"

She'd like most things, if he asks like that.

"Maybe." She tries to move to the bed, but he slides his knee up and in-between her legs, and the friction has her moaning again. If he fucks her against the door, they might break it down. That would be quite the sight. Maybe she'd earn a reputation, after last time. Mark was with her last time.

"I almost left today."

He lets her hands go and pulls on her hips to lead her to bed. "I'm glad you didn't. I'll make it worth it." He lowers his mouth to her breasts as he pulls the bra down to uncover them. Reaching behind her, she undoes the clasps and he takes the cue to pull back and take off his own clothes. He pulls a condom from his pocket and strokes his hard cock.

"Take it off," he demands as she takes off the rest of her clothes. "Get on all fours." He orders, and she does. She wouldn't like this all the time, but she's in just the right headspace that she's enjoying this right now. She jerks in slight surprise as he kisses her ass cheek. He spreads her legs apart a little bit and slides a finger into her pussy. Lily pushes back into his hand.

Then he licks her asshole.

Lily clenches the bed sheets as she opens her eyes. How does she respond to that? It doesn't feel bad but it doesn't feel good either. Maybe she just needs to give it a chance like when Mark was licking her calves. Is this something Mark likes too?

"Oh," she sighs as he slides another finger into her pussy and steadily pumps. The sensations start to build on each other, and Lily closes her eyes to enjoy them.

"That's it." He groans as she pushes back into his hand. Lily moans out as he gets faster, and in practically no time at all she clenches around him as she comes. He pulls away to bite her ass cheek and Lily squeaks with a moan. She arches her back as he places a hot heavy hand on it.

"Let me in," he's gentle as he lines up the head of his cock to her pussy. Lily moans again and pushes backwards, swallowing a few inches. He groans and pulls her hips further backward so he sinks all the way in.

He starts a hard steady rhythm that turns Lily's mind deliciously blank. She closes her eyes to groan out and she imagines Mark watching from the doorway. What would his face look like? Would he be horny or happy? Would he want to join? How would he feel if she didn't notice him?

Amos gently thrums his fingers against one of her ass cheeks. He's probably going to slap it. It's nothing she hasn't done before. Except he spanks her so hard that she pauses as pain shoots up her body. Her ass throbs. Well, that's a turn off. Lily shifts on the bed beneath her, opening her mouth and he spanks her again. She cries out in shock and he groans from the sound. She doesn't want to break the mood, but she's not going to enjoy this if he hits her again.

"No spanking." She pants, and he runs his fingers over where he spanked her. Her ass warms and tingles where his fingers press. He continues to fuck her, rough and fast, like he's racing her towards orgasm. She hopes she comes again before he does. She never had to worry about that with Mark. He pushes her further down into the mattress and it's just the right angle to send her crashing into her next. Amos jerks against her a few times as he comes, and then Lily finds herself sitting on the bed in a daze. She puts on her bra and her skirt as he pulls on his pants, but he walks over to her with his shirt in hand.

"Why don't you wear this for a little while," he slides his polo over her head and gives her a hand to stand up. He kisses her forehead as he pulls her hair out of the shirt. "I'll come back for it soon, okay?"

She hums in response. She doesn't want to be claimed, but she wants Mark to see her in his shirt. Amos grabs the bed sheets and throws them in the hamper as she opens the door. He grabs her waist as she does. "If you ever want more of me, all you have to do is ask." His teeth graze the small of her neck and Lily shivers. "Or don't ask, just come plant one on me."

They split there and she contently collapses on the closest couch. She's not alone for a second.

"Have fun?" Mark slides next to her on the couch. He doesn't seem jealous at all, and somehow that makes her bitterness feel wrong. Did she want to fight? No. She doesn't. He wraps his arm around her.

"It was great." She snuggles further into him. "You?"

"I had some fun with a couple friends before you got here."

"No, I saw it." She's less bitter about it now that she's had her own fun. She's still hurt, but what should she have expected? They aren't even dating, let alone exclusive. They met at a swingers' club. It's just another aspect of his life that she's not used to. This isn't like the kink though; she can't learn to share him. Her questions do seem to be answered now.

"Oh yeah? Is that why you disappeared into that room? I turned you on?" He nudges her shoulder. Lily nudges him back instead of answering and Mark leans back into the couch, bringing her with him. Mark launches into conversation about his work as Lily stares off into the distance. This is wrong, right? This feels wrong. Sleeping with other people isn't something you do in a relationship, or a situationship, or whatever this is, right? Her stomach slowly sinks and her orgasmic buzz fades.

"So," Lily ventures, interrupting him. "is this something you think you'd always need?"

"What do you mean?" He asks slowly. Is he rethinking everything he thought happened today? Should he be?

"Well," she's glad she can't see his face, because it might stop her questions in their tracks, but she has to know. "You said you had trouble dating because you couldn't find a domme." He hums his affirmation. "Is part of the problem that you swing?"

"No." He shifts behind her, and moves his hand up and down her back, "With the right person, I could give up swinging. It's the kink I can't live without. Swinging is just fun for right now." He takes a curl in his hand and kisses the top of her head. "I think I could give almost everything for the right person." He murmurs. Lily lets out a breath. Could he be thinking that about her? She wants him to be. She could be. She's just got to learn how to hit him. She should just ask. Say something.

"Do you—"

"Here she is," Amos announces. He's there with a friend. Lily stands and Mark's hand lingers on her leg. Is he jealous?

"Right, thanks for the shirt." She grabs the hem of it and Amos kisses her again. Mark is right behind her. Is that a good thing? Amos' friend is there too. She pulls back with a nervous smile, and he pulls his shirt off of her.

"You're welcome." He leaves his big warm hand on her hip and his friend gives her a once over. "If you are up for it, Amber and I would love to take you upstairs."

"Oh!" Lily glances at Amber, who slides her hand around Amos' waist. He's insatiable! Lily's cheeks warm as she tries to formulate a response.

"No rush honey, we're here pretty often and you're always welcome to join."

"Or," Amos glances at Mark and then back to Lily, "if your friend wants to join he can."

"Wow," Lily shifts between them. "Um, thank you." She stammers. Amos and Amber exchange a smile. "Maybe next time."

"Sure. Whenever you want, just come lay one on me."

Lily sinks into the couch when they leave. "Oh my god." She repeats a few times, hiding her burning face into her hands. Behind her, Mark rubs her shoulders.

"Are you okay?"

"They just—I didn't—and you" Lily breathes out. "I've never even had a threesome." Mark laughs and Lily crosses her arms. "Whatever! This is only my fifth time here, I'm not ready to be Mrs. Sex!"

"So next time?" He teases.

Lily hides her head in her hands as Mark starts laughing. "Let's talk about anything else," Lily's cheeks blaze.

"I got the underwear gig."

Lily squeals and throws her arms around him. "Congratulations!"

He hugs her back and his warm arms against her skin turns her on enough that she's ready for round two, which is surprising but not unwelcome. "I mean, it's not huge, but it's something."

"It means some dude is going to be staring at your six pack and thinking about how unrealistic of a standard that is." She pokes his stomach as she smiles. "I'll have to buy a pack."

"I don't think it's ending up there, I'm only getting a couple hundred bucks for it."

"Well, I'll buy whatever it is you end up on. I'm happy for you!"

"Thanks!"

She doesn't end up playing with Mark at all, but she spends the rest of the night on the couch with him and somehow that's so much better. Maybe she doesn't have to define this right now; she can just enjoy it.

<u>Chapter 19</u>

"He's right, isn't he?"

"That you are inexperienced, yes. That you don't deserve Mark, no." Tala repeats for what must be the tenth time. Tala's getting annoyed, but Lily can't stop the spiraling thoughts. Derrick's words haunt her, and she spent all weekend looking up BDSM videos and blogs, taking kink quizzes, and hoping that something inside of her will click on with every new website. He can't be right. He might be. It's barely 9 AM and she's ready for today to be over already.

"Darling, just text him."

"Fine, Fine, I will!" Lily huffs.

I want to go climbing again. Are you free during the week? She sends about 20 minutes later, which is a cop out but not really. They can't have a serious conversation over text, and she can't hint at one without him wanting to know more.

Miss me already? He responds immediately with a string of emojis. Lily smiles, but it fades quickly.

I'm actually planning to climb after work today so I can meet you at your house at 7. He sends a minute later.

See you then.

"Lily!" Jeff pops over her cube. "Looks like we have a potential solution involving the triple redundancy idea, but when I told the process engineer about the change, she almost screamed. She's called a meeting, and it starts in about 10 minutes."

There goes her entire day.

She doesn't get out of work until 6. She almost cancels on Mark, but she can't risk Derrick getting in between them. By the time she makes it home, she's exhausted, and she'd take a nap if it wasn't for the fact that Mark is already on his way. She's not quite sure what happened in those nine hours of meetings, but she knows that tomorrow she'll have to sort it all out.

"What happened between you and Derrick?" Mark asks as soon as she opens her door. Lily sighs as she finishes putting her shoes on. "He wouldn't tell me much, just that you needed to do some thinking and I should stay away from you for a while."

"We had a disagreement." She's unsure of how much she wants to reveal. "I expressed an interest in taking classes at The Playhouse and learning how to be a better Domme for you, and he thinks that I'm not a good choice for you since I'm not experienced."

"You wanted to take classes for me?" He smiles shyly as he steps into her house.

"I do. You disobeyed your Dom for me?" Lily meets him halfway when he leans down to kiss her. Lily closes the door as they move back into her house.

"I did. I'm crazy about you, and this. I wasn't going to just stay away."

"Mark." Questions bounce around in her head in between kisses. Would Mark leave Derrick for her if she asked? Is that even a question she can ask? Part of her doesn't want to know. She bites his lip as she pulls his hair.

Mark moans into her mouth, and Lily smiles as she detangles herself from him. She pointedly looks down to the tent in his pants before stepping back. "Looks like you better get that under control or everyone at the climbing gym is going to see it."

191

Mark groans out before placing his head on her shoulder. "Are you sure you need training?"

Lily gives him a gentle swat on the ass to get moving, and grabs her keys to lock up. Lily pauses as she looks at the keys, thinking about Derrick's warning, but she shakes her head to clear it. As long as they keep going like this, she buys herself time to learn.

The ride to the gym is filled with pleasant conversation, but Lily can't help the anxiousness that settles in her bones. This might already be in its final stretch. The climbing gym is rather empty, and Mark warms up with some pull-ups while Lily gets her rentals and signs up for the top roping class. She's the only one taking the class today, so Mark volunteers to partner up with her. The knots are easy to learn, the phrases are easy enough to remember, and she only runs into a problem when she climbs her first wall and has to let go.

"Just jump off!" The instructor shouts up at her.

Lily's hands tighten on the holds instead of letting go. "Mark?" She calls, looking down the fifteen feet she's already climbed.

He chuckles. "I've got you."

Lily stares at the wall in front of her. What if she tied the knot wrong? What if Mark tied it wrong? Falling from this height winded her before, and that was on the thick padding. She could break her ankle from this height. Maybe she could climb down a few more feet to reduce the risk of injury, and then she can jump. "I can downclimb,"

Mark laughs beneath her, not even trying to hide it anymore. "Just let go, Lily!"

Next to her, a kid shouts with joy as she reaches the top of the wall, yells to the adult with her and kicks off the wall. Kids aren't afraid of anything, Lily rationalizes. It's perfectly normal to be scared of getting hurt.

"You can do it."

Lily's arm starts to cramp. She takes one off to shake it out, and her other hand starts to slip. Lily lets out a startled yelp as her hand slips but the harness catches her with ease. Lily kicks out against the wall as Mark starts to lower her, but her heart races until her ass touches the mat beneath her.

"I don't know if I like this any better than bouldering." She stands.

"It'll get easier, the first one is the hardest. Now switch."

"Not really into switching." Mark mutters.

Lily playfully slaps his arm. "Behave."

Mark grins and unclips his section of the rope as Lily unties hers. They switch. He ties his figure-eight in a few seconds as Lily clips in. She double checks each step with the instructor and then moves to Mark's to check his. She pulls on the knot just in case and finally declares him good to climb. The instructor nods and with a 'climbing' and 'climb on' Mark starts flying up the wall. Lily can barely take in the rope fast enough to keep up with him.

"I think you're high enough now!" Lily calls up as Mark clears half the wall. He stops climbing and turns to her, releasing one hand to wave to her.

"Take!" Mark calls and Lily double checks that she's taken all the slack.

"Got you."

"Falling!" He grabs the rope and kicks off the wall. Lily tightens her fingers on the rope to make sure that he doesn't fall. He looks down at her as he swings out from the wall, kicking off of it to avoid scraping the hold. "Are you going to let me down, dear?" He asks playfully after a few seconds.

"Right!" Lily calls up. She grabs the clip and tilts it slightly to slowly let him down.

"You can go faster than that. My youth is wasting away."

"Great." The instructor nods. "You are ready to climb, just make sure that you keep checking in with each other and grab someone if you have any questions."

"So, which one are you climbing first?" Mark looks up at the walls as he cracks his knuckles. The instructor leaves.

"The easiest one." Lily laughs.

Mark finds an easy wall for her, and after tying in, Lily gives him a mock salute and then starts to climb. He compliments her form and Lily turns her focus to getting to the top piece. It's difficult, and her hands throb as she pulls herself up again. Finally, with an exclamation of triumph, she steps up onto one of the last pieces.

"Take!" Lily shouts with glee as her hands wrap around the final hold. She did it! The rope shifts against her back as Mark tightens the slack.

"Got you." Lily nods and takes a deep breath. She prepares to let go.

The instructor was wrong. The second time is scarier than the first. Lily looks down again, and is suddenly not happy that she was able to climb the whole wall. She tightens her grip, but it's only a matter of time before she is too tired to hold on anymore. Her fingers aren't strong enough for her to check her ropes again with one hand.

"Falling!" She doesn't let go. Fuck, not again.

"Lily?" Mark asks after a few seconds. "Are you coming down?"

"I'm okay!" She's not okay. She's going to fall and get hurt.

"Do you trust me?"

"Yes."

Mark should be a safe bet, but she's still going to get hurt.

"Okay, what about yourself? You double checked everything. It's going to be okay, but you have to let go."

"What if I fall?" What if she lets go and gives in and all that's waiting for her on the bottom is pain? There are so many elements out of her control, and trying to control it more isn't going to help. Her eyes warm.

"I'll catch you." He promises. "I'm not going to let anything hurt you."

That's as good as she's going to get, isn't it? She's already up here, she's already done all her checks. She's just got to do it, she's got to do it and let go. "Falling!" She shouts as she lets go. Sure enough, she's only falling for the barest of seconds before the harness catches, and then Mark lets her down slowly. Once the rush fades, excitement creeps in.

"Good job," he encourages as her feet touch the ground beneath her, "next time, we'll just try to make sure you remember how to let go." Lily playfully shoves him, and he stares at her in mock offense.

"My best suit, and you've ruined it with chalk."

"Then maybe you should take it off." Lily fumbles with her knot.

"I didn't peg you for an exhibitionist." He winks as he steps into her space.

"I'll peg you right here." Lily grabs his harness, and uses the excuse of unclipping him to also run her finger along his shorts over his hardening cock. He closes his eyes as she does so. "You dirty boy." Lily gives him a quick kiss that is just a tease at this point. "Now go pick the wall you want to climb next."

"Yes, miss." He smiles as he walks away, and Lily shakes her head as she looks back to the top of the wall she jumped off of.

Too bad relationships don't have a safety net. Soon enough she'll have to let go of Mark and there'll be nothing there to catch her.

Chapter 20

Mark asked to come over and picked the movie to watch, but he's been quiet and reserved all night. The few attempts Lily makes to get him to talk are met with hesitance, so she leaves it until the end of the movie. Mark lifts the remote to shut off the TV and Lily sits up to stretch. Her shoulders are still sore from yesterday's climbing, and she groans as they pull.

"Did you want to stay the night?" Lily yawns.

He shakes his head. "You've got your customer meeting, and I've got an early morning," he shifts to the side so he can look up at her, "I moved my clients up to the morning, and it looks like a new gig came up for the afternoon."

"Not the underwear one?"

He shakes his head again, but he doesn't seem as happy as she expected. Something is wrong. How does she get him to bring it up? "Congrats! Everything's finally coming together for you!"

He smiles, but then frowns. He closes his eyes and turns to face the TV. Lily waits for him to respond, to tell her all about his new modeling job or what's bothering him, but he doesn't. She reaches out to touch his shoulder and ask if he's okay, but he lets out a breath as she touches him.

"Derrick asked to collar me." He blurts. Lily's heart leaps up into her throat and she can't respond. She jerks her hand back. What can she say?

She's too late. Mark has been wanting this collar since before she's known him. Now that she's started trying to be a better dominant for him, he's being collared by another. She wanted to win Derrick over, so that she wouldn't burn a bridge with him by dating Mark. She wanted enough time for Mark to decide he wants her over Derrick, so she could have him. Derrick has moved up the timetable and cut her out of the running before she even had a chance. She's the one that initially brought this up to Derrick, the one who suggested Mark wanted more. She brought this on herself, really.

"I'd been waiting for it for so long, but it surprised me." He continues once the silence starts to drag. Mark doesn't turn to look at her, and she's glad for it. She should be happy for him; should smile and congratulate him and maybe even ask what it looks like and if she'll see it at the next play party. She shouldn't be blinking back tears, digging her nails into her thighs, and trying not to scream. When did he ask? How? "I guess part of me never expected it to happen." He shifts, pressing his back further into the couch and leaning his head against it. "I'm really excited that it did though." He sounds unsure, and so Lily swallows her pounding heart to be supportive. They are friends.

"How did he ask?" She forces herself to ask.

His shoulders are slumped and his knee keeps bouncing. "Well, it was more of an offer. You know I asked him forever ago, but he said he'd been thinking about it too. He asked me if I still wanted it."

Lily takes a second to process the hesitation in his tone, the bouncing of his knee, and the fact that he won't look at her. He's not excited. He's unsure. "Don't you?"

"I did."

Lily moves towards him, hanging onto his wistful tone, daring to hope.

"I don't know if I want it anymore."

She looks down into his face and places her hands on his cheeks. He closes his eyes. Could this be true? Could she have a chance at this, at him? He lets out a shaky breath and it gives her confidence. Her fingers tremble around his face. He finally opens his eyes and looks up.

"What changed?" They lock eyes and Mark hesitates. Lily can't help a small smile as she shifts to her knees above him. "Are you unsure because of me?"

"Yes." Mark confesses.

She doesn't want him to take it, she doesn't want him to belong to anyone but her. She imagines a future where he is hers: where he kneels for her at parties and she has the confidence to hit him and turn him into the best kind of crying mess. She swallows and her hands tremble as she lifts them up off his face.

If Mark had his way, she would brush her thumbs over his cheeks and tell him that she wants him. She'd confess that she's new but she's eager, and that she wants all of this with him. She'd ask for his patience, his help, and his love. She'd ask her puppy to stay.

But then he'd say yes.

Her smile fades off of her face. Mark's been wanting a collar for longer than she's known him, and now he might be throwing away everything he's ever wanted so that he could choose a future with her: but would he be happy with her? She's not the domme he wants, and there is so much she has to learn before she could even really try to do all of the things that make him happy. He broke his own heart leaving his ex because she couldn't do it. Wouldn't she be the same? She can't do that to him.

What if it's like Derrick said, that this is shiny and new and that she'll be bored of it soon, that she will leave Mark with yet another broken heart at the end of this? She still can't even hit him.

What is she doing?

"I think you should take the collar." Lily hates herself even as the words come out, but she has to do this. She can't let him do this.

"What?" The hurt in his voice should stop her but it doesn't. He pulls away from her and the couch.

"I mean, it's what you've always wanted, right?" Lily wants to sound friendly, she tries to sound friendly, but her voice comes out sounding empty.

"So you don't want…" Mark trails off, and she knows what he's going to ask, and she won't lie and say she doesn't want him, so she stops him.

"I don't have anything to do with this."

"You…" This time it's not hurt, but accusatory. "You don't have anything to do with this?"

"What do you want me to say?" Lily gets off the couch and moves away from him; getting louder.

"I wanted you to say no." Mark shakes his head. His eyebrows furrow.

"You've been wanting this forever!"

"I want you!" He yells, and in all the ways that Lily longs to hear it, it breaks her heart. She never thought she'd be here with him, scrambling for reasons they shouldn't be together.

"Well, you shouldn't!" She stammers, eyes roaming through her kitchen so she doesn't have to look at him. Even in his hurt, in his anger, the lines of him are beautiful. "I mean, I'm not a real domme anyway! What if you decide you want this and it turns out I'm just a tourist," she spits the last word out, hating that Derrick has managed to worm his way in her thoughts so thoroughly. "I can't even hurt you!"

"You can't hit me," Mark corrects, his voice high and hitching, "but you sure can hurt me." Mark stands up and storms towards the door and Lily steps towards him.

"You can't be mad at me for telling you to go for what you want!"

"I want you!" He shouts. "I want ice skating and rock climbing and movie nights and all of that with you!"

Tears spring into her eyes, but she closes them and shakes her head. "You said that you don't want a vanilla relationship, so obviously you want more than that! You want the puppy play and the orgies and the beatings and I can't give you that!"

"What do you want?" He interrupts, "all this is you trying to tell me what I want, but you haven't said what you want." He clenches his jaw, "or what you don't want."

"I…" She wants him, and this, and she wants to storm across the room and jump into his arms. He'd probably catch her and crush her to him as he kissed her. He'd carry her over to the island and fuck her there. She'd apologize as she kissed him and he would talk about how much he's wanted this. They would spend the night in each other's arms talking about the future. They'd certainly become a couple after this. She'd be able to love him so easily, and she thinks he could love her too. Nothing really has to change with them, they could do what is making them happy and—would they keep going to the club?

Of course they would. It would be more nights of them fucking other people, of Mark seeking his pain thrills with other people. It would be a constant feeling of not being enough for him. Of making breakfast with him and kissing the bruises other people put there. It would be a life of being part of Mark's love life, but never the whole of it. She'd hate it, once it wasn't shiny and new to be in love with Mark. She'd hate the sharing and the inadequacy. Her and her little red riding crop could never be enough for the man she saw beaten on the cross. When she thinks of that future, it's clear that when it comes to wanting it…

"I don't." Lily finds she can't say much else.

"You don't." Mark repeats skeptically. When Lily doesn't answer right away, his whole posture changes. His shoulders slump and he swallows before clearing his throat. "You don't?" His voice cracks.

She could tell him. She doesn't have to be this vague, and maybe it's more hurtful to do it this way, but she doesn't. Her throat is full and heavy and it's hard to speak without bursting into tears and that won't help the situation at all.

"I don't." She repeats, hating that her voice also breaks.

"You…" Mark starts, pointing a finger at her, but he lowers it and doesn't finish his thought. "Was it just…" Mark trails off again before deciding he's had enough. His entire expression changes, and his body language shifts. He stands straighter as his face sets into hard lines. She can practically hear as his defenses are raised one by one. It bothers her, and makes her want to reach out to him, but she doesn't. He walks over to the door and puts his shoes on and Lily does nothing. She clenches her jaw and fist so hard her palm stings, but she does nothing. When the door closes behind him, Lily lets out a breath as her chest heaves and the tears spill from her eyes. She sinks against the nearest wall and sobs.

She did the right thing, right?

Her sleep is restless at best that night and when Lily looks into the mirror in the morning, her eyes are so swollen from crying that makeup will only make it look worse. She runs the cold water over her eyes to try and reduce the swelling, and she takes some pain meds to try and counter her headache. Maybe she deserves this, for hurting Mark the way she did, but she did the right thing. A little hurt now will save them from a lot more hurt later.

It's new for her though, breaking up with someone she wasn't even dating.

Lily pulls her hair back into a ponytail and stares at her face. She'd call off of work if not for the customer meeting, and she'd go to work late if she could be confident that the presentation would be done, but she's sure that it's not. At least rushing for this project should take her mind off of her personal problems.

She starts making breakfast and lets her thoughts wander to last night. She was right. She had to be. She let Mark go and do what he—

"Ow!" Lily yelps as she pulls her hand back from the cutting board. She clenches her cut finger in her other hand and makes her way to the sink to wash it. It stings, and she is lucky that it's just a small cut, this could have easily been a trip to urgent care, and then her whole day would be more off than it already is. Lily wraps a paper towel around her thumb to apply pressure as she curses in her head. What use is she going to be to the team today if she can't even get herself together?

Unbidden, her thoughts turn to Mark. He was so caring when she was winded from her fall. He'd likely be running to get a bandage if he were here. Tears spring to her eyes again and she blames the cut. She looks over to the counter where the cutting board is, but all she sees is Mark's face as he pressed her against it. She turns to the living room, but she stepped on him right there. He crawled across this floor for her.

No more thoughts about Mark. Lily will just get breakfast at her job's cafeteria. She doesn't want to be in her house, and she can't think about Mark anymore. Today has to go right. She can't lose her project too, not after all this time.

She wraps her finger up and puts on a nice suit with a skirt. She picks her favorite heels, tries to hide her red eyes with makeup, and drives to work.

"What the hell happened to you?" Tala stands as Lily walks by her cube.

"Good morning, Tala."

Tala raises her eyebrows in question. "Most certainly not. Are you okay?"

Lily shrugs her shoulders and then drops her bag on Tala's extra chair. "Is this about your meeting today? Did you bring your makeup? I have to fix whatever you thought you were doing."

"I did."

"Let's go, then." Tala gestures to the bathroom and walks with her to it. "So what happened?" Tala asks as she opens Lily's makeup bag and hands her a wipe.

"Mark was offered a collar."

"Oh geez, that sucks." Tala pulls out lipstick and blush. "I'm guessing he took it?"

"Well, not exactly, but probably by now." Lily purses her lips before continuing. She blinks fresh tears away and takes a deep breath. "He told me he was having doubts, and then I told him to take it."

"You WHAT?" Tala almost shouts, and Lily winces.

"Okay," Lily holds her hands up defensively, "hold on." Lily takes another breath, but its shaky and it doesn't look like there's any hope of getting Tala on her side. "Mark's been wanting this since before I knew him, I wasn't going to stand in the way of it."

"Did Mark want you to be in the way of it?"

"Yes." Lily confesses. Disappointment and annoyance fight for control of Tala's facial expression.

Tala puts her hands on Lily's shoulders and sighs. "Okay, I say this as a friend, because I love you more than anything. What the hell is wrong with you?"

Lily sputters. "What?"

Tala starts applying Lily's foundation. "I mean, we've had no less than five conversations about how you were learning, and good enough, and how you guys were dating and when he confesses—because I'm assuming it was him who did—you turned him down because you decided he didn't actually want you?"

"When you put it like that…"

"There is no other way to put it." Tala's blunt. She snaps the tube shut. "I don't understand you sometimes, for all that you have to communicate with people, you don't listen. You get this idea in your head about what's best for people, and then you never let anything sway you on that, not even them."

It's different though. Mark's already had a vanilla relationship fall apart. It will hurt them both a lot more if she wasn't up to the task later. It's not like being kinky is a small change, or something she could fake for him. Tala grabs the eyeshadow and Lily closes her eyes.

"So, what do I do, then?" Lily whispers. "No matter how much I want to be, I'm not a domme yet. I might never be. So I watch him grow tired of teaching me? I see him go to other people for his needs because I'm not enough. I'd hate it."

"Or you could trust him." Tala's voice is hard, but her hands are gentle on Lily's face. "Trust that when he says he's willing to wait and teach you he will."

"I don't want to ask him to do that." She can't ask him to do that.

"Sounds like he offered." Tala moves on to her cheeks so Lily opens her eyes again. "I'm with you all the way, always, but I think you made a mistake. I think you need to go to Mark and confess your feelings and you need to talk to him about your doubts, and then you listen, and you trust him."

"It's not going to work." Lily frowns. "He's already tried dating someone who wasn't kinky enough. Can we just leave this alone for now?"

Tala grabs her lipstick. "For now." Tala finishes the rest of her makeup in silence, and hugs her tightly before she leaves. "You should come over for movie night tomorrow."

"Love you."

"I love you too." Tala squeezes back.

Lily turns to look in the mirror and lets out a sigh of relief at Tala's magic. She packs her makeup bag as Tala's words float around her mind, but Lily did the right thing, for both of them.

Jeff spots her leaving the bathroom and speed walks towards her. "Have you read your email?"

"What? No. Sorry, I haven't even had my coffee yet. Please don't give me any bad news today. I'm already scrambling for ways to save the program."

"I'll walk with you," Jeff offers, and Lily nods as she makes her way to the cafeteria.

"So, what's up?"

"You know the triple redundancy layout we've been experimenting with..."

"Yeah." It's their only hope. That or Lily's persuasion.

"Well, if you open your email, you'd see that the reliability team cleared the design late last night."

"Oh that's good." Lily nods as they enter the cafeteria line.

Jeff grins. "Wow, you really need coffee."

"So next we have to—" Lily stares back at him. "Wait."

"There it is."

"The reliability team…" Lily trails off. If the team is done, then…

"Yep!"

"Yes!" Lily shouts as she hops and turns to face him. "That's amazing! Have we told the team?"

"Everyone's on the email. We're drafting new slides for this afternoon."

"That's amazing, my goodness."

"And all before your morning coffee," Jeff jokes, "I told you, you just had to trust us, we wanted this to work out just as much as you did."

"This is great."

"Did you want to meet to figure out what I should put together for our part?"

"I'm free all morning." A weight lifts off of her shoulders. "I'll set something up after breakfast."

The day passes in a brilliant rush of engineering. She doesn't even do much talking. She lets her team and their experience shine through and the customer gives them another two months to build parts and get results. A whole two months!

Lily pulls up her phone and freezes at Mark's name at the top of her message history. She shuts off her screen and places the phone down as the rest of the team celebrates, but her smile isn't as wide as it was before.

It would have been worse had it gone on longer. It would have been so much worse if she'd already fallen in love or planned a future.

***

Tala and Aleeyah giggle with each other in the kitchen as Lily grabs another cookie. They are doing their best to include her, but the awkwardness of third wheeling is killing the night for her. It's a work night. She can just make an excuse and head out without much of a fuss.

Her chest aches as Aleeyah leans over to whisper into Tala's ear. It would have been amazing to go on double dates and just hang out with them and Mark. Lily looks away and sighs, pulling her legs closer to herself. He could have been here now. Mark and Tala could've bonded over ice skating falls before getting hot chocolates and seeing a movie. Aleeyah would laugh with her over scary rock climbing heights. They could have board game nights and nights at the Playhouse. Tala could have teased her about 'chocolate' endlessly.

Burning wetness stings at her eyes and a knot appears and tightens in her throat. Now that she's had a taste of him, of dominance, of climbing dates and ice skating memories she doesn't want to go back to eating alone and only having time in her life for work. She can clearly remember the change in his face with his acceptance and the way he looked when he thought she didn't want him. She wasn't listening to him, and he shut down.

What would Mark have said if she gave him the opportunity to talk; if she told him about her insecurities instead of pushing him away? Would he have wanted to wait for her, to teach her? Would he simply have gone to his knees and offered her everything? It would have been amazing until she was standing with her crop and cold feet. Great until his offers to teach her bled into resentment that affected their whole relationship. There's no way to know.

There is one way.

"I need to go talk to Mark." Lily stands from the couch. "I have to actually talk to him."

"Good." Tala responds from the kitchen.

"You should." Aleeyah encourages.

"No." Lily stresses, remembering Mark's schedule and how he's certainly at his gym right now. She could drive straight there and... "I *need* to go talk to him."

"Now?"

"Yeah." Lily smiles, making her decision. "I'm going to go talk to him now."

"He might not want to talk to you now." Tala holds her hands out, looking a bit more cautious than Lily is feeling. Aleeyah walks up to her.

"I know, but I have to try." Lily is undeterred. "If he doesn't want to talk to me then that'll have to be fine, but I have to try."

"No." Aleeyah grabs Lily's wrist softly and shakes her head. "It's not a good idea to go right now."

"What?"

"She's right. Don't rush this. He'll probably be around on Friday or you could text him and ask him to meet up." Tala places her hand on Lily's shoulder and Lily crumples, falling into the couch and grabbing a pillow.

***

She's barely been able to focus on anything all week. She won't be much better until she knows whether or not she's… lost him.

The week is unfortunately longer than her nerves last. By the time she pulls into the Playhouse's parking lot, she's full of doubt. Their last conversation went so poorly. The last time they were here it wasn't together. Her heart races, and her head throbs. What's changed? What makes her think she can hit him? What makes her think she can do this? She parks behind his car, and she can't convince herself that he isn't there. She taps the steering wheel a few times as she tries to build her confidence, but she honestly doesn't know what she'll do if this doesn't work.

It has to work.

She drafted a dozen messages she couldn't send to him over the week. She couldn't take the chance that Mark wouldn't respond. He still might turn her away. She glances at the time and shuts off her car. No one is going to stop her now, not even herself.

He's inside talking to Derrick and she takes a minute to take him in before he notices her. From where she's standing, he looks like hard angles and sharp edges. His muscles make deep harsh cuts in his skin, and it looks like she could cut herself if she reached to grab him. He moves his hands as he's talking, and they are fast and harsh, like he's angry at the whole world. Even the way he holds his shoulders, stiff and unyielding, makes him look intimidating. He's not wearing a collar. Lily wants to turn away, but this is Mark, and she knows him better than that. She clears her throat. Mark pauses and turns slowly, like he already knows it's her. He says something quickly to Derrick and then takes a couple steps in her direction.

"Lily." Even his voice is full of sharp edges that threaten to bleed her if she lets them. She knows it's on purpose, and its likely defensive, but it still hurts. "What are you doing here?"

"Mark," Lily starts, reaching out for his hand, "I came to talk to you. I'm really—" he pulls his hand away.

"Now is really not a good time." He looks away from her. Lily pauses. She swallows as she shifts from one foot to the other. She briefly considered he wouldn't want to talk to her, but she didn't imagine it would feel this bad when he didn't, like her chest is suddenly too small and she can't breathe.

"When would be a good time?" She asks softly, fearing the answer.

"I don't think there is a good time." He bites. Lily takes a breath but doesn't speak, and Mark turns around and walks away from her. Lily takes another shuddering breath.

"Okay." Lily blinks rapidly to stop her tears from falling. "I'm going to head out, and I'll wait for you, for however long you need me to."

Mark stops walking and Lily stares at his back, "and you don't have to talk to me again if you don't want to, about this or about anything." Her voice cracks, so she clears her throat. "I just wanted you to know I'm sorry. I should have listened to you instead of assuming. I just want you to be happy."

That's all really. Lily stares at Mark's back, but he doesn't turn back to her, so she turns away from him. It hits her now, how stupid this was. He's here with Derrick, his dom, and she came to surprise him. For what? A romantic confession in a swingers' club? Lily glances around with blurry eyes and sees the others staring at her. She cried the last time she was here too. They both slept with other people the last time they were here. Lily lifts her head and tries to control her tears so she can walk out with her head high, but once she's out the door she runs to her car. At least she knows now.

***

Lily practices her edges absentmindedly on the ice. Her skating playlist blasts in her ears and her thoughts are finally blissfully quiet. It's been a few hours already, but she's not ready to go home. Her legs and lungs burn, but her eyes are clear, and her heart is finally calm.

It's been a week since things with Mark ended, if they ever really began, but she thanks him for bringing her back to the ice. He doesn't know that, of course, and she can't really tell him, but it's nice, nonetheless. Tala and Aleeyah have been in damage control mode, but Lily is drained. She silenced her phone for the day. She'll deal with the world tomorrow.

Despite it being Saturday, the rink is mostly empty now, and she uses the time and the space to carve her feelings into the ice until the buzzer kicks her off. She turns towards her bag and promptly trips over her toe pick as she spots a familiar figure. Lily catches herself before she falls. He waits for her at the bench.

"Is this a good time?" He's looking at the ice. "Tala said you'd be here, but—"

"Mark." All of the words in two languages leave her. Her fingers fumble with her laces as her heart pounds. What is he here for? Surely, he wouldn't tarnish her ice rink with a fight.

His face falls. "I'm sorry. I can go."

She grabs at his sleeve before she realizes it and she clears her throat as she holds the fabric in her fingers. She sits to untie her skates and he sits next to her silently, waiting. The usually easy space between them is now awkward and stiff. What should she say? She slips into her shoes and walks out the front door, and he follows.

"Why did you go to the Playhouse on Friday?" He asks as the door closes behind him. It's not accusatory but sounds as tired as she is.

"I don't know," she admits. "I wasn't getting you back, because we weren't dating, but I want to be." Lily sighs. "I hated the thought that you might think I didn't want you, because I do. And I couldn't get it out of my mind that—"

"You want me?"

"I do," Lily confesses as she reaches her car. "There are so many things we'd have to talk more about but I do."

"You lied to me, then," he's harsh and unforgiving, "when you said you didn't."

Lily can't help but to step into his space and take his hands in hers. "Don't think for a second that I don't want you." Lily closes her eyes and shakes her head. "I don't want the swinging. It broke my heart to see you that night at the Playhouse. I know we weren't exclusive, and I fucked Amos right after out of spite. We aren't even together and I can't stand the thought of others having you. I don't want to spend my life kissing the bruises other people give you because I can't hit you hard enough. I don't want to watch you grow tired of teaching me and leave me."

"Lily…" Mark tries to stop her, but she has to keep going.

"I wouldn't feel like enough. I can't just be a part of your love life." Lily pauses as Mark's fingers wrap around hers. "That's why I was so desperate to come to you, I had to tell you that."

"So, you weren't just using me for the sex." His voice goes soft and quiet. It must be important to him.

"Of course not." Lily blushes. "I just didn't want to see you throw away what you've always wanted because of me when I couldn't fit into the spot I thought you wanted me in. You'd been talking about collars since I met you. How was I going to stand in the way of you finally getting one when I wasn't absolutely sure that I was ready to go down a kinky path? If that's what you wanted, I had to let you go."

"I wanted you more." Mark answers. Lily pauses at the past tense, and part of her wants to turn and run away. She's silent as Mark rubs his thumbs over her hands, sure that her heart will leap from her throat if she tries to speak. "What *do* you want?"

"What?"

"You still haven't said what you want."

"I guess I haven't." Lily sighs out. "I want you. I want ice skating and rock climbing. I want more steak dinners and breakfast on the couch in our pajamas. I want us to laugh over my failed attempts at dominance until I get it right. I know it's not going to be easy. I'm going to have to trust you and listen more, but I want to try."

Mark nods but doesn't speak for what drags on like hours. "Derrick only asked because Michi is finally pregnant, which is great news, really." Mark clears his throat. "He's looking for stability in his life and it didn't feel genuine when he asked. I was hoping you'd tell me not to take it because I was hoping we were genuine."

"We are genuine." Lily confirms.

"I wanted you to tell me not to take it. I wanted you to tell me not to be Derrick's submissive, but to be yours." Mark pauses, and Lily doesn't know what to say, because she can't ask him for that. "But it was unfair of me to think you'd do that, since I know you are so new to exploring all this. I was using that collar to pressure you. I'm sorry." Mark sighs before rubbing the back of his neck. The question burns in her throat, but she can't ask. "I didn't take it. Turns out I never wanted a collar, I wanted to love someone enough to be collared. I wanted someone to love me enough to ask." He swallows and looks away. Lily gives him the space. "I ended things with Derrick. I need both."

"I can do the puppy play and the teasing. I can learn the impact, but I'm not like Derrick. If that's something you need—"

"I don't need all of it." Mark interrupts. "I need some of it, but I don't need it all. If I—if we—I don't need to swing. I don't need more than one person. I need attention. I—" Mark presses his forehead against hers. "I want to be yours. I want you to think of me in the mornings and give me kisses goodnight. I need to know you won't leave when it gets hard or when I get difficult to be around. I need to submit and I need the spankings but we'll learn together. I want you to grow with me and you never have to do anything you don't want to."

"I don't want to let you go." Lily whispers.

"Then don't." Mark tilts his head, slides down, and captures her lips in a kiss. Lily presses her lips harder to his with a small noise and he playfully nips at her mouth as his hands let go of hers to crush her to his chest.

Chapter 21

"Now, why don't you be a good boy for me," Lily says softly, enjoying the way Mark squares his shoulders and lowers his gaze, "and get down on your knees."

"Lily," Mark slowly kneels in front of her.

"No," she crosses her legs in her chair and brings her red riding crop into view. He lowers his gaze further to the floor.

"Mistress," he breathes the word out in one long sigh of submission, almost as if to say finally.

Lily smiles. "Now, that's a good boy."

Despite buying the crop months ago, this is the first time that Mark is seeing it, and she's happy he isn't making a big deal about it. It makes her nervous to think that she's competing with his years of experience, but he's tried to reassure her that she's not. She's still learning. She's been watching videos, and taking classes at The Playhouse, but this is the one step she's been unable to take before. He's been hinting at wanting to try again. There is a difference between asking for and accepting his submission, and actively being a dominant that will hurt him.

He's always searching for the little moments to offer his submission, something Lily has become more aware of in the past weeks. He always sits on the floor next to the couch unless she invites him to sit with her, and will spend movie nights kissing her feet and rubbing her legs if she lets him. He likes putting his head on her lap and getting head scratches or belly rubs, which is super cute. He likes cooking for her and getting the praise that she gives to both him and the food. She is consistently finding more things she likes, and is exploring with glee.

Last night, he brought her a glass of water while she was working. She hadn't asked for it, and he hadn't asked if she wanted it, but she nodded as he placed it down. Then he lowered himself down, not quite kneeling, chin up, neck exposed. *Do you need anything else?* He'd asked. In a moment of clarity, she realized that she didn't, but he did.

She's a soft domme. At least she is right now. There is more to Mark's submission than service, and he's been patiently waiting for her, and just her, to want to pick the crop up again. Once she does, she's going to open up another side of him: the pain slut, the brat, and the supper sated mush of a man that impact play brings out of him.

He's done so much for her, and she wants to be able to do this for him. Lily builds Mark's anticipation up by slapping her hand lightly with the crop. Mark takes a deep breath, and the room fills with anticipation.

"Stay there. I want to look at you."

"Yes, Mistress." This time, the word flows out of him with need. He's never referred to her with that much reverence before. It turns her on, just to know how much this means to him. She stands to walk around him, and she continues to tap her hand with the crop. She does want this too, if she is honest with herself. All the ways that she is scared to hurt him fade when she thinks of the sated man he becomes from the pain. He won't run from her because of it, he will kneel to her; he will love her for it.

It starts with anticipation. He's been wanting this from her, and now he's so close. She thwacks the crop on the chair next to him. Mark trembles and Lily smirks. This teasing is something she doesn't need to feel insecure about. She loves when he trembles in front of her, especially when she doesn't need to touch him for it.

She brings the crop down to gently touch his clothed shoulder and he almost flinches at it. She doesn't touch his skin, but moves the crop over the shirt on his back. Mark takes a deep breath as she does so. She stands behind him, and runs her free hand up and down his back.

"Take your shirt off." She steps back, and he quickly pulls his shirt over his head and lets it fall on the floor next to him. She rewards him with a "good boy" and the feel of the crop gently tracing the lines of his back muscles. He lets out a small sound she'll cherish, but she doesn't dwell on it. She gently lowers the crop to his covered ass, before walking around him and bringing it up to his neck. "Tell me, puppy, what are you thinking?"

"I'm so happy right now, I was hoping we'd try this again soon,"

"You have so much experience with this," Lily walks back to his front, "with pain."

"Yes, Mistress." He looks up to her briefly, before lowering his gaze again. She brings the crop to his neck. He swallows. She uses the crop to push his head back up to look at her.

"I've been unfair to myself, thinking that I needed to match what everyone else has done to you."

He stares into her eyes but doesn't speak.

"I've been unfair to you, thinking you'd demand it from me during our first time."

He's silent, and she lifts the crop to his cheek, crosses his lips, and brings it down to trace the outline of his pectorals. She looks down to his pants, and she sees the imprint his hard cock makes in them. "I think I know what you want." Lily whispers.

"Tell me." Mark shivers, his voice equally soft.

"I think you want me to try, and I think you are willing to help."

"Yes, Mistress." He confirms. "I said I wanted you to grow with me."

"So here's my plan." She lowers the crop to her side. "You get naked, and on the bed, and I'm going to join you shortly. I want to tease you with the crop, and then we'll see how some light impact goes."

"I think that's an excellent plan, Mistress."

"But first," she moves her foot in front of her and in his range, dropping her voice into the mix of tease and demand that exactly matches the way she saw in a video. "You are going to ask for it."

He drops to the floor to kiss her heel. "Lily, my Mistress, you honor me by letting me ask."

Lily cannot deny the way her nipples harden and her insides ache. "Will you please use this poor sub as practice for your impact play?" He nuzzles her ankle in a way she hadn't thought sexy before this moment. "Will you please hurt me?" He peppers kisses from her ankle to the toe of her heel.

Lily doesn't respond. She's speechless. Every kiss, caress, and plea turns her on further in a way she hadn't expected it to. She is surprised to find she wants nothing more than to hurt him in all the ways he's asking for and then wrap him up in a fluffy blanket to watch a movie. She remembers the way he snuggled into the couch with a content sigh after a beating, and she wants to recreate the scene in her living room. Mark's ask turns into a beg, and he places an open mouth kisses on her ankle that shoots a bundle of excited energy to her clit. Lily draws her foot back quickly, and he lowers his hands to his side as he quiets.

"I will." Lily's voice is thick with arousal and desperate for his touch. "Get naked and wait for me on the bed," she orders. Mark undresses in a desperate scramble, and almost runs into the bedroom. Lily takes a second to breathe as her pussy clenches around empty air.

Focus. This isn't about her, and this isn't about sex. This is about turning Mark's ass a nice shade of pink.

She takes another few seconds to compose herself before walking into the bedroom. Mark is there, laying on the bed on all fours, propping his ass up for her to see. Lily walks up to him and steps out of her heels. She uses her hands and the crop to gently tease his back and sides to start.

Lily taps on the inside of his thigh, and Mark spreads his legs for her. She takes the crop and slides it the rest of the way up his thigh and then over his cock, and his hips roll with the sensation. He lets out a small whimper. What would he do if she tapped this against him lightly? She moves the crop down his other thigh before retreating.

"Where do you like being hit?" She asks. "Anywhere I need to stay away from?"

"I love my ass and thighs being hit," he arches. "My back is a good spot, but not on the sides. It tickles when it's light and feels weird when it's hard. Stay away from higher than my shoulders and lower than my knees for now."

Based on the pain chart she downloaded the ass and thighs would be best for today.

"Safe word?" She asks, even though she's unlikely to come close to him needing them.

He leans into the crop. "Gimbal."

"You really trust me," Lily murmurs, as she runs the crop higher up his thighs to press against his swelling cock. Her heart swells as she softly smiles.

"I do." In that tone it almost sounds like a vow.

"I won't, but I wonder how you'd react if I tapped you right here." He doesn't flinch away or speak, but he lets out a needy moan. It surprises her, and she files that away to be readdressed in a few years. She teases until she can see a glorious drop of precum on his cock, and she swipes it up with her finger.

"Do you like the taste of your own cum?" She walks around so she can hold her finger up to his face. He closes his eyes and opens his mouth, but Lily doesn't let him taste it. She waits for him to open his eyes before licking it herself, and Mark whimpers. Lily walks around him again and then finally, brings the crop down onto the skin of his ass. It's a lot lighter of a hit than she was hoping for, but Mark doesn't seem to mind.

"Thank you, Mistress." Mark breathes out.

Lily brings it down again, and again. He thanks her each time, but she is hoping to build on intensity until he is moaning, and instead she is losing the head space of her teasing.

"Thank you, Mistress," he repeats, but she can hear the humor in his voice as he asks, "May I have another?"

"Quiet." Her hands clench around the crop in her hand. She brings the crop down onto his ass again, and flushes with shame as she pulls back at the last minute. The tap is gentle, and Mark's shoulders shake with silent laughter.

"Mistress," he tries again and she smacks the bed next to him as hard as she can. Mark settles onto the bed.

"I'm warming up so you just lay there and wait." She shifts. "Please. This is the best way you could serve me right now."

"Yes, Mistress." He coos, but she is reminded of his bratty behavior from before, where Derrick spanked him hard to get him to actually settle. She brings the crop down again. This time she hears a dull thud and smiles, but Mark doesn't look impressed.

"Thank you, Mistress."

"Don't say it every time," Lily whines, "it's too much pressure."

Lily lifts the crop again, but she lacks a follow through, and the thud is dull and light. "Damn it," Lily starts to laugh. "Why is this so hard?" Mark doesn't shift until she sits on the bed next to him and taps it, and then he falls onto the bed and turns to look up at her. "I know I'm not actually going to hurt you," Lily continues, "and yet each time I feel myself pull back."

"Anything I can do to help?" he asks.

"I don't know." Lily admits, "I want to make you happy."

"You do make me happy," Mark sits and give her a soft kiss before pulling back. "And I do need this, but I'm not expecting you to hurt me off the bat."

"I know."

"So, I want you to hit me the way you hit the bed, how do we get there?"

"I just have this idea that hitting you harder will actually hurt you, and I can't help the idea that…" Lily trails off and gestures ineffectively with her hands.

"I think you actually need to hit me." Mark comes into her space and drops his voice down. "It's just like my first ice skating fall, everything gets easier after it."

"So you think the first hits the hardest." She clenches the crop in her hand. "What if it's like rock climbing, and each one is scarier than the next."

"Either way, it's fun isn't it?" Mark shares a breath that Lily thinks will turn into a kiss, but then he pulls back and gets on all fours again, Lily turns on the bed to face him.

"Now, my dear Lily, my mistress, will you please hurt me?"

"Once upon a time I promised you a second sore bottom." She smiles as she stands again. Lily traces the crop from his shoulders to the swell of his ass and then gives it a gentle swat. She gently taps his ass all over before jerking her wrist and hitting him again.

"Thank you," he stretches out on the bed. It sounds like he's thanking her for more than the single hit.

"Thank you." Lily places her hand on his hip as she hits him again and she hopes he hears 'I love you'.

"How am I doing?" She asks a minute later,

"You are teasing." He wiggles. "Can you try a little harder?" Lily nods and hits him just a little bit harder.

"Harder." Mark preens, "That's a good warm up teasing strike, but I'm ready for more." Lily pulls back and her next strike is even harder. When she hit herself with this force on her arm it hurt. She hopes it's enough. It's not, and she spends the next few minutes getting incrementally harder with her strikes.

"Harder." Mark wiggles his ass.

Lily stammers as she pulls the crop back. "Harder? That was pretty hard, I thought." Mark shifts slightly, spreading his legs a little and lowering his shoulders. "Please," He tries, and Lily shifts her gaze from his ass to the crop. "Trust me."

"Okay, but you'll tell me if it's too much."

"Yes. Now please, Mistress, hit me."

Lily brings the crop down once more, and this time, she follows almost all the way through. The sound is louder than the rest and she smiles. "How was that?"

Mark makes a desperate needy noise and pushes his ass towards her. "Just like that, please."

"Just like that?" She repeats, grinning as she brings the crop down again. "Good?"

He moans. "Golden."

"Excellent." She moves to a new spot on his ass to hit next. It's not enough to truly satisfy him yet, but it's enough to build a foundation on, together.

<u>Epilogue</u>

"Breakfast is served." Mark drops a kiss on her forehead as he hands her a plate and sits next to her on the couch. The image on the TV switches to a close up of her rocket. Lily yawns into her hand before popping a strawberry slice into her mouth. It's earlier than she'd usually wake up, but that's time zones for you. Mark's practically vibrating in his seat, and she doesn't have the heart to tell him they'll be there for a while before it actually launches.

"Thank you." She leans into his side and he wraps an arm around her as he picks at his fruit.

"This was your headache project, right? The first one you led?"

"Right," Lily blanches at the memory. "For a while there, we didn't know if we'd make it to this part."

"Now you're actually sending people to space."

"I'd worked on projects before this one you know," she teases, "but this was the first one that was mine."

"I know what you mean. The vitamin ad wasn't my first, but it feels that way."

He bought a dozen copies of the magazine the day it came out. He was in a picture on the bottom banner, twisted and flexing so hard she had to look twice to make sure it was him, but he was on the cover. He grinned for weeks, and then the next ad came in, and the next one.

Ally Marr

The journalist on screen details all the recent work that's gone into the rocket. Lily's name doesn't come up. Her company's name doesn't come up. It's not her moment. She didn't expect it to be. Yet sitting here in her pajamas and fuzzy socks with Mark is just as fulfilling as leaning on the railing and feeling the wind blow her hair back with Jeff. She doesn't know all the checks they are running and she doesn't hold her breath to see if each one goes right. She leans into Mark and turns to kiss his cheek and nuzzle into him.

"Don't fall asleep on me." His voice is soft.

"I won't." Hers is softer.

The morning is quiet, the sunrise barely peeks through the blinds, and Mark is warm. It's perfect.

The plates go in the sink. Lily grabs a blanket to cuddle under. Mark counts down with the TV. Smoke billows outwards and Lily squeezes Mark's hand as the rocket launches into the atmosphere.

"Make a wish," Lily murmurs as the screen turns white with oversaturation. Mark grins and makes a show of rubbing his chin and not so subtly rubbing his bare neck. Lily pretends not to notice. There may or may not already be a collar hidden in her closet.

"Do you think it'll come true?"

"Mine did." Lily nudges his shoulder and glances back at the TV.

THE END

Acknowledgments

It's been a lifelong dream of mine to publish a book, and part of me can't believe I finally did it. This book has been years in the making, and it wouldn't have been able to cross the finish line without a few special people.

Morgan, you are the best writing friend a girl can ask for. Thank you for letting me throw any and every idea at our proverbial wall, and for helping me find the gems in all the noise. So much of this book has been influenced by your feedback and support that I can't imagine what it would have been without you.

There have been so many people who touched this novel, from my editor Shana to the numerous alphas and betas who all shared my love and devotion to my world and characters. I cannot possibly thank you all in a page, but you have my love and my thanks!

Anyone who picked this book up and glanced at it, skimmed it, or read it: THANK YOU! This journey has been hard, but it's all worth it to get a story that was once a vague idea into something I can share with you. If you liked it or loved it, I'd love to hear from you on any socials or even AllyMarr.com.

Last but not least, my husband Tim. You are my very own happy ever after. It can be hard to write about something you do not know, which is why I'm grateful I know love so well. You've always been supportive of my work, and have gone out of your way to try and help me find inspiration in the little ways everyday people share their love. The magic I feel with you is the magic I hope to capture in my books.